HIS TO PROTECT

THE CHAINED HEARTS DUOLOGY

BOOK 1

ASHLEY DAVIS

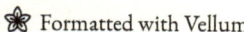

To the ones who survived what was meant to break them
&
The ones who dream of being chased through the woods by a masked man

CONTENT WARNINGS

This story contains themes and situations that may be difficult for some readers. Please take care of yourself while reading, your mental health is the most important thing.

Potential triggers include:
- Violence and terrorism
- Kidnapping and captivity
- Guns, knives, and combat scenarios
- References to torture and past trauma
- PTSD, anxiety, and panic attacks
- Strong language
- Suicide
- Explicit sexual content
- Loss of a child/spouse (off-page)

While these elements are part of the characters' journeys, your well-being as a reader matters most. If at any point you need to step away or put this book down forever, please do.

On a brighter note: If you are having trouble visualizing Riley's apartment on base or his bunker layout, there are blueprints included in the back to help you visualize the world more clearly.

PROLOGUE

Six weeks. Six long, grueling weeks Jeremy sat, racking his brain for a way out. That was until the opportunity presented itself in the form of a six foot two Russian man with a score to settle. It only took one bad day for Jeremy to warm up to Ivan, quickly considering him a brother.

He tried to ignore him at first. Tried to keep to himself and wait for his parents to bail him out. They always did. The day they came to visit him was the day everything changed. He sat waiting, quietly watching through the bulletproof glass window as his mother picked up the phone and told him with tears in her eyes that they couldn't get him out this time. He had never been so angry. The glass shook as he slammed the phone down, screaming at her for ruining his life. His mother flinched away, tears welling up in her eyes as he was ushered back to his cell.

Jeremy returned screaming until his face turned red. His knuckles bloodied, spattering across the wall of their shared cell. Ivan took him under his wing that day. The anger simmering in Jeremy's eyes reminding him of himself when he was young. The two became close, and soon enough Ivan introduced him to a handful of other inmates. All with the same thick Russian accent and matching tattoos, most on their chests while Ivans was plastered onto his neck. A large, hairy beast with fangs. Horns like the devil stretching out of the top of its head with a mouthful of razor sharp teeth, bared in an almost grin.

Jeremy tried his best to ignore the fact that the men were clearly in some sort of gang, but he had no idea just how deep that gang really went. He spent weeks with them, slowly learning Russian, opening up to them about how he was framed and thrown in jail. He confided in them. He just needed to get out and he was going to hunt down the one who got him tossed in jail and take their life before fleeing the country to start over. That single statement, the trust behind those words told Ivan everything he needed to know.

Days later, Jeremy awoke to a fist slamming into his nose, instantly breaking it. The sound of bone crunching threatened to send the contents of his stomach back out. A flurry of punches and kicks followed. His ears ring as a thick metallic liquid fills his mouth. Whilst being ripped from his bed Jeremy tried to fight back. His fists swing at anything he can see before his eyes swelled shut. The pain shooting through his body was almost unbearable as another foot connected with his ribs. A raspy scream escaped his lips. Just when he thought this would be what killed him, the punches stopped. Jeremy laid there, not daring to move as he listened to the footsteps shuffle down the corridor, the soft whispers in Russian going with them.

That fateful night was almost three weeks ago. An initiation of sorts, that's what Ivan told him when he returned from the infirmary. He had refused to turn them in, in turn, he sealed his fate as one of them. The last thing he needed to do was meet the head of their organization. The two of them sat in a secluded room that a pair of scraggly guards took them to. He explained that they are not quite a gang, more like a large group of people fighting for the greater good. They follow a man named Dmitri, who has been paying off the guards to keep them comfortable until he can get them out, and if Jeremy wanted to leave with them, he would need to win their leader over.

———

Nervous jitters flood him. The sharp bite mixed with the dull hum of the tattoo machine Ivan is using to tattoo his chest helping to calm his nerves. In a matter of minutes Dmitri would arrive and decide if he was good enough to join him, or if his life would end that day. He sent a prayer up to a god he doesn't believe in and hopes the tattoo is enough to prove his commitment to his new found family.

"So, you're the outsider my men have grown so fond of?" A scratchy voice with a thick accent bellows. Footsteps echo in the silence, growing louder until a short, stocky man steps into the room. A pair of piercing blue eyes, one a lighter shade from the scar running through it, scan over him, curiosity peaking when they settle on the half done tattoo.

"I would get up and shake your hand if Ivan wouldn't kill me for delaying his work, he made it very clear this is very important to you." He says with a smooth smile. A small chuckle escapes Dmitri's lips, seeing why everyone took a liking to him so quickly.

"What else did Ivan tell you?" He asks, carefully watching Jeremy for his reaction. To his surprise Jeremy stays calm, shrugging his shoulders just enough to not mess up his work in progress.

"Only what I'm allowed to know. I know you are very important to a lot of people, even if you have to make hard choices for the greater good. I also know that like me, you're hunting for someone who fucked your plans up too, and I think I have a plan that can be help both of us get what we want, but I need to get out of here first." The silence that follows was enough to make him worry that he has overstepped. A loud, rumbling laugh burst from the man standing in front of him.

"Tell me this plan, then I will decide if you are worth the trouble."

"I was framed. A woman I have known my entire life, someone I thought was family, turned me in, blaming me for a crime I didn't commit. I thought she cared for me, but instead I was thrown in jail and left to rot. I need to hunt her down and you have the resources to do that." Jeremy stops, eying the short man picking fuzz of his tailored suit, looking for any reaction, good or bad.

"And just how would that help me?" He sneers, his patience growing thin.

"You're looking for someone too right? And he's looking for you by finding people you associate with? Well, you find her for me, have some of your guys spread the word that she's going to be meeting you, tell everyone what she looks like. It seems to me that is the kind of information that would get back to your man and he would go looking for her, when he does you can grab him."

Dmitri's eyes narrow, taking in his words and giving each one careful thought. He begins a slow lap around the room, Jeremy's eyes never leaving him as he does. He knows it will work, he just needs Dmitri to know it too.

"And how do you know this little plan of yours will work?" The pacing stops. He watches as Ivan finishes the beastly tattoo now adorning his chest.

"To be honest, I don't. I have never been involved in

anything like this. It's one of those things that's just stupid enough to work." The wobbly metal chair scrapes across the floor as he stands, pulling his bright orange shirt over his head.

"What will you have me do with this woman when I finally get what I'm after?"

"I don't want anything to do with her. Kill her, keep her, give her to your guys. I don't care, consider her a gift. She was family to me once, but it's too late now. I have no family."

"You do now boy." Dmitri says. A cruel smile spreads across his wide mouth. "Well then, it's about time we go hunting"

CHAPTER 1

"How can you be sure they're here?" Mikey yells, firing his gun once more before ducking back into the safety of their room.

Riley leans around the corner, reloading his rifle and firing, this time hitting one of the men at the other end of the hall. Small chunks of concrete rain down on their heads from a grenade explosion somewhere above them. They look at each other, a silent understanding the other team must be having one hell of a time clearing the upper floor.

"I'm not, but I'm not leaving without looking," Riley yells back.

This fight has been going on for too long. They never imagined these men would be more skilled than the ones at the last compound.

Riley glances around the narrow hall, watching as each member of his team leaves their cover to fire at their enemy. A loud groan rumbles from his chapped lips, knowing he doesn't have time for a firefight. He needs to make it to the cells before his team blows the building, or worse, Dmitri kills all the prisoners.

"How long until impact?" he yells to no one in particular, firing down the hall again. He hits his target, the man falling to the floor, unmoving.

"17 minutes, 54 seconds, sir." another man yells. "If you're going to do this you need to go now!" he adds.

Riley leaves his cover, firing two more shots with another man hit, his blood spraying the crumbling concrete wall behind where he falls. Only three left. He knows he's clear to take one or two of his men to clear the cells while the rest of his team handles the last of the people engaging them.

"Mikey, you're with me," he states, clapping a hand on his shoulder.

"Cover us," he yells to the last of his team firing on the enemy, giving them the cover they need to slip into the stairwell. Once clear, they start down the stairs, trying to get to the third floor before time runs out.

As soon as their boots hit the landing, Riley slows, hoping the building holds out long enough to do what he came to do. Only sixteen minutes left before everything turns to rubble. He cracks open the door leading into a narrow hallway and peers in. Only seeing two guards, he assumes everyone else has left their post to go help in the fight raging above them.

"Two guards; I'll take the one on the right, you take the left," he says, watching Mikey nod in agreement. Riley takes a deep breath and quietly counts to three.

Their guns fire simultaneously and the guards hit the ground with a sickening thump. Riley waits, counting the seconds in his head. When he gets to sixty and no reinforcements show up, he motions for Mikey to follow close behind. They maneuver into the hallway, broken fluorescent lights flicker while the smell of blood and urine overwhelms their senses. An explosion rocks the building, reminding him just how little time they have.

"Any idea what cell we're looking for?" Mikey asks, looking at the rows of doors on either side of the hall.

"No... Just start opening. If anyone's alive, tell them to run."

Riley rushes to one side and pulls the first cell open. The heavy metal groans as he pulls the weight of it back, the stench of death hitting him before he has it half open. Peering inside, he sees a man, or what used to be a man, laying on the floor. A dark-brown stain of old blood coats the floor around where he lays.

The next three cells are the same. Lifeless bodies of people who died undeserved, gruesome deaths. As he approaches cell number five, he hears the muffled whimpers of someone still clinging to life.

He pulls the door open with so much force he feels it in his bones. With his gun ready, he steps into the room, his flashlight illuminating the faces of a man and woman huddled together in the corner, covered in what he hopes is just mud. He screams at them to go, to get as fast as they can as they rush past him. He tries to shake off the disappointment of not finding the one they are here for, telling himself these people are still prisoners who deserve to be saved just as much. Riley backs out of the room, storming to the next cell, ready to get this mission over with. Doors six and seven come up empty, he is about to give up, knowing they only have about 10 minutes now, when he hears screaming.

"Help! I'm still in here," the stranger yells. "Please, let me out!"

The man's screams echo through the empty hall. The only other sound is Mikey opening more cell doors. The gunfire grows quiet, causing Riley's stomach to turn into knots.

"Finish that cell and find out what the fuck is going on!" Riley yells, opening the cell. He's met by a rail thin man covered in fresh cuts and deep purple bruises, but seemingly okay. Riley shouts at him to get out, warning him of the incoming missile. The man wastes no time running toward freedom.

"Wait! Are there any more people here?" he asks. The desperation in his voice rings clear.

Owing Riley his life, the man tells him there is one left, the door at the end, before he turns and runs.

"Six minutes, sir," Mikey says. "They have more firepower than we knew about. Delta Team had to fall back. The rest of our forces are trying to keep a path clear for us, but we need to move."

Riley sprints to the last cell, knowing he's out of time, and rips the door open. He only has seconds to take everything in. A blanket as a makeshift bed, the floor stained with a mix of fresh and old blood, the overwhelming stench of urine, and in the corner next to the door, a small bucket full of what he knows all too well are torture tools. He scans the rest of the room, and there, chained to the floor, is the woman they came for.

CHAPTER 2

Liz drags herself across the floor, fighting back the bile clawing its way up her throat. She tries to get as far as possible from the puddle of piss the last guy left, but she can only make it so far before the cuff around her wrist forces her to give up. She knew she shouldn't have fought back the last time. She was warned what would happen if she continued to fight but, against her better judgment, she decided pissing him off was worth the beating. If only she had seen the chains first, she may have made a better choice.

The loud pop of gunshots ring out in the distance causing Liz to flinch, the rusted metal of the too tight cuff slicing deeper into her wrist from the sudden movement. It was a typical night: some pissed off man came in, took their anger out on her as usual, and then shooting started. She thought some idiot made the mistake of trying to escape and paid for it with their life or the shit hole's limp-dick leader was throwing a temper tantrum.

When the man put down his knife and ran out, she knew something was wrong. Two more gunshots, so synced it almost sounded as one, echoes down the hall, ripping her from her thoughts. Someone is firing a little too close to the cells for her liking, confirming her suspicions this isn't a normal night.

The telltale sound of bodies hitting the floor has her propping herself upright, trying to save what little strength she still has. Something is happening in the compound and this may be her best chance to escape.

The man in the cell next hers starts screaming for someone to help him, like anyone here would care about letting him out. If they go down, they sure as hell aren't going to take the prisoners with them.

Liz opens her mouth to tell him no one is coming to save them when she hears the heavy cell doors opening. It starts at the end of the hall, and she starts counting.

Six... seven... eight.

Closer and closer until the ninth door opens. The man who was screaming starts thanking the gods, meaning hers is next. She only has a few seconds to think, to figure out who is here and what they want. No more shots have been fired, at least not where the prisoners are kept. Are they taking hostages? It seems like the only logical answer.

"I'm not letting these assholes take me," she says to herself.

Liz reaches for the small, jagged bone she's been hiding in the crack of the floor under her tattered wool blanket, part of the last real meal she had. If you could call a single, boiled chicken leg and a spoonful of rice a meal. Their newest form of torture, withholding food until she's too weak to fight back, only giving her enough food to stay alive. Lucky for her, they were so busy gossiping about what they had planned, they didn't even notice the bone was missing. Liz spent every moment she had grinding it into the concrete floor, sharpening it to a point that would easily pierce her captor's neck.

Slow, heavy footsteps echo down the hall, approaching the

cell. Something is very wrong. For months, Liz has listened to the steps of everyone who would come into her cell, learning what each person sounds like, and those aren't the steps of anyone who's come before. Gripping the bone so hard her knuckles turn white, trying her best to hide it, she silently makes sure she has room to swing. This was meant for him. If he was going to kill her, she was going to make sure he suffered the same fate.

Her anger builds knowing she will never get that chance. The locks on the door disengage and the heavy metal groans open. Liz closes her eyes and tries to slow her breathing. All she needs is this man to get close enough to make her move.

"Are you alright?" His voice is deep and scratchy like he's been yelling, yet somehow, it's almost comforting. "Can you walk?" he asks, taking a few small steps toward her.

Another man starts shouting from somewhere down the hall, urging him to hurry. Liz takes a small, slow breath, desperate to keep her fear at bay. She has been held prisoner for months, she knew what to expect from the men holding her. These men are new, and the thought of what they may do to her sends a shiver down her spine. Her cell was the last in the hall, meaning they have taken all the others out. Her mind races, her heart matching its rhythm.

Where are they taking everyone? Did they just kill them? Who are these men and why are they here?

The man steps closer, his footsteps growing louder. If she dared to open her eyes, she would be face to face with a pair of bloody boots. The smell of iron and dirt making her fight back vomit all over again. Suddenly, a second set of footsteps approaches her cell, much faster than the man standing before her.

"She's dead, just leave her. We need to move," the second

man says, a hint of sorrow in his voice. "Reaper, they are waiting on us," the same man says, much more firmly this time.

Reaper? Oh yeah, this man is definitely just here to finish me off. she thinks to herself. All she needs is for him to bend down and she will make him meet the inspiration behind his little nickname.

"She's still breathing, weak, but alive. Could be drugged," the first man, Reaper, responds.

"She's barely hanging on. She's out cold. Even if she wasn't, look at her. She is too weak to walk herself out. You need to let this one go, sir. You'll die if you don't leave her."

"You know I can't do that. Even the ones they killed weren't beaten this bad. Go without me, I'll catch up. I'm not leaving her here." Reaper uses a tone that says his decision is not up for debate. "What the hell did they do to you?" he whispers, more to himself than anything.

Her breathing slows, trying to calm her nerves so she can do what needs to be done. When the scratchy blanket she's laying on moves, and she feels him pick up her hand, Liz realizes she needs to see what is happening. Slowly, her eyes open, assessing the situation as fast as she can. The man towers over her, even crouching down. He tugs at the short chain connected to the cuff on her wrist, just long enough for her to move to the bucket they so graciously left her to relieve herself, not long enough to allow her to fully stand. He silently mutters to himself about needing to break the chain. Her eyes snap shut before he catches her watching. It takes all the mental strength she has not to yank her arm away, every movement has the cold metal cuff sliding against her already torn skin.

Liz is forced to look one more time, trying to find a weak spot. As she scans his body, she notices guns strapped to his denim-clad legs, a knife the size of her arm across his bulletproof vest, and a large rifle slung over his back. She drags her eyes to his face, only to see he's wearing some type of mask. It looks like a skull, but where the teeth should be there are something like fangs reaching to the bottom of his face, and two horns extending off the top. Finally, she sees what she was looking for; there is a small spot on his shoulder not covered by his vest. It may not kill him, but it should buy her a few seconds to run. A moment later, he pulls at the chain holding her to the floor, sending little shards of concrete into her hair. She's free. It's time. She takes a deep breath and starts counting.

One...

Two...

Three...

She opens her eyes, letting out the breath she had been holding, when his eyes snap to hers.

"Shit," Liz squeaks.

"Hey, you're safe, I'm going to get yo—" is all he can get out before she swings at him with every ounce of strength she has left.

He screams and Liz feels a warm, sticky liquid pooling around her hand. She keeps her grip, pulling the now slick chicken bone straight down, causing as much damage as she can. She wills her useless legs to stand, the feel of his skin tearing sends a wave of nausea through her.

The man stumbles back and Liz scrambles to her feet. One look at the gash in his shoulder sends her over the edge and all the vomit she had been trying to keep in comes rushing up. He doesn't give her time to be sick before he's on her.

"Did you just fucking stab me?" he screams, looking down at his shoulder.

He grabs the chain still attached to her with one hand, her free hand in his other, before slamming her into the wall. If he wasn't still supporting both her arms, she would have collapsed from the impact.

"LET GO OF ME!" she screams, trying to tear herself away. "I'll fucking die before I let you take me," she tells him, throat raw from the near constant screaming.

He drops her arms and she stumbles toward him, not used to being on her feet after being chained to the ground so long.

She musters as much energy as she can and tries to rush around him, desperate to be free, but she's too weak. She foolishly tries to shove past him, and he grabs her, throwing her back onto the floor. Her skull cracks against something hard.

"Fucking asshole," she whispers, barely loud enough for him to hear.

This man is easily over six feet tall, solid muscle, and obviously highly trained. Meanwhile, she's been chained to a floor, beaten, and starved for weeks, not thinking about their differences before deciding to fight him off. She starts to stand and he steps toward her.

"I'm trying to fucking help you!" he yells at her, a mix of panic and fear in his eyes.

She can barely hear him over the ringing in her ears. Somehow, she manages to stand, ignoring the black spots taking over her vision. He takes another step and she starts swinging, trying to do anything she can to make it to that door. He easily steps around her flailing arms, but she doesn't stop, using every last bit of energy she has just to keep from passing out.

"Enough!" he yells. He grabs one of her arms to try and stop her attacks.

She sends her other arm at his face, trying to do anything she can to hurt him. Screaming in frustration when a loud bang from the hall draws his attention, distracting him long enough for her fingers to brush against the mask. The horns on top may be strong enough to impale him again.

She stretches her arm, determined to rip his mask off his face. He's holding her arm just far enough to make her struggle to reach. When her fingers curl around a small ridge on the side, she pulls. She's so determined she doesn't even see his fist swinging at her.

Her head snaps back at the impact, and she falls, pain radiating through her body. She watches helplessly as he bends down, pulling her into his arms. Her eyes flutter closed before everything fades to black.

CHAPTER 3

Liz opens her eyes to find herself in a small bed, the smell of bleach heavy in the air. A thin white curtain surrounds her to create a makeshift room. She tries to lift her head, but the throbbing forces her to stay down. She attempts to get her arm under her so she can sit up, but something stops her from moving. She panics, that familiar feeling setting in.

She knows this feeling, she's had that weight on her for the last few weeks. They've chained her to another bed. Forcing her eyes open, she sees her wrists handcuffed to the rails of a gurney, sending her spiraling. Her breathing quickens and her ears ring. She's trapped, not caring about the consequences, she starts to pull.

What could these new captors do that the old ones didn't? Every day for twenty seven days strange men and women would come into where she was being held and beat her senseless. Fists, feet, random objects they brought with them, it didn't matter as long as it ended with her screaming, begging them to stop. Then, and only then was she allowed food. The more she fought back the worse the beatings would become. Eventually they didn't stop until she was knocked out cold, that's when she started to lose track of the days. They didn't break her then, and she sure as hell won't let these new captors break her now.

A sharp hiss leaves her lips as the fresh set of shackles dig into her already cut-up wrists. The noise alerts two guards stationed outside of the curtain. Within seconds, they are on the other side, yelling for a doctor.

A man wearing a white coat steps in behind the guards. Liz takes a few deep breaths, her eyes frantically scanning the who she assumes is the doctor. He's a short man, no more than 5'4, heavy set, with short graying hair. If she has a chance at fighting anyone off, it would be him. Her eyes flick back to the two men staring at her, suddenly missing her cell and the comfort of knowing what is going to happen.

"Glad to see you're awake," the man says, flashing her a curt smile before turning to one of the guards and whispering something inaudible.

"My name is Dr. Bennett. Do you know where you are?" he asks.

She shakes her head. Her mouth is too dry to even think about forming words. The bright lights of what she can only assume is some type of medical room, causes the pounding behind her eyes to grow more intense. She fights to keep them open, to take in every detail of where she is. If she's lucky she can find a way out. Liz pulls on the cuffs again, trying to get enough leverage to sit herself up.

"If you keep trying that, I'll be forced to sedate you again," he says, writing something on his clipboard.

Again. That one little word sends a chill down her spine. Liz thought she had just been knocked out from that man in the mask, not drugged. What had they done to her while she slept?

If she lets herself run through every possible thing they could have done she will never stop. Liz was only a child when she learned that in order to survive you need to ignore your feelings. Pain, fear, anger, it doesn't matter, shove those feelings so deep inside your mind you become numb to them. She sighs and puts her head down, clearly not a battle she is going to win. Looking around the small room, there are no decorations, no signs of other people, just the incessant beeping of the machines they've hooked her up to.

She glances down, seeing tubes coming out of both arms, deep purple bruises forming where they entered. Somewhere in the room, outside of the too white sheets, she can hear the faint ticking of a clock. She lifts her head back up and scans the room, craning her neck trying to find the source of the ticking.

"Time?" she manages to get out, her voice deep and scratchy. The doctor looks down at his watch, before continuing to mark down whatever he was reading on the machines. Her anger re-ignites as if she will somehow manage to escape by knowing the time. She has no way of knowing how long ago they took her. If she knows the time, she will at least be able to have some idea of how long they keep her locked up.

"Please?" she chokes out. She looks over at him, his brows pinched together, something akin to annoyance on his face.

He lets out a heavy sigh, rolling his eyes like a simple question is an inconvenience, before finally answering, "2:36 a.m."

Liz lets her eyes close and lays her head back down, not having enough strength to thank him. She thinks to herself, *I didn't get dinner before everything happened.* The pounding in her head intensifies as she tries to work out how long it has been. Liz figures it has only been about ten hours, too tired to think more on it.

Exhausted and in pain from her struggle with the masked man, she doesn't try to stop the sleep that consumes her.

She's awoken some time later to the two guards grabbing her ankles. She's up in an instant, attempting to pull her legs away. The smaller of the men turns, yelling for the doctor before returning to pin her legs down.

"Don't fucking touch me!" Liz screams, throat burning and raw.

She tries to swing at the man, only to have the metal around her wrist stop her. She feels her skin rip back open, fresh blood dripping down her arm, staining the white sheets under her. The doctor rushes back over to her, syringe in hand. Her eyes widen at the sight of the needle, panic taking hold and refusing to let go. She tries to squirm as far away as the restraints will allow before he can inject her with the mystery substance. Liz knows she can't afford to be unconscious again, so she pulls her legs up as far as she can, attempting to curl into a ball. She does anything she can to make it harder for them to grab her.

"What the hell are you doing?" a female voice shrieks.

All three men look up, too caught up in the commotion to hear her entering the room. She steps fully behind the curtain and shoves past the two guards, giving them a look of shame as she does. She looks Liz over, eyes full of pity.

"Does someone care to explain just what the fuck you are doing?" she asks, turning to where Dr. Bennett stands. He opens his mouth to mutter an explanation, but Liz quickly shouts over him.

"They grabb—" she says before one of the guards steps toward her bed, causing her to flinch away.

The movement didn't go unnoticed. The woman whirls on him, ready to unleash her full wrath. He takes a step back and apologizes before removing himself from the space. The woman turns back to the bed and gives Liz a slight nod. She takes it as an invitation to continue explaining what happened.

"They were... touching... me," she says, each word making her throat burn.

"I was told to have her restrained and brought to the interrogation room once she wakes up," Dr. Bennett cuts in. "I was just following orders," he adds.

The woman looks him over and orders him to step outside the curtain, following close behind.

"What the hell kind of doctor follows orders to restrain and sedate a scared woman who just got rescued from a fucking terrorist organization?" she hisses at him, unaware Liz can still hear. "We don't know what this poor woman has been through, and you just sent two large men into her room to put shackles on her? Did you consider what could be going through her mind before rushing in ready to sedate? Do you even care about the trauma that poor thing is experiencing right now" She doesn't give him time to answer before starting again.

"What do you think he's going to do to you when he finds out what just happened? That man is going to kill you." Dr. Bennett stutters, not able to form a coherent response.

"That's what I thought," she says smugly.

Her heels click on the floor as she walks back in. Pulling a chair over to the bed and sitting down, looks through the chart the doctor had been filling out. She shakes her head, clearly disappointed with what he has marked down. She takes a few minutes to look over everything before setting the chart down and double checking all the machines. After what feels like an eternity, she turns and looks at Liz.

"I'm sorry for their behavior. They have orders to have you shackled and brought to a new room as soon as you awoke, but they also have been told to leave you until someone could come be with you."

Liz can't help but stare at the woman darting from beeping machine to beeping machine, a quiet confidence in each movement. Dressed in a pair of slacks, classic white blouse and her rich brown hair pulled expertly into a french twist, she looks like she belongs in an office rather than a pop up hospital room.

"Unfortunately, you stabbed a commander, and from what your file says, continued to try and fight him? I'm impressed, but due to your prior attack, there is no way we can let you be unrestrained," she says with genuine kindness behind her deep brown eyes, before walking over to grab the shackles the men tried to put on her legs. She sets them on the rolling over-bed table perched at the end of the bed.

The clanking metal causes Liz to break out in a cold sweat.

"I know you are in shock right now, but you are safe. May I?" she asks, motioning to the end of the bed. "If it's going to be too much for you, I can try to find guards more comfortable escorting you."

Reluctantly, Liz shakes her head no. There is nothing in this world that would make her agree to putting chains on her ankles. The woman just nods in silent understanding.

"You will still need handcuffs. I am going to remove this side from the bed. When I do, I need you to slowly move your hand to the other side so I can put it on your other hand. Then I will take the other one off," she explains, watching to make sure she isn't becoming overwhelmed.

Liz dips her head in agreement. She holds her hand as still as possible, trying to avoid any movements they may find threatening. After being chained to the ground, beaten and starved for god knows how long, they are still worried she will somehow overpower them. Anger stirs in her chest. How can anyone look at her and worry for their own safety rather than hers, she wonders to herself. This woman claims she is safe, yet still insists on restraints, all because she fought back when cornered. That sentiment alone makes her want to scream, to act like the monster they are treating her as, but that will only prove them right.

The woman removes the cuff and allows Liz to move at her own pace, placing her hand next to her other one. Just like the first, Liz stays as still as possible while she gets the cuff put back on. The woman moves on to the tubes protruding from her arms, apologizing when Liz hisses from the sting of the IV being pulled out.

"Can you stand? The morphine should be kicking in anytime now, it will help with the pain." She reaches behind Liz, trying to help sit her up.

Liz winces when the woman's hand touches her back, bits and pieces starting to come back from the events leading to this. She closes her eyes and tries to remember everything that happened.

She remembers stabbing a man in a mask then being thrown into a wall. She wouldn't be surprised if her entire back is one giant bruise from the impact, along with some broken ribs. After a moment, and a lot of pain, she manages to sit up fully. The woman helps guide her legs off the side of the bed. The second she stands, they buckle from the weight. Whole body screaming in pain, she wishes the masked man had just killed her.

"I'm going to call the guards back in. They won't hurt you, they are just going to escort you to the new room and get you settled," she says, sadness flashing across her face.

The woman knows something she isn't saying. Maybe she can't, or maybe she's just as evil as the rest of them. Liz starts to suspect this is a routine with all the new females they take—

bringing in the mean men just to have a kind woman come in and make things seem safe.

There is no point in fighting back, she is too weak, too frail after her time as a prisoner. Perhaps it's for the best, after all, Liz has spent her entire life fighting and it's only carried her from one shit show to the next. She nods her head and waits for the men to take her to her new prison.

CHAPTER 4

ootsteps echo through the empty hall as the two men towering over Liz lead her to a new room. She looks around, taking in as many details as she can. All she sees is the white walls of the small, narrow hall made bright by the harsh fluorescent lights. There is no sign of life anywhere.

Liz looks up, spotting the security cameras tracking her as they walk by. She reaches down, pulling at her tattered shirt, a sad attempt to save some of her dignity.

The two men glance at each other, sneering when they realize what she's trying to do. They slow to a stop in front of a set of doors, opening the one closest to them, and commanding her to go in.

She's frozen in fear, unable to step back into another small, locked room. One of the men shoves her, sending her stumbling forward. Once inside, she looks around, noting the small metal table with what looks like a metal handle jutting up from the middle and three chairs. Two of the three walls are bare, nothing on them but damage and rusted stains. The third wall is in better shape, holding a giant mirror. There is a small security camera in the corner next to the door, aimed right at the table in the middle of the room. It looks like a room straight out of a bad cop show.

One of the men instructs her to sit. She drags her aching bare feet across the cold floor, forcing herself forward. She gets to the table and gently sits, the cold metal biting into her, causing the bruises across her body to ache.

"Hands," one of the men snaps.

She gingerly lifts up her arms and sets her hands on the cool metal table. Tears well in her eyes. She has no fight left, even if she did, she is wildly out numbered. The other man wastes no time running a new set of handcuffs through the handle attached to the table. He roughly slaps the cuffs around her arms, leaving her confined to her seat. The first man leans over and whispers to the other before he leaves the room, slamming the door behind him.

"Stay quiet, someone will be in to deal with you soon," the man still in the room says before letting himself out.

Liz forces herself to take a shuddering breath. Two sharp breaths in, almost as if she had been crying and struggling to breathe, followed by a slow exhale. She read somewhere that doing this tricks the body into calming. She repeats this two more times. Her mind may still be racing, but her heart no longer feels as if it's going to explode. She drags her eyes to the mirror facing her, not recognizing the person looking back.

She has never seen herself look worse. Her long, black hair is nothing but tangles, grime, and dried blood. Once vibrant, green eyes are dull and full of despair where they sit above sunken cheeks. Cuts and bruises cover what she can see of her body. She has two a black eyes and a split lip. She can't tell if the injuries are from her fight with the masked man or from the daily encounters with her previous captors.

"Just fucking kill me," she says, putting her head on the table so she doesn't have to see her reflection anymore.

She has no idea how much time has passed when the door opens and a man and the woman from the other room walk in. She scans them over, trying to figure out who these people are. She guesses the man is in his late fifties, wearing an army green coat covered in different colored badges. The woman is about ten years younger, still looking out of place. She is too put together to be in the dingy room.

"Welcome to Fort Stryker," the man says, pulling out a chair and sitting down. The woman doesn't say anything, just slides into the seat next to him, a look of disappointment on her face. "We have a few questions for you about Dmitri and his operation."

The man folds his hands and puts them on the table, eyeing Liz like he couldn't believe the sickly woman in front of him was the one who stabbed a man twice her size.

Liz gives him nothing, just stares at the metal table, counting all the dents and scratches marring the surface. She wonders how many others like her have been held here, questioned and tortured even though they had no information to give. Her guess is too many.

"My name is Paula, we just have some questions for you. I will try to make this fast so we can get you some food, okay?" Paula says in a quiet gentle tone, not trying to startle Liz further.

"Before you start getting special treatment, why don't you tell us who the hell you are," the man says. Paula's lips purse, she looks as if she wants to reprimand him, but never does.

Liz drags her eyes up to meet the mans, seeing the determination in his eyes she quickly looks away.. Her body relaxes slightly. Unsure if it's the medicine kicking in or if she just knows it doesn't matter if she cooperates or not. She lets out a sigh, already knowing the outcome of the interrogation. Maybe this time they will kill her quickly instead of making her suffer. Liz focuses on her hands, twisting the small length of chain nervously, the soft clanging filling the silence.

"No," Liz says to them, steeling herself before continuing. She slowly drags her eyes back up to his. "Assholes like you don't care about my name, just what you think you can take from me. It's only a matter of time before you kill me, so why ask? Just take me out of here and put a bullet in my head. Save us all the trouble, because I'm not telling you shit," she says, laying her head on the table, hoping it's enough to make them leave.

"I will get the information out of you one way or another. You're not leaving this fucking room until I get it," he yells, slamming his hands on the table.

Liz startles, lifting her head back up to smirk at the man with the same attitude that got her beaten by her last captors. She couldn't stop it if she tried. Liz has never been able to control the need to antagonize men who treat her with disrespect, even when it results in blood and broken bones. With that, he gets up and storms out of the room. She never thought it would be so easy to make him show his true colors, but it's a relief.

"Scott!" Paula shouts, getting up to chase after him.

The door slowly closes. Liz only allows herself a moment before moving her head over to her chained hands and drying her eyes. Time ticks by, only the sound of boots scuffing and murmurs outside the door to keep her company. They must have guards stationed outside, and she's sure there is someone on the other side of the mirror, getting some sick enjoyment out of seeing her in this state. The door swings open and the man walks back in, taking his seat. Liz looks around, no sign of Paula anywhere.

"I think we got off on the wrong foot. I apologize for my outburst," he says. When Liz doesn't try to speak or acknowledge he returned, he clears his throat and continues.

"My name is Scott. I'm a General in the U.S. military, more importantly, I'm head of an elite special operations unit called Nemesis." He's clearly trying to get some sort of reaction from Liz with his willingness to share information. "We rescued you from the base of Dmitri Komarov, our current enemy number one," he says to Liz, making sure to emphasize she was rescued.

She keeps her head down, determined to ignore the man in front of her. After the way he's had her treated, she has no intention of allowing him to know anything she's been through.

"I don't know your role in all of this, but you have been in his compound for a while. He has kept you alive for a reason. I know you have some information on the way he runs things," he says before adding— "You also stabbed my best commander. I can have you locked away for the rest of your life, but if you tell me what—"

He was cut off by the door being thrown open with enough force to send it crashing against the wall. The sound makes Liz jump, her eyes snapping to the entrance only to see the masked man from her last cell storm into the room. Liz feels like the air is sucked out of her lungs, her blood running cold. He doesn't even glance at her, instead, he goes straight for the general.

"What the fuck are you doing with her?" he yells, and Liz swears she can feel the room shake.

The general is out of his seat in an instant, trying to go head-to-head with the masked man. If the general thinks he can intimidate him, he's an idiot. The man is at least a foot taller with an aura of "fuck around and find out" about him. Even with all the gear piled on his body, she can tell he is pure muscle, whereas the General looks like he hasn't seen a gym in the better part of twenty years.

"Stand down, Riley, that's an order," the man yells up at him. "She has information we need. If she was a prisoner why would she attack someone trying to save her? She's working for him. I will have her locked up for the rest of her life," he says, trying to hide the tremble in his voice. He glances to the door, hoping his guards will come in. He may be the General, but Riley is clearly feared by everyone around.

"She was fucking scared!" he yells, stepping closer to the man cowering in front of him. "I made myself clear, she is mine to protect, no one was to speak to her without me. That order was for you too general."

That's the first time Liz allowed herself to really look at him. His torn shirt has been replaced with a black-hooded sweatshirt. She eyes his shoulder. The image of his torn skin and blood dripping down her hand sends a wave of nausea over her. She doesn't bother letting herself feel any remorse. Maybe he was trying to save her, but she wasn't willing to risk it.

"You're out of line, soldier! You're going to throw away your career for a bitch who tried to kill you?" he shouts at Riley.

"Hey! Fuck you," Liz shrieks at him. Both men glance at her in shock at her outburst.

The air in the room stills. Everything goes quiet as Riley looks at his general. He takes a step closer, his broad chest almost touching the general's face, and looks down at him.

"What did you just call her?" he asks, too calm.

The general pales, taking a step back. He looks at Liz again, who's glaring back at him like she's rooting for Riley to tear his head off. The general made it obvious he fears the man in the mask, and that man doesn't want her harmed, for now.

The general finally turns and walks out the door, telling someone she can't see to make sure he gets his information, before finally scurrying away. Liz listens as his footsteps fade before finally turning her attention to the man who saved her.

His mask is different, only covering the bottom half of his face: plain, black carbon fiber extending just enough to cover his nose. Short and scruffy dark blond hair shows, and when she finally dares to look at his face, her gaze lands on the piercing caramel eyes staring back at her, softening when they meet hers.

She silently curses at herself for not looking away, her stomach turning to knots, but she can't tear her eyes from him. There is something in the way he looks at her, something safe. Her fight or flight instinct has always been impeccable, since the day a man approached her at a park as a child. She kicked him and ran away, listening to that instinct ever since. Now, it's silent, there is nothing, no sensation screaming at her that this man is dangerous despite knowing he is.

Another man walks in, Riley breaks their eye contact, his expression hardening back up. The man is a few inches shorter than his friend, wearing jeans and a tight t-shirt. He smiles at her before walking over to the table and sitting down.

Riley shuts the door, and he lets his shoulders finally relax. He strides back to the table, Liz analyzing his every move. He doesn't try to sit, instead stands on the other side of the table, arms crossed, his ominous demeanor making it hard for her to not shrink away.

"My name's Mike. Big guy over there calls me Mikey," the man says, pointing his thumb over his shoulder at Riley. He clears his throat, and before he can start to talk again, Riley steps around and sits in the chair next to Mikey.

"What's your name?" he asks, eyes softening when he looks at her. She doesn't know why, but she's compelled to actually answer. Maybe it's the fear he will make her life hell, or maybe it's how he defended her to the general, but she feels like she owes him something.

"Liz," she says, "or Lizzie, I guess."

"It's nice to meet you, Lizzie. I'm sorry it's not under better circumstances." Mikey says, smiling at her. She looks back down at her hands, quietly fiddling with the chain, not willing to give these men more than she has to.

"Do you have any family looking for you?" Riley asks. Seeing the pain flash across her face, he quickly changes the subject. "How did you end up in Dmitri's cells?"

"And how long have you been there?" Mikey quickly adds.

"Just try to tell us what you're comfortable with, you have my word that we won't push it," Riley says when she doesn't respond.

The torn shirt she's wearing slips down her shoulder as she adjusts uncomfortably in her seat. She can feel Riley's eyes lingering on her exposed skin but when she meets his gaze he quickly looks away. There is something in the way he carries himself that she can't quite read. Her eyes narrow, watching with caution as he slips out of his chair. He paces the room, needing to let out a little energy before he goes and finds the people who brought her here.

"Commander?" Mikey asks.

His pacing continues, seeming to get more and more angry about something he is keeping to himself.

"Riley!" Mikey tries again. This time he stops and looks at Liz. She's eyeing him with more curiosity than fear.

"Did anyone offer you a change of clothes?" Riley asks.

Liz becomes painfully aware of her clothing, or lack thereof, all over again. As she goes to cover herself, her arms are stopped by the chains holding her to the table, the loud bang of metal on metal filling the small space.

"Food? Water? Anything? Or did they just force you in here and chain you to the fucking table?" Riley shouts, causing Liz to jump. Not sure what will set him off, she shakes her head no.

"I think I made them mad," she whispers. Agitation is still plastered on his face, but when he looks at her his eyes are concerned, not angry.

"What do you mean?" he asks. He follows her gaze when her eyes shoot to the door, knowing they aren't truly alone.

"You're safe with us. Even if they could hear you, me and Riley wouldn't let them near you," Mikey says.

Liz nods her head in acknowledgement. "When I woke up, they were grabbing me. I screamed at them and some doctor ran in yelling about sedating me," Liz chokes out, each word burning her raw throat. "That woman who was here, Paula, she came in and yelled at them, and they seemed angry. After they brought me here she said if I answered them I could get food, but it just pissed that Scott guy off," she quietly adds.

"I bet that's why he made her leave." Mikey says, turning to Riley.

"Did they hurt you?" Riley asks, his tone pure ice. Her eyes flick back to the door and he gets his answer. Still, he waits to see if she will tell him anything.

"No," she says, unable to meet his eyes. "The big one pushed me in here and wasn't too gentle putting these on," she says, lifting her wrists. "But, that's all he did."

His eyes narrow on her wrists covered in small cuts, and where there aren't cuts, her skin is raw from cuffs. He looks at the table, seeing the smears of now dried blood sends him into a rage all over again.

"Mikey, watch her. No one comes near this fucking room until I get back," Riley says.

Mikey immediately stands and walks out the door, leaving just the two of them. Riley looks at her, opening his mouth to say something before deciding against it. He simply opens the door and storms out, leaving her scared and alone once again.

CHAPTER 5

Sometime later, Liz hears footsteps echoing down the hall. She sits back up, thinking the general was coming to try again, but the door opens to reveal Mikey and Riley. Liz doesn't know whether to be scared or relieved.

They walk into the room, and she notices Riley has his hands full: a plate and bottle are in one hand and what looks like clothes in the other. Her eyes linger on his hands. His knuckles are red and cut like he had just been hitting something. Riley tosses the clothes onto the table and carefully sets down the plate and bottle of water.

"Can you move your hands enough to eat?" Riley asks, looking at Liz staring at him.

Not wanting him to see how scared she is, she rolls her eyes before quickly raising her arms a few inches off the table, the metal snapping her hands back down.

"Does that answer your question? Even if I could, I'm not eating that," Liz manages while staring Riley down. "If you want me dead, you can tell your little boss to stop being a coward and come kill me himself. This little good cop bad cop thing won't work on me."

"Oh, she's feisty. I like her," Mikey says, slapping Riley on the shoulder before turning back to Liz. "You look like you haven't eaten in weeks, and you've been shivering since we walked in the room," he says. "At least drink some water, maybe put on some real clothes so you're not freezing."

Liz is taken aback by the genuine concern in his voice, but she's not going to give in so easily. She knows she can't trust these men, no matter how much her gut screams at her she should.

"If you think I'm going to put on a little strip show for you, you're as stupid as your boss. I would rather die than be humiliated like that again." She looks Riley in the eyes. Her words must have struck a nerve because she could have sworn she saw sadness flash in his eyes. She sits back in the hard metal chair, trying to hide the wince as she does.

"I think you're forgetting, I've already seen all of you, love. Who do you think carried you out of that shit hole?" he says, looking her over. Liz looks away, hoping her cheeks don't give away how embarrassed she is. "But I understand. We're not trying to put you on display."

Riley turns to Mikey and whispers something she can't quite make out. He quickly gets up and leaves the room. No more than a few seconds later, the mirror on the wall is illuminated, revealing a small room full of boxes with Mikey in the middle.

"He's going to guard the doors, and I'm going to cover that camera. You," he says, turning to look at her, "will be changing into those clothes."

"And if I refuse?" she asks timidly.

"I'm not going to force you into anything. The choice is yours and yours alone."

Uncomfortable with his kindness Liz lifts her hands again, hard enough to send a fresh wave of pain up her arm. She rattles the cuffs to remind him she can't move.

He lets out a big sigh, his patience growing thin. "If I take the cuffs off, are you going to attack me again?" he asks, almost playfully.

"Why don't you come over here and find out," Liz muses, her tone lighter than before.

He looks at her, his eyes lighting up with the challenge. If she didn't know better, she would think he's smiling under that mask.

"I'm going to un-cuff you, and you're going to behave," he says firmly, watching her, challenging her to be a smart ass now that he's offered some amount of freedom.

She opens her mouth to say something before thinking better of it and snaps her jaw closed.

He steps toward the table, pulling something out of his pocket, leaning over her with a small key in hand. She hopes he doesn't notice when her hands start to shake in anticipation. She can't remember the last time she was allowed to be unrestrained.

Riley slides the key into one cuff and slowly turns it until Liz hears the soft *click* of the lock releasing. She holds back her tears, she won't let these men see just how close to broken she is. The second lock *clicks* free, but she doesn't dare move her hands.

Riley moves to the other side, gently opening the cuffs and pulling them off, setting them on the table between the two of them.

"I'll keep them off as long as you don't try to attack me again," he says, his voice playful again.

Liz looks at her tender skin. She almost forgot what her wrists look like without hand-cuffs. She peers over at Riley, quickly averting her eyes. Something about him is different from the other men who had taken her. He almost seems like he genuinely cares about her safety.Her mind starts to race.

The sounds of Velcro and boots stepping across the floor pulls her from her thoughts. Liz looks up; Riley's back is to her while he pulls his vest off, slightly wincing from the pain in his shoulder. She takes the opportunity to pull her hands off the table, rubbing at the soreness in her wrists, checking on the bruises and raw skin.

"Camera's covered, you're safe to change," Riley says.

She looks around, making sure there are no other cameras. Then checks the glass window, making sure the room is still empty. When she doesn't see anything watching her, she quickly pulls the tattered, oversized t-shirt over her head and drops it next to her. Wearing nothing but a ripped pair of panties, she takes a deep breath before quickly removing those too as she fights to keep the panic from setting in. She is naked in a room with a man who can easily overpower her if he wants. That terrifying thought sends her heart racing.

"Might be a little big, but it's the best I could do in the middle of the night," Riley says to her, his back still turned.

Liz picks up what looks to be a man's undershirt and pulls it over her head, sucking in a sharp breath from the pain. As soon as the shirt is on, she's hit with the smell of sandalwood and cardamom. She quickly grabs what's left: a pair of gray sweatpants, clearly meant for someone much bigger than her. She slides one leg into the pants, then the other, but once she has them pulled up, they immediately fall back down. She looks for a string or anything to tighten them, finding nothing. Liz simply rolls them down, hoping the extra fabric bunched around her waist holds them up enough.

She slides back into her chair, making sure it makes a noise as she does. Riley lowers the vest and sets it on the floor before turning to see her putting her hands back near the anchor on the table, waiting to be re-cuffed. His anger reignites seeing her submit like that. Liz looks up at him, noting the anger in his eyes.

"Thank you," she whispers, thinking he's angry with her for not saying it sooner.

His eyes soften, and walks to the door, opening it for Mikey to rejoin them. Mikey looks at her, noting her hands and how she is waiting patiently to have her handcuffs replaced. He glances at Riley who gives his head a small shake.

"Please eat," Mikey practically begs, sliding the small plate of food toward Liz. "You haven't eaten since we got you here."

"No," she says to him, ignoring the pleading in his tone.

She pushes the plate back to the men in front of her. Without hesitation, Mikey grabs the sandwich, taking a large bite before throwing it back onto the plate and sliding it back. Liz just looks at him, eyes wide with shock. She opens her mouth to say something, but he holds up one finger, silencing her while he chews. He swallows, then grabs the water, twisting the cap off and tossing it onto the table. He pours a big swig of the water into his mouth and sets the bottle back down, pushing it to the other side of the table. "We told you the food is safe, darlin... Eat," he says before quietly adding— "Please."

"Aren't you going to put the handcuffs back on?" Liz asks, hands still in the middle of the table next to the anchor. They both look at her with a mix of amusement and pity.

"Are you going to stab me?" Riley asks, stepping close to where she sits. "Again," he quickly adds, amusement dancing in his eyes.

"I haven't decided yet," Liz says, batting her eyelashes at him.

She knows the men are growing tired of this back and forth with her. It's only a matter of time before they snap and show her just how horrible they are. If only it was as easy to make them snap as it was the general. At least if they treat her how she's expecting, her anger and distrust will be justified.

"Okay, how about we make a deal," Riley says, sliding into a chair. He wants to get this over with so he can finally get some sleep. "If you eat, I will tell you whatever you want to know. Where we are, who we are, anything."

She takes a second to think this over, looking between the two men. What if they are really trying to help her? Something in her soul is screaming at her to trust Riley. Just being in his presence sends a wave of calm over her. She thinks to herself, before reaching over and picking up the sandwich, she brings it to her mouth and takes a small bite before setting it down and looking back at Riley. He stares right back, neither one willing to look away first. Mikey clears his throat in an attempt to break the tension.

"So, what do you want to know?" Mikey asks, growing a little concerned about the stare off happening beside him.

Riley finally breaks and glances at the food still sitting in front of them. Liz smirks, proud of herself for not letting him intimidate her. Little does she know, he would have stared into her eyes all day, but she needed the win, needed to be stronger than him.

"What's with the mask? You had one when you attacked me in the cell, too" she says, taking another bite of sandwich, embarrassed by the small moan that escapes. It's been so long since she's had real food, not thrown onto a dirty floor so she can "eat like the animal she is".

"Really?" Riley says, raising his eyebrows. "We give you free reign to ask anything and that's what you want to know?" He wanted to add that he didn't attack her, but the split in her lip has him keeping his mouth shut.

"There's more," Liz responds. "But you said anything. I want to know why you hide your face. Are you that ugly?" she asks, taking another bite of the sandwich. She chews, glaring at Riley, waiting for his answer.

"Quite the opposite, love," Riley says. "I wouldn't be able to get anything done around here if women could see my face," he adds, winking at her.

She swallows the food, not satisfied with the answer, and crosses her arms, leaning back in her chair. She asked a stupid question on purpose, to see how they would answer. If they aren't going to hold up their end of the deal, then she's done. Seeing the change in her demeanor, Mikey shoots Riley a look.

"He wears a mask because of what happened when he was held prisoner, but that's not my story to tell," Mikey says.

Liz sits back up, curiosity peaked at his words, but senses this isn't something to push. She takes another bite of food, carefully thinking of her next question.

"Are you guys ga—"

"No," Riley interrupts. "Just partners on the team. He watches my six, I watch his, everyone stays safe,," he adds.

"Do you have any real questions? Or are you just going to keep fucking with us?" Riley asks, watching Liz.

She knows her time is running out, so she thinks about what she really needs to know. She finishes her food, and takes a deep breath, readying herself to ask the questions she doesn't want to know the answers to.

"Are you really in the U.S. military? If you are, why was your general threatening me? I couldn't fight off one of you, let alone two, even if he didn't have me restrained. And what's the deal with the guy who took me?" she asks, her voice much quieter.

She can sense the hesitation in the men sitting across the table. A realization settles into their expressions.

Riley leans over and whispers something to his partner. Mikey gets up and excuses himself before walking over to the door and leaving. Once the door clicks shut, Riley sits up straighter and really looks at Liz. Even now, with the little attitude she's had with him, he can see the fear in her eyes.

"Technically, yes, we're really in the military. This is Fort Stryker in Nevada," he says, looking around the room. "Myself, Mikey, and a select group of others form an elite special operations unit overseen by the general you met earlier." He looks anywhere but at Liz, not wanting her to see the anger behind his eyes at the mention of his boss.

"The man who took you is named Dmitri Komarov, leader of a Russian terrorist organization who has been attacking the U.S. for years now but keeps managing to escape our team. As for why he took you, that's what we're trying to figure out." He finds her watching him, trying to figure out what his deal is, and if he can be trusted. He catches her eyes flicking to the door, no doubt waiting for Mikey to walk back in.

"I sent him away, I thought you might be more comfortable talking to just one of us. Maybe if you can tell me what happened, we can figure out why he was keeping you."

She thinks on his words for a minute, trying to discern what he truly wants to know. He makes it sound like Dmitri should have just killed her long ago.

After a prolonged silence, she reaches for the water and takes a small sip, pacing herself, uncertain of when they will allow her another. Finally, she looks at Riley and asks— "What do you want to know?"

CHAPTER 6

That was the last thing Riley expected her to say. He thought she would fight him about it, or worse, go silent again. Riley takes a moment to think about what they need to know. He watches as she takes a sip of the water, another small moan escaping her lips, and her eyes flutter closed. He looks away, not wanting her to see how much he enjoyed seeing her like that. He shakes off the thought, feeling like a monster for being attracted to her after everything she has been through. He adjusts in his seat and looks over at her.

"I know you aren't involved in Dmitri's operation, but he kept you around for a reason and you did stab me," he says, looking down at his shoulder, "so now the general is convinced you're working for Dmitri. He thinks you're a threat."

"I stabbed you because you're a stranger who came into my personal space. I didn't know what you were going to do to me," Liz quietly states. She inhales deeply, her thoughts spinning as she glances at the hidden wound she gave him. She can't help but feel bad for attacking the man who tried to help her, even if she didn't know that's what he was doing at the time. "I'm sorry," she says to him. "For stabbing you," she adds, guilt plastered over her face.

"Don't—you're right. You were alone and scared. Shit, I punched you, knocked you out, and brought you here, left you alone with those two assholes, and the general. You should probably stab me again," he says, amusement dancing across his caramel-brown eyes. "Just tell me what happened," he adds with a small chuckle.

Liz looks around nervously, taking a few more breaths before finally calming her nerves enough to start. "That's the thing. I don't know what he wanted with me. I was grabbed by two men outside of a bar and woke up in that dirty ass cell," she says, hands starting to shake. "The day I woke up, he came into my cell and told me he would make me pay for 'humiliating' him."

Liz abruptly stands, pacing around the cold room before continuing. She takes a deep breath, steadying herself. The small concrete room suddenly feeling too much like the cell she was held in for so long.

"At first he would come into my cell and ask if I was ready to apologize, and when I wouldn't answer, he would hit me. If I tried to fight back or hide, he would have someone hold me down, nothing I couldn't handle, reminded me of my childhood honestly."

Riley stays quiet, tracking her with his eyes: back and forth, across the small room, then back again. He forces himself not to react to what she tells him, knowing he will only scare her more. So, he sits, waiting for her to start again.

"He did that for twenty seven fucking days, thats when he came in and told me he's tired of waiting for me to come around." She still paces the small room. "You don't need to know what he did, or tried to do, but it was the first time I really understood the severity of what I got myself into. Everything up to that point was fine, it sucked, but it wasn't any worse than I'd had before. That day I fought with everything I had left," she says, stopping her pacing and sliding to sit on the hard floor. She pulls her knees to her chest, pain etched all over her face.

"After that, he made one of his guys chain me to the floor, to make sure I couldn't fight back again, but that was the last time I saw him. He would let his guys come in and do what they wanted to me. Hit me, kick me, cut me, whatever they felt like that day. Then they started drugging my food, making me sick." She looked up at him before averting her gaze, not wanting to let him see the tears filling her eyes.

"When I started refusing the food, they just stopped bringing it. For days at a time, they would starve me until I was so hungry I would eat whatever they brought." She glanced up, seeing the hate behind his eyes. She started to shake, knowing what would come next after someone looked at her with that much anger.

"I didn't mind being starved, really. At least when they withheld food, they wouldn't come in at all. They made sure to get me as weak as possible before they came back." It was then she finally let the tears fall. She sniffles and quickly wipes her face, attempting to stand.

"How long were you starved this time?" Riley asks, his voice pure ice. He gets up and walks to where Liz sits, each step echoing around the small room. He crouches in front of her and asks again—"How long?"

"How long have I been here?" she asks. "It was five days, I think, before you came in."

Five fucking days without food or water, seven counting the two days she's been here, he thinks to himself. He needs to get her out of the room and get her some real food. Not surprised she can't stand back up.

He stands and extends his hand to her. She looks at his arm, eyeing it like she's waiting for it to strike. Liz needs to make a choice, trust this stranger and hope he truly does want to help her, or shove everything she feels so far down she's numb to the world and let them end her life. She slips her hand into his and he helps her up.

He walks her back and helps her sit in the chair again.

"Thank you," she whispers before snatching her hand back.

He sits on the table, something telling him he needs to stay close. Just then, a cracking noise cuts through the silence. He looks over at his vest and groans, sliding off the table to pick up his radio.

"What?" he says.

The radio crackles. GENER... AL... IN... BOU... D the voice cuts through the static.

"Shit," Riley says, walking back to the table, roughly sitting in the chair closest to the door.

"The general is on his way, and he's going to be expecting information," he says, voice dripping with annoyance. He glances at the door, not knowing when it's going to open. "If I don't tell him something, I don't know if I can stop whatever he has planned for you." He turns back to see her trembling in her seat.

Out of time, the door handle turns and the general steps in, slamming the door behind him. He ignores Liz and simply asks Riley—"What did she tell you?"

Riley stands and stalks to where the general is waiting. They talk, too quiet for Liz to make out anything they are saying. She looks just in time to see the general crane his neck around Riley so he can peer at her. His eyes widen when he takes in the sight of her sitting there, wrists free of restraints, and fresh clothes on her body. He shoves past Riley, storming toward the table. Liz cowers in the chair, waiting for the blow that doesn't come.

"What the hell is she doing unrestrained?" he shouts, turning on Riley. "That woman is working for our number one enemy, and you let her go free!" he yells as he grabs the handcuffs still sitting on the table.

Riley sees Liz, legs pulled into her chest, her too thin arms wrapped around them, making herself as small as she can, shaking in anticipation of what she expects to come next. He forces himself to calm, not wanting to be the reason for her fear and steps around the general, putting himself between the two of them.

The general eyes Riley, noting his back turned to Liz and his face starts to redden. He extends the cuffs to Riley. "Put them back on, Commander," he says, shoving the handcuffs into Riley's chest. "That's an order."

Riley grabs the handcuffs and tosses them across the small room. He turns to the general, who looks like he's going to have an aneurism. The general starts to sputter but Riley cuts off his ramblings.

"She hasn't done a damn thing to deserve being in hand-cuffs." Riley shouts, unable to control his anger any longer.

"She stabbed you!" he yells.

"She was scared!" Riley shouts right back.

"You're going to deny a direct order from your commanding officer to protect Dmitri's whore?" Spittle flies from the general's mouth.

Suddenly, it feels like the air has been sucked out of the room. Liz hadn't realized how many little noises there were until it all stopped. Her heartbeat quickens in her ears. She struggles to breathe. She doesn't know Riley, but he has been fiercely protective of her. Whether it's genuine, or a ploy to gain her trust, Liz doesn't care. Right now, he is the only thing keeping her safe.

"Careful, General," he says, an eerie calm taking over. "Your authority has limits, and it stops where my tolerance ends."

The general swallows hard, taking a step back.

"You ordered me to get information, and I followed those orders. She wasn't involved in his operation, and I won't allow anyone to treat her like she was."

General Scott lets out a big breath, not expecting Riley to rush to her defense. He looks around Riley again, noting Liz hasn't tried to move in the time he's been in the room. He turns back to Riley and smirks. "What are you going to do? Keep her with you at all times? Are you willing to put your position on the line to prove she's innocent?" He sneers, thinking he's won.

"If that's what it takes, then yes. Mikey and I will supervise her at all times," he says, silently hoping his friend isn't going to be too upset. "Sir," he adds with a smirk hidden under his mask, noting the shock on the general's face.

"Fine, you gentlemen can play babysitter to that—woman. I expect eyes on her at all times," the General says, choosing his words very carefully. "But if anything happens, you will be stripped of your rank and I will get the pleasure of handing you a dishonorable discharge" He makes it a point to add on the last bit, a desperate attempt to land a final blow. He turns and strides for the door, before reaching for the handle, he turns back to Riley. "Get her to your quarters before the whole fort wakes up, and make sure she stays there until I say otherwise."

With that, he opens the door and walks out. As soon as the

general's gone, Riley lets out a sigh and hangs his head. He only allows himself a moment to breathe before facing Liz.

"Well, you heard him. Are you ready to go see your new prison?" he asks, joking. Seeing the sadness on her face he adds— "Sorry, not funny. I'm going to try to get you home as soon as I can."

Reluctantly, Liz gets up and follows him out the door.

CHAPTER 7

When they turn the corner into the narrow hall leading to the housing unit Mikey is perched against the wall waiting for him. He places his thumb onto the small pad next to the handle and waits for the three clicks. He opens the door, and gestures for Liz to enter, Mikey keeping a safe distance behind. He goes slow, giving her time to go into the dark room on her own terms. Riley sees her hesitation, hears her breathing quicken like she's on the verge of a panic attack.

He doesn't let her get to that point before he reaches around her and flips a switch on the wall next to the door, illuminating the small, apartment-like room. She takes a single step and looks around the space, taking in every detail.

There's a small couch in the middle of the room with a kitchenette behind it, a small wooden table and three chairs against the back of the couch, and a window on the wall opposite the main door. The last wall has a TV mounted between two doors. Three beeps chirp out as the door gets locked from the inside.

Riley clears his throat, pulling her from whatever thoughts are running loose in her head. Striding over to one door, he turns the handle, and swings it open.

"This will be your room for now," he says, walking into the room and flipping the light on, Liz follows close behind. There isn't a lot to see: a small bed, a nightstand, closet, and another door.

"It's not much, but it's better than the cell Scott wanted you tossed in," he says, walking to the other door and opening it to reveal a small bathroom, a sink and toilet on one wall, shower on the other, and a second door directly across from the one they are standing in.

"We have to share a bathroom, but both doors lock from the inside," he says, engaging the lock.

Instead of opening the other door leading to his bedroom he ushers her. His focus shifts from showing her around to making sure she is handling the tour alright. He knows the feeling of adjusting back to a regular life after going through some shit, Riley can only hope she will place even the smallest kernel of trust in him to help her.

Riley steps out of the room and walks to where Mikey has made himself comfortable on the couch and turns on his heels. "I have access to all these rooms, locked or not, so please don't do anything stupid." He starts for the door, stopping just as he steps out. "Oh, and one more thing, the doors and windows need my code to open them. If you set that alarm off an entire military base will end up at my door, so please just behave and let me work on getting you out of here." The door closes slowly behind him, leaving Liz to poke around the room.

Riley walks over and plops down on the couch, entirely too exhausted to deal with his friend. His head rolls back, resting on the plush cushions of the couch, eyes drift close while a sigh escapes his covered lips.

"Do you think she's going to be okay?" Mikey asks, getting up and heading for the kitchen. He opens the fridge and digs around. Finally finding what he is looking for, he grabs two beers, handing one to Riley before plopping himself back down.

"I don't know. She's been through a lot. I ran her prints while I was getting patched up and couldn't find any record of her. It's like she doesn't exist." He takes the beer before sliding his mask down to take a long sip. He sighs again, knowing he will need to get more information from her before the general will allow her to leave.

"I mean, if anyone is going to help her through what happened it's you. Does she have any family? She's gotta have someone out there looking for her," Mikey says, watching as Riley shakes his head. "How the hell is there nothing? You think she could be working for him?"

They look at each other, wondering if they made the right choice in trying to help her.

Riley walks over to the door leading to his room. "I need to wash this blood off, keep digging. I'm taking a few days off to keep an eye on her. Let me know if you find anything," Riley says before walking into his room and shutting the door. He strips off his ruined gear and tosses it into a messy pile on the floor.

Thinking about what he just got them into, he paces over to the bathroom. Seeing no light on, Riley walks in and turns the shower on. He checks the temperature of the water, making sure it's warm before stripping off his mask and briefs and getting in. He turns the knob and lets the scalding water run over him, washing away the dirt and dried blood. He makes it fast in case Liz needs to use the bathroom, although he has a feeling she won't even attempt it if she hears life anywhere in the small apartment.

He steps out, wrapping a black towel around his waist, going right to the sink to brush his teeth. Once he's finished, he quickly leaves the bathroom, pulls a new pair of briefs out of his small dresser, and puts them on before collapsing into bed. He lays face down for a while, unable to keep his thoughts from drifting to the woman in the other room. He hadn't even given her a toothbrush.

With a loud groan, he forces himself up and over to the closet, his large footsteps too loud in the empty apartment. He digs up an extra toothbrush, then walks back to his dresser, grabs another undershirt and pair of sweatpants before walking to the bathroom. He sets the supplies in a pile on the sink, hoping she will understand it's for her. Satisfied, knowing she will at least have a change of clothes, he walks back to his bed and climbs in, sleep taking hold in an instant.

When the sun rises, Riley lightly knocks on Liz's door. When she doesn't respond, he opens her door and quietly steps into the room. He looks at the bed, expecting to find her still asleep, but the bed is still untouched. He starts to worry, scanning the small room, not seeing her anywhere. What if she left in the middle of the night and he didn't hear her? No, he would have heard. Years of combat and near constant attacks had made him hyper-aware of any noises, and if he did miss it, the blaring alarms would have woken the entire base.

Making quiet, controlled steps around the room, Riley scans everywhere to find her. Hidden in the corner, blocked by the small bed is Liz, curled into herself on the floor. If it wasn't for the shallow rise and fall of her chest, he would have thought she was dead. Unsure of what to do next, he walks over, hoping his footsteps are enough to alert her to his presence. When that doesn't work, he gently nudges her with his booted foot.

Liz startles awake, shooting forward, hands up like she's ready to fight whoever dared wake her. Her breathing rapid, she scans the room, recalling her surroundings. She looks at Riley, her eyes wild and filled with a mix of panic and anger.

"What the fuck is your problem?" she says to him, taking a wobbly step to where he stands. Riley throws his hand up in surrender, smiling under his mask, happy to see she still has some fight left, even if she is just fighting him.

"Sorry," he says with a soft chuckle. "I knocked, but you didn't answer. I wanted to make sure you weren't dead." He takes a step back as he lowers his hands. He looks her over, trying to make sure she's okay. His eyes dart to her wrists, then back to her face, lingering on her split lip. Guilt hits him like a truck. She had been through so much, and he attacked her like every other man she had encountered in the compound.

"Mikey is here, with food," he says. "He's going to stay with you while I'm gone." He turns to walk away but stops himself and turns back. "I'm not going to force you to be around us, but I hope you will at least get some food." Turning back, he walks through the door, shutting it softly on his way out.

The second the door *clicks*, Liz rushes over and locks it, more for her peace of mind than keeping them out. She leans against the door in an attempt to steady herself. Feeling like an idiot for using the small amount of energy she had to run across the room. She slides her body to the floor and lays back down, hoping the men in the other room won't come knocking again.

After twenty minutes of waiting for Liz to come out, Riley gives up the small kernel of hope he had. He gets up, grabbing his gym bag. He crosses the small living room and punches in a code, disengaging the first lock.

"Just give her space," he says to Mikey, turning the little knob of the second lock. "She looked pissed when I went in," he adds before unlatching the third and final lock.

He pulls the door open and steps into the bright hallway, the heat of the base instantly making him break out in a sweat. He looks back at the door with the woman behind it, before his door swings shut.

Mikey lets out a sigh, getting up and walking to the small kitchen. He reaches into the cabinet above the sink and takes a plate out before deciding against it and puts it back. He goes into the cabinet next to it, hoping there are still some paper plates from the last time Riley fed their team. He moves a few things around, and right next to a stack of red solo cups, he finds the small stack of paper plates. He pulls both out and starts piling on food. Not knowing what Liz likes, he just puts a little bit of everything before grabbing a cup and filling it in the sink.

He walks across the room and gently knocks on her door, hoping he doesn't startle her. "Hey, darlin," he says to the door. "I know you're not going to come out, but I brought food," he says, praying she will answer him.

He stands in the silence for a minute before walking over to the table and picking up the plate he made. He walks back and sets the plate on the floor, then the glass of water. He knocks one more time, knowing she won't answer.

"Riley is gone, so it's just us. I'll leave it next to the door if you change your mind." He wonders if she can even hear him. In one last attempt to get her to open up, he says, "I'm going to step out to make a call, don't die while I'm gone."

Liz listens to Mikey plead through the door, wondering why they care so much about her eating. She knows they will just lock her back up for not knowing anything about the man they are looking for, so eating will only slow down the inevitable.

She listens to his steps as he crosses the room, straining to hear anything else. One lock, then two. She pushes against the floor, forcing herself to sit. Once she hears the third lock, she reaches for the door. She pulls it open just enough to see the plate of food through the crack, closing the door quickly before Mikey can return. Liz lowers herself back onto the floor, falling asleep to the sound of her stomach rumbling. She wakes some time later to the sounds of talking. Pressing her ear to the door once again, she listens.

"How is she?" Riley asks.

His eyes go right to the door, hoping Liz is still alive. He tosses his gym bag into his empty room.

"She didn't touch the food I left, so I'd say not good," Mikey responds, watching Riley from the couch as he walks over to Liz's door, lifting his hand to knock before deciding against it.

He walks back and throws himself onto the soft cushions of the couch, letting out a deep groan.

"If we can't get her to trust us, the general will have her thrown in a damn cell with his guys watching her 24/7," he says to Mikey, still watching her door as if he can see her behind it.

"You got her to talk to you last night," Mikey says. "Just do that again." He stands, pulling his phone out of the pocket of his jeans. 5:18 p.m. Mikey starts for the door. "Scott's not going to let this arrangement last for much longer. If she stays quiet, he's going to use that. We both know he will turn her fear into an admission of guilt then let his men do what they have to do to make her talk. You need to get her to tell you something," he says to Riley before opening the door and walking out.

CHAPTER 8

Liz listens to the men go back and forth about her; she can't stand them talking like she's not in the other room. Unable to take their pity any longer, she scoots herself up onto the bed. Sitting on the plush mattress doesn't feel right, like she's not supposed to feel comfort anymore. She throws her head back in frustration before sliding herself back onto the hard tiles. It's not fair and deep down she knows it. Her whole life had been one, long disaster. Sure, there were amazing moments sprinkled in, but for the most part it was Liz vs the world. Trauma seems to follow her like a lost puppy.

The way Liz sees it, she has two options; let what happened consume her and give into their demands, inevitably ending up locked up once more, or, deal with the horrid things she's been through with a 'fuck you' attitude and find a way out on her own terms. The beauty in trauma is there is no one way to handle it. Some get lost in it, unable to separate what they experience from the reality of getting away, some turn to drugs and alcohol to forget, some even take care of themselves, seeking professional help to overcome what has happened to them. Liz on the other hand, has been perfecting her own way since child-hood, a chaotic mix of bullying herself into thinking things aren't as bad as she thought, sarcasm, and having a fight or fight instinct, rather than fight or flight.

Liz knows she needs to be stronger than whatever tries to break her, that is the only way she manages anymore. Being stronger means she gets to win and in the end she always wins. There has only been one battle where she didn't come out a victor, even still, she is going to make sure it ends her way, a small victory. She can get through this, Liz just needs to keep reminding herself she made it out. They may be holding her hostage again, but what she just endured for god knows how long was worse than anything they can do to her now. Even being held by a Russian terrorist she didn't break, she fought back until the very end.

Her eyes drift closed as she replays their words over and over again. That dickhead of a General won't let her go until he knows she's not involved, and she can't prove she wasn't while they don't trust her, they won't trust her if she won't talk to them, she won't talk until *she* trusts *them*. It's obvious now Riley is telling the truth about trying to help her, the question is, is she going to let him? *Mikey had said Riley was also captured at some point, he knows exactly what is going on in my head, is that the reason he's trying so hard?* Unable to fight off the sheer exhaus-tion from the last few days, her thoughts slow, letting her drift into a fitful sleep. She didn't sleep long before the nightmares started.

She jolts awake, clasping a hand over her mouth to keep from screaming. She remembers all too well what happens if she screams. Her wild eyes scan every inch of the room, her delicate body covered in a thin layer of sweat, breathing heavy. The phantom weight of handcuffs transports her back to Dmitri's encampment. It takes a few minutes for her to remember where she is, not in her old cell chained to the floor, but in her new one. Thoughts shift from memories of what happened to her own mental battle of convincing herself it wasn't that bad and the sooner she gets over it the sooner she can get her life back on track. She can't stay, as long as she is not on her own she will never be able to move on, suddenly the harsh realization of what she needs to do settles in.

"Great, just fucking great," she groans to herself before standing back up, pacing circles around the small room. The small apartment wasn't what she was expecting when the general said she would be staying in his quarters. Picturing a warehouse house type set up, with rows upon rows of neatly made bunk beds, Riley's apartment came as a shock. It was nice, almost cozy, with a much too familiar smell that put her on edge. He had very few decorations and it was clear he didn't spend much time living there. Trying to remember every little detail, she anxiously picks at her cracked nails while she continues her circles.

The rooms are small, with only one window in the whole place. Although the kitchen more than likely has knives, there is no doubt in her mind that Riley removed them. The moment she saw the window her composure almost flew out of it. It had been so long since she was allowed to see the outside world, even if it is just a sliver. Her cell had a small barred window at the top of one wall. She was never able to see anything out of it, where they chained her she couldn't even see the sky, but rays of sunshine always told her when a new day in hell started. The door had beeped after they went in, followed by soft *clicks* of locks engaging. He could have been lying about the alarms, but a nagging feeling in her stomach tells her it was the truth. She is locked in, for now. There is only one thing she can do. Liz is forced to push everything away and play nice with Riley. She does not need to trust him, but he needs to trust her, and there is only one way to gain that. A new found determination fills her and she walks to the door, knowing her only way to freedom is sitting outside the room.

CHAPTER 9

"Hi... Sorry," Riley says, putting his hand back down, reluctantly backing away from the doorway. "Everything okay?" His deep voice is full of concern.

Looking up at him like he said something crazy, Liz takes a small step back. "You mean, other than being forced to stay here until some asshole in a fancy coat decides I'm not a threat to him? I'm fucking peachy," she says, flashing him a fake smile.

"At least you have enough energy to be a smart ass," Riley says, rolling his eyes.

He knows he should feel bad for antagonizing her but making her mad is the only time he's seen life in her eyes since she attacked him in that cell. He does a slow sweep over her body, once again checking to make sure she isn't hurt, or more hurt than she has been.

Liz wraps her arms around herself, all too aware of the thin white shirt that doesn't leave anything to the imagination.

He tracks her arms with his eyes, quickly looking away when he realizes what she's doing. "I was just coming to try and convince you to eat something," he says, noting her change in attitude. He turns and walks back into the living room, wanting to give her the space she needs. "One of my men is on the way with some food," he says, glancing at the time on the tv again. "You like burgers?"

"Yeah? I guess," she says, more a question than an answer. Liz takes a deep breath, counting to five in her head before stepping into the small living room, the brightness from the window causing her head to throb again. She peers over, spotting a white box attached to both halves of the window, silently wishing Riley had lied about the alarm.

"I..." She stumbles over the words, trying to say the right thing to not upset him. Liz tries and fails to stop herself from blurting out the only thing on her mind. Blowing out a breath in frustration, she finally blurts— "Why are you being nice to me?"

"Do you want me to be a dick instead? Force you to do what I want?" He sits on the couch, pulling out his phone and typing something into it before sliding it back into his pants pocket.

Something about the way he said that sends chills through her body. "You know that's not what I meant!" she says, voice raising slightly. "I just don't get why you're going through all this trouble. Why not just let that little guy in the jacket lock me up? Better yet, why not just kill me yourself since everyone thinks I'm involved with what's his name. Seems like it would save everyone a lot of trouble."

Riley throws his head back and lets out a deep laugh. Liz just glares at him, wondering what she said that can possibly be that funny. He looks over to see Liz watching him, her green eyes simmering with anger.

A sharp knock cuts through his laughter, pulling their attention from each other. Riley gets up from his spot on the couch and walks over to the door, cracking it open. As he bends down to pick up the bag of food, he can still feel Liz's eyes on him. He turns, confirming his suspicions that she's still watching him.

"Easy, love. I'm not laughing at you," he says, walking over to the small table behind the couch and setting the bag down. "I've just never heard anyone refer to the general as... what did you call him?" He rips the bag open and starts pulling out things in foil wrappers, plopping one at each seat at the table. "Oh yeah... that little guy in the jacket."

Done with the conversation, Liz turns and storms back to her room.

"Wait," Riley calls after her.

She stops, giving him an undeserving chance to continue with whatever bullshit she knows is about to come out of his mouth, reminding herself that she can't shut down if she's going to gain his trust.

"Look, I'm sorry, okay?"

Arms crossed, Liz waits for him to finish the apology she knows she deserves.

"I shouldn't be fucking with you after everything you've been through, but that's the only time you seem to care. When you're not mad at one of us, you look like you're just waiting to die"

He finishes putting out the food before going and grabbing a few things from the small refrigerator. Riley sets them both on the table and sits down, ripping into his burger. Immediately, Liz is hit with the scent of meat and fried deliciousness.

"It's been three days, that means eight since you've had food. Please, eat something," he says, looking at her, eyes pleading. He kicks the chair from under the table so it slides out.

She isn't sure if it's an invitation or an order. Despite her best efforts to ignore him, Liz takes a few steps toward the table.

She watches him with genuine curiosity as he takes a large bite of the burger, noting something off about him.

"Is your mask different again?" she asks with a puzzled look, letting her empty stomach guide her decisions.

Riley puts his food down and looks at her. Having no idea how to answer, he silently sips his beer.

"You look like you're trying to be Batman." She pulls the chair the rest of the way out and gently sits, her whole body aching with the movement.

"I'll take that as a compliment," he says smirking, picking his food back up and taking another bite.

"Don't. Batman's trash."

Riley nearly chokes, quickly hitting himself in the chest a few times to make the food in his mouth go down. He drags his eyes up to hers, full of amusement. Before he has the chance to come up with a response, she opens her mouth and asks—

"Is that why you have some weird hero complex? Because you idolize him?" She asks.

"Oh that's just mean. Has it crossed your mind that maybe I'm just a soldier, trying to do what I swore an oath to do and keep you safe? There is no hero complex, just a man trying to make sure you don't starve to death."

"If I do eat, what are you going to make me do in return?" Her melodic voice is laced with fear.

"What makes you think I want something in return?" he asks, trying not to appear hurt that she would think he's expecting some sort of payment.

"Men like you always want something in return," Liz says, barely more than a whisper.

It's then he realizes she's willing to do it, she's willing to give him anything he wants in exchange for a meal and basic human decency. He looks over at the broken woman, reminding himself it's only been three days since he's rescued her. No one knows the extent of what those bastards did to her, and she doesn't know he would never take advantage of someone like that.

"Love, you've never met a man like me. Those men, the ones who get off on hurting women, the ones who expect you to bow to them for giving you the smallest amount of kindness... those men fucking fear me." Fire rages in his deep amber eyes. "I'm never going to ask for anything I wouldn't give myself. I just need answers. I told you, you're safe. I've already dealt with a few of the men who hurt you, and if you ever feel like telling me more, I will deal with the rest."

Liz watches him, not able to tell if he's being honest, she simply waits.

Riley reaches back into the bag and pulls out a small paper box full of fries. That gets her attention. He holds the box out to her, hoping and praying she takes the food. It's been so long since Liz has eaten real food, she decides whatever he demands in return will be worth it. She doesn't give herself time to change her mind before grabbing a fry and popping it into her mouth.

Riley watches Liz eat, her eyes fluttering closed, wondering how long it's been since she had food she actually enjoyed. He sets the box down and slides it over to her, hoping she will eat the rest.

"I have an idea, since you're willing to be out here," he says, her eyes snapping to his, knowing it was coming.

"Nothing like that, love. Just an answer for an answer." He waits for her to object, when she doesn't say anything, he continues. "I'll answer any questions you have, if you answer some of my questions."

"I already told you; I don't know anything about that Russian guy you're all obsessed with. All I know is I pissed him off and suffered for it." She pops another fry into her mouth.

"I know," Riley says, taking a large swig of the beer in his hand. "But maybe if we know more about you, we can figure out what he wanted with you. Your choice, I won't force you into anything."

He continues to eat his food, giving her time to think about what he said. Letting her decide if she's willing to place the smallest amount of trust in him or not. He glances over when he hears her toying with the wrapper on the burger.

"Okay," she says, noting the instant relief on his face. She stays silent, not moving as she waits for him to ask his first question.

"How old are you?"

"32... You?" Liz responds.

"35... What's your full name?"

"Elizabeth Daniels." She thinks for a minute, debating on what she should ask. "Same question." Her eyes narrow, glaring at him, fully expecting him to refuse an answer.

"Riley Corson. Why ask personal questions you don't care to know the answer to?"

"That counts as your question. You obviously worked hard to hide your identity. I mean c'mon, you're wearing a mask in your own room. It would be stupid to not to know your real name, if that actually is your real name. I may need to see some I.D" she responds, shrugging her shoulders.

Hoping her smart ass response doesn't upset him enough to take the food back, she watches as Riley reaches into his back pocket and pulls out his well worn leather wallet. A small plastic card gets plopped down in between them while Liz takes a too large bite of her burger. Her face twists in disgust.

"Oh come on, it's not that bad of a picture," Riley teases

"Are there tomatoes on this?" she asks, quickly chewing and swallowing the bite in her mouth. Frowning, she sets the burger down and pulls the hidden tomato slice out, tossing it onto the wrapper.

Riley chuckles, shaking his head, out of all the things she's been through, this is the one that gets her? A damn tomato? He thinks for a second, popping in the last bite of his cheeseburger.

"That counts as your question," he says. Liz opens her mouth to object. "And before you waste another one, yes, I am pretty proud of that," he says, a smug grin returning to his face.

"Ass," she mutters to herself. She plucks a fry out of the box and throws it at him.

Fear covers every inch of her face as soon as the food left her hand. It's been so long since she was treated with any sort of respect, she took too much comfort in the sheer normalcy of it all and slipped up. Something about Riley is oddly comforting. Maybe it is the lightness in his eyes, or the way she can tell he's smiling, even with his mask, but instead of actively forcing herself to stay on edge, she let herself exist for a moment, and it's going to get her killed.

She watches in horror as it hits him in the chest before falling into his lap. He stares at her in disbelief as she shrinks back in her chair, cowering for what comes next. Riley slowly reaches down and picks the fry off his lap, eyes never leaving hers, and tosses it in his mouth. Her jaw falls open, in utter disbelief he would simply eat it and not punish her.

"You still owe me an answer," he says before she can over-think anything. He gives her a second to take another bite, now that her food is tomato free. Hoping his next question doesn't ruin everything, he leans back in his chair and asks— "Do you have a family?"

The pain on her face is almost enough to make him end the whole thing, let her eat her meal in peace. He knows if she has family, he can contact them and force the general's hand to let her go, but the tears well up in her emerald eyes and make him wonder if it's worth it.

She tips her head back, closes her eyes and steadies herself. "A husband and daughter."

Silence fills the room; Riley isn't sure how to keep going after that. He got the answer he was hoping for, but something about it seems... off. He continues watching her, breaths deep and intentional. He knows she's trying to pull herself out of something. It's painfully clear to him that this isn't her first time wrangling her emotions. She takes another breath in through her nose before blowing it out. She reaches up and wipes away the tear that has slipped out, hoping he didn't notice.

"What happened to you yesterday? When you came back your hands were red and bloody" she asks in an attempt to forget the last question.

Riley looks down at his hands, still red. Happiness swells in his chest to see her eating. How is he supposed to explain what happened without scaring her? She already thinks he's just as bad as all the other men she has encountered.

"I told you; I dealt with some of the men who hurt you. I didn't expect you to notice," he says with a slight shrug of his muscular shoulders. A sad attempt at being nonchalant.

She eyes him cautiously, trying not to look scared.

"Does that bother you?" he asks coyly.

"No... I just thought you were the good guy, but you beat up who I assume are your men, just for being mean to your prisoner."

"I never said I was a good guy. There is a reason even the general is afraid of me. I do what I have to do to the people who deserve it and protect the people who don't. They disobeyed direct orders and got less than they deserved for it." Riley takes another long sip of his nearly empty drink.

Liz looks away, thinking about everything he just told her. Part of her wants to be thankful. He stood up for her and made sure they won't hurt the next person. The other part is scared that at some point, she will face the same consequences for attacking him.

"Is what your friend said true? About me not existing?" she says, noting the shock on his face.

He had no idea she had been listening when they were talking. He sits up straighter, trying to figure out how to explain what is going on.

"Yes and no. I ran your prints, and nothing came up. When you told me your name, I tried that with your prints and still nothing. I didn't have high hopes with just your first name, but still, your prints should have matched a birth record. You obviously exist, but someone worked damn hard to make it seem like you don't. Unless you gave me a fake name,"

"Oh," is all she can manage. Not sure what to say, she had a life, a long time ago, but still a life. There should be photos, a marriage license, birth record of when her perfect baby girl entered the world, but it's all just gone. That's not the answer she was expecting him to give. Maybe she imagined it all, maybe being held prisoner damaged her more than she thought.

She's so entranced in her thoughts she doesn't notice the locks beeping and a man stepping into the room.

"What the hell are you two doing?" Mikey says, startling Liz.

She jumps, frantically looking around for something to use as a weapon. She looks at Mikey, the look on his face, and schools her face back into a calm expression, before looking at Riley and saying— "That counts as yours, you know."

Riley knows she cheated, but he lets her have it, curious to know what she's going to ask him next. Mikey walks to the table, not trying to spook Liz any more than he already has.

Riley watches her, eyes never leaving Mikey. Not sure if she is okay with him being here or not, Riley turns to Mikey and explains what they have been doing. Mikey slides into the chair between them and Liz wraps her arms around herself, trying to not let her discomfort show.

"If you really are trying to help me, will you teach me to fight? Like really fighting. What if he comes looking for me? If he finds me ... I don't want to be helpless again." Liz blurts before she loses her nerve.

They both look at her in shock. Riley isn't sure what he was expecting, but it wasn't that. He looks at Mikey who is smiling like an idiot, clearly pleased with her question.

"I... Uh... Maybe?" Riley manages. "The general will be pissed. I know he will insist you're hiding something if you believe Dmitri will come back for you. It might take longer for us to get you out. You will need to stay hidden around base, but I guess it wouldn't hurt. I'll have conditions."

Liz lets him finish, wondering what he means by "conditions". He has been good to her so far, but it's only been a few days. The thought of what he may demand causes her heart to race. Seeing the panic in her eyes, Riley is quick to explain.

"You need to take care of yourself. No more begging you to eat. If you're going to train, I need to know it's not going to kill you, got it?" he says, observing her as she overthinks every word, nodding her head. "Alright, your turn, next question."

"Is it really safe to shower? Or are you just waiting for me to be naked and vulnerable so it hurts more?" Liz asks, unable to look at the men at the table, not ready to see how angry they are.

"You're safe, love," Riley says as gently as he can. "One last question," he says, knowing this one may very well ruin all the progress they've made. He needs to know, it's been all he can think about since he heard the way she spoke to the general.

"Why do you antagonize the people who want nothing more than to see you dead? You said you have a family, but since you've been here, you've literally told us to kill you. I just don't get it."

A mix of rage and hurt fills her eyes. He knew it was a bad idea, but he was too stupid to let it go. Fighting back tears, she stands so fast the chair falls over, the crash deafening in the quiet. She doesn't say a word, just storms to the room, slamming the door behind her.

Liz stomps over to the bed and lays down on the plush mattress, letting all the tears she's been holding back fall. She sobs deeply into the pillow, waiting for one of the men to come punish her for what she did. She waits, not caring about the blows she knows will come, until she has no more tears left to cry, and sleep claims her.

CHAPTER 10

A soft knock on the door sets Liz on edge. She quickly sits up, rubbing the sleep from her eyes, swollen and red from crying. She glares at the door, not ready to face the man on the other side. He knocks again. Thinking it's Riley waiting to dish out her "consequences" after the outburst, she stands and slowly opens the door only to see Mikey on the other side.

"It's after noon, darlin. We let you sleep all day. Time to eat," he says to her with a smile.

"You let me sleep for an entire day?" she asks, shocked.

"You needed the rest. Now, you need to eat, go shower, and I'll make you a plate." He turns, leaving Liz standing in the doorway, dumbfounded.

Liz closes the door, re-locks it, and double checks it's locked before walking into the small bathroom. She makes sure both bathroom doors are locked, jiggling the handles three separate times to be sure.

In the mirror above the sink she can see her hair is a matted mess, the bruises on her neck and shoulders fading to a disgusting shade of yellow. The fresh bruises on her face have bloomed into a bright purple and the split in her lip is starting to heal. She pokes at her lip, wincing as she does. Blowing out a breath, she turns to the shower, reaching in and turning the handle. The shower clunks and water sprays out of the shower head. She keeps turning the handle, hoping to get it hot enough.

Once steam starts to form behind the glass door, she strips out of the borrowed clothes she's been wearing for days and trembles. She hates how scared and vulnerable she is, heart racing, eyes darting around the small room, waiting for someone to come in and watch her. She shakes off the thoughts, checks the locks one final time and tries to focus on getting clean.

Liz lets the burning water wash over her. With her head leaned forward, she watches the mix of blood, dirt, and water swirl around her feet. Quickly remembering she has nothing of her own, she grabs the first bottle of soap she sees and squirts some into her hand. She scrubs her hair as hard as she can stand, nails digging into her scalp, trying to get the dirt and blood out of her hair. When she can't take anymore, she moves on to her body, lathering up her hands, rubbing the soap all over, and getting herself as clean as she can as fast as she can.

She steps out of the shower, looks around, and spots a black towel on a rack leading to Riley's room. Snatching it, she gets just dry enough to put clothes back on. She wraps her soaked hair in the towel and bends to grab the clothes she has been wearing when she sees a folded pile on the sink. She stares in disbelief. Riley must have left them for her. Tears spring to her eyes when she sees the black shirt sitting on top of the pile instead of a white one. She grabs the clothes and puts them on, then it hits her why the apartment smelled so familiar.

She picks up the old clothes and puts them up to her nose, breathing deeply. Her nose crinkles and she throws the clothes back down. It's hidden under the smell of being worn by her for days, but there is still a faint scent of sandalwood and cardamom, just like the clothes she just put on. The tears she was fighting back start to fall, touched he would give her his own clothes.

She grabs the toothbrush, ripping open the box, needing to focus on anything but the man whose clothing she's in. She globs some toothpaste on the brush and starts scrubbing.

When her mouth finally feels clean, she takes down the towel from her head, looking at the tangled mess in the mirror. She looks around for a brush, anything she can use to tame her hair. When she finds nothing, Liz rakes her fingers through her hair in an attempt to get the tangles out. Realizing it's no use, she picks up the old rubber band and reties her hair. Before leaving, Liz cleans up after herself. The towel gets rehung where she found it, and she folds the dirty clothes before placing them in the small hamper.

Mikey is sitting at the table eating lunch when Liz finally leaves her room. He looks over at her, not expecting her to actually come out. She looks around, a look of disappointment flashing across her face when she doesn't see Riley anywhere. She may not trust him, but he has been kind to her and she has spent more time with him. Mikey gives her a knowing smirk before getting up and pulling out a chair for her.

"Still wearing Riley's clothes?" he says, confirming the thoughts she had in the bathroom as she walks to the table and sits.

"Is there something else I should be wearing?" she asks. "I can go put on the scraps I came with if you want."

Mikey stifles a laugh, just happy she's not a walking corpse like the last few times he's seen her.

"I'll talk to Riley about getting you some clothes," he says, eyeing her bare feet. "And shoes," he adds.

Mikey stands and pulls out his phone, punching in a number before walking to the other side of the living room, just far enough for Liz to not hear him. She sits at the table, quietly picking at the small pile of food he set in front of her.

"Hey! What's your shoe size?" Mikey yells from across the room. She stops chewing and looks at him with a puzzled look.

"Um, seven, I think," she says, going back to her meal.

She watches as Mikey keeps talking to whoever is on the other end of the phone. He hangs up and walks back over, sitting on the couch in front of Liz. She glances at Riley's bedroom door, wondering if he's in there. Mikey is quick to notice where her attention goes.

"He got called to the general's office," he says to her with a smirk.

She quickly averts her eyes back to the food in front of her. "Thanks, I was so worried," she mutters sarcastically into her food.

"Joke all you want, but I see how you are with him. You think I don't see your guard slip when he's around you? I can see it in your eyes, you know you're safe with him." He chuckles again, lying down, propping his feet up on the arm of the small sofa.

"Or, heres a wild fucking thought, I was locked up by men who beat my ass for breathing wrong, and i'm trying to avoid that happening again," she shoots back, ignoring the truth in his words.

"You know damn well he would never do that." He states, leaving no room to argue. Mikey doesn't shout, doesn't get up to defend his friend or intimidate her, simply states what she already knows.

"Okay, so Stockholm syndrome then," Nothing could explain why she feels the way she does, but Mikey is right. Some tiny piece of her knows she is safe with Riley, some inexplicable feeling she refuses to acknowledge. He lowers himself back down with a huff. Mikey knows she is lying to herself, but it's up to her to admit it.

"You still mad at him?"

Liz thinks for a minute. Was she ever really mad at him or just mad at the situation? She picks up her empty plate and brings it to the trash, dropping it into the black bag, thinking of how she can answer him.

"That question was fucked up," she says to him, unsure of what she should be doing now that she's done eating.

"It was," he agrees, "but he just wants to understand you so we can help."

"Maybe I don't want his help. Maybe I just want to leave." She walks into the living room, looking at the empty seat on the couch, and debating if she should sit or not.

"Doesn't matter, darlin. The general is a huge dick, and Riley is your only shot at getting let go," he says, watching her pace. "That's why he's with the general, the second you said you have a family he's been pushing to find them so we can get you home. I think that's the only way the general will agree to let you go."

She stops her pacing, looking at where he's lounging on the couch. "Is Riley going to be in trouble if no one can find my family?" she asks, a small pang of guilt going through her.

Mikey eyes her as he sits back up. "That depends, did you lie about having a family?"

She stays silent for a while, wrapping her arms around herself before silently walking to her room. She stops, taking a deep breath, and forces herself to say one more word before closing her door.

"No."

CHAPTER 11

L iz groans as she stands, reluctantly walking to the door, and silently kicking herself for knowing just how Riley knocks.

She cracks the door and drags herself back to sit on the edge of the bed, she needs to know what he will do. The little voice in the back of her head screams at her to trust him, but she isn't sure she can trust that voice any longer. The first day he brought her, he made it abundantly clear he can go in and out as he pleases, but will he?

"Can I come in?" she glances over at Riley nodding slightly, trying not to show the pure shock of asking for consent. Gentle footsteps make their way in, stopping just inside the doorway. The comforting scent of his cologne dances around her room. She looks away and waits, ready for him to yell at her.

Riley closes the door behind him in an attempt to give them some privacy. Liz notes that his mask changed again. This time it's just a ski mask with only the bottom half of a skull. He's in the same black hoodie from the other day with the hood pulled up. She wonders to herself what the deal is, wishing she had asked the other day instead of storming off.

"I brought you dinner," he says, trying to keep things as casual as he can, sure she is still furious with him. He takes a step further into the room, smiling to himself for seeing her finally on the bed instead of the floor. It's a small step in the right direction. For now it's all he can ask for.

"I talked to the general, and the good news is he agreed to let us teach you to fight. I think he's hoping you will kill one of us in the process," he says, hoping it will get some sort of reaction from her. "The bad news... is he's insisting we confirm your story, find something about you on some sort of database before we can let you go. Hopefully it will only take a few weeks."

"Weeks? You're going to keep me prisoner for weeks?" she shouts. She stands from her spot on the bed and storms to where he's standing, glaring up at him like she wants nothing more than to stab him again.

"Look princess, unless you gave me a fake name and have been lying this whole time, someone wanted you gone and did a hell of a good job of making that happen," he shouts back, instantly regretting it. He takes a steadying breath and a small step back to give her space and says—"I'm doing everything I can to help you, but it's going to take some time."

She doesn't back down. There is just something about him she can't explain. Deep down she knows he won't hurt her, even if she did snap and scream at him.

"Are you fucking kidding me? I was chained to a floor and beaten every fucking day only to be taken by you and locked in a new fucking prison by some asshole with a complex, and you think I would lie about who the fuck I am?" she practically screams, taking a few steps in his direction until they were almost touching. Her fists are balled at her sides, fighting the overwhelming urge to swing. "And I'm not your fucking princess," she snaps, emerald eyes burning.

He doesn't respond, but simply takes a small step forward, forcing their bodies together. She sucks in a sharp breath, looking up at him. Her senses are overloaded at the closeness, the smell of him, the warmth of his body, the rightness of it all is too much. Unsure if she wants to push him away or pull him closer, Liz focuses on not doing anything she may regret.

When she doesn't back down, he lowers his head until his masked mouth is next to her ear, and whispers— "Come eat dinner, princess." He turns on his heels and walks out of the room, leaving her standing there, mouth open, to process what she's feeling.

She takes a moment to compose herself, trying to shake off the goose bumps Riley left her with. She silently counts to five before striding for the door and walking out. When she enters the main room, Mikey and Riley stop talking and look at her, a dumb smile plastered on Mikey's face. She eyes them, wondering what they could have been talking about.

"What's up with him today?" she asks Riley, pointing her head at Mikey. Riley looks over at him, seeing the smile on his face.

"He's just hungry," he says, pulling containers of food out of a box.

Liz walks to the table, her eyes catching on the big bags sitting on the couch. She ignores them and sits at the table, the smell of the food making her salivate. Mikey and Riley join her and start making plates. Riley loads up with grilled chicken, mixed veggies, and roasted potatoes before he sets it down in front of her.

"Um...Thank you?" she says, eyeing him, wondering why he's being so nice after she yelled at him in the room. There has to be more to it. Never in her life has she been lucky, certainly not lucky enough to be held hostage by someone who truly wants the best for her.

Liz and Mikey eat in silence while Riley does something on his phone. She keeps peeking over at him, wondering why he isn't eating. When they finally finish, Liz picks up their plates and brings them to the trash. She hopes being helpful will keep Riley from being too mad at her for the outburst. The guys just watched her in awe, cleaning up was the last thing they expected. When everything is picked up, she quietly thanks them for the food and heads back to her room.

"Not so fast," Riley says, causing her to stop and turn around. She looks at him with a mix of confusion and fear seeing the excitement in his eyes. "Those bags are for you. And before you say anything, you don't owe me shit," he says before she can say what he knew she was thinking.

She walks back to the couch, looks at the bags, and then back to Riley. Suspicions rising, Liz wraps her arms around her slender body, not willing to risk touching anything.

"I just guessed at what you needed, check the bags and let me know what else you want me to grab," he says, walking over to the fridge and taking a beer.

Liz peeks into the first bag: a shoe box and some basic toiletries. Tears spring to her eyes. She moves a few things around in the second bag, spotting a few pairs of leggings and a hooded sweatshirt. When she gets to the third, the first thing she sees, sitting right on top, is a tiny red ball of lace. She reaches into the bag and pulls it out, holding it up for him to see. "Really?" she asks, dropping it back into the bag.

Mikey lets out a sharp whistle, clearly impressed with Riley's selection.

"I don't know what you wear. That's just what I pictured

you in," he says, shrugging his shoulders. Liz's eyes widen at the confession while her stomach turns to knots.

Mikey slinks toward the door, not wanting to witness whatever is about to happen. Riley sees him reach the door; he puts his beer down and turns to beg him to stay, but before he can stop him, Mikey opens it and slips out. He lets out an audible groan and leans against the counter, knowing she is going to hate him more than ever.

"Excuse me? You think about me... in my underwear?" Her face reddens.

He pushes off the counter and walks over to her, getting almost as close as he had before, her whole body grows warm while her legs grow weaker. Stockholm syndrome, she reminds herself. She has not been around a kind man since the last time she has seen her husband, and her body is doing a piss poor job of reacting to being around one.

"I can't help it. Every time I see you wearing my clothes..." He reaches out and tucks a stray lock of hair behind her ear, letting his hand linger.

Liz lowers her head, blushing. She should be pulling away from him, but the warmth of his hand on her skin spreads over her body. She stands frozen.

Riley slides his finger down her jaw, tucking it under her chin. He gingerly tips her head up, forcing her to look at him. "I can't stop myself from thinking about what you're not wearing under them."

Liz's big green eyes go wide, looking up at him full of lust she will never admit to feeling. She takes a step back, clearing her throat, not ready to think about the feelings this man stirs up in her. She keeps telling herself it's just Stockholm syndrome. Repeating it over and over again, hoping if she says it enough it will become true. It has barely been a week and she is his prisoner. There's no way she can actually be attracted to him, then he goes and says things like that while looking at her like he wants to make her forget every horrible thing she has ever had the displeasure of experiencing.

"I'm sorry... I shouldn't have—"

"Thank you, but you really didn't have to do all this," she says, cutting him off and gesturing to the bags. She wants nothing more than to never speak about what just happened. The pain in his eyes was obvious during his apology, he feels like a monster. Realization washes over her. Monsters don't feel like monsters. When a man is truly evil they thrive on their victims fear, they don't feel bad for it. She starts getting choked up so she says the only thing she can– "I would have been fine figuring something out for myself."

"If you want to keep wearing my clothes, you can just say that. I'll never tell you no." He teases to see her blush again. Riley looks away, cursing himself under his breath. There is something so captivating about her, he can't help himself.

"You're still an ass," she says, smiling at him, the first genuine smile she's had in years. "But thank you, I promise I'll find a way to pay you back."

"I'm not letting you pay me back, love." Riley reaches over and picks the bags up, swiftly carrying them to her room.

Liz quickly follows. As soon as they step over the threshold of the room, Liz becomes painfully aware of how small the space is. She shifts on her feet, waiting for Riley to leave.

"We start training in the morning, so make sure you're ready," he says and walks out, closing the door behind him. The room suddenly feels too empty with him gone, so Liz does the only thing she can, and starts unpacking the bags. All the things Riley bought her were pretty normal: black leggings and plain shirts, sweatshirt and some basic hygiene things. She takes the things for the bathroom and brings them to the door, setting them on the floor just outside the room.

She gets to the last bag, dumping it onto her bed: a couple sports bras fall out along with a pile of underwear and a small silk robe. She picks up the robe and hangs it in the small closet. Liz picks up the underwear to put them in the dresser, trying not to think about the fact Riley picked them all out for her, when she finds a small bottle of red nail polish.

Her heart starts to race, painfully aware she shouldn't be feeling the emotions stirring within her. Liz tries to focus on anything else, but the thoughtfulness of that one small bottle sends tears rushing to her eyes. She grabs all the soap, finds the towel she used that morning and walks into the bathroom. Liz puts the soap in the shower and sets the towel on the floor before making sure the door to Riley's room is locked. She turns the shower on boiling hot before stripping and getting in.

She attempts to move quickly but ultimately decides to take full advantage of everything Riley bought her. She plucks the pink razor from the floor and shaves every hair from her body. She starts to think back to being locked up, when one of the "doctors" would come in and wax her for no reason other than humiliation.

She takes a deep breath, sliding the razor up her leg, relishing in how good it feels to do something because she wants to. She finishes and moves on to her hair, washing it twice. Liz quickly lathers up her new loofah and scrubs her body, the scent of vanilla and cashmere filling the small space. Once she is done, she climbs out, instantly missing the heat.

Liz wraps up in the towel and gives herself a once over in the mirror. Her eyes are slowly fading into a sick yellow hue instead of deep purple and her split lip looks like nothing more than a bad scratch. She rushes back to her room to dry off. She rifles through the drawer she stuffed all the underwear into and pulls out a random pair, stuffing her legs into them before putting the robe on and cinching it tightly around her waist. She's amazed at how soft and luxurious it feels against her finally clean skin. Wrapping her hair in the towel, she goes back into the bathroom, making sure to grab all of her things from the shower.

The next hour is spent brushing three months' worth of tangles from her hair. She managed to finish just as a headache set in. Liz quickly pulls it into a French braid, surprised when the end reaches her lower back. When she is satisfied with what she has accomplished, she heads back to the bathroom, her feet pattering across the floor. She was about to open the door, just wanting to brush her teeth before bed, when she hears the sink turn on. She glances down at her body, only clad in a pair of panties and the silky robe. Not wanting Riley to see her like that, she walks back to her bed and crawls in. She let herself enjoy the feeling of the soft, plush mattress for only a minute before beginning to overthink everything that happened.

Every word, every look, every touch they exchanged replays over and over again like a bad movie, sending her into a deep sleep.

CHAPTER 12

Liz wakes up feeling better than she has in a long time. Between the refreshing shower, the full night's sleep, and all the food given to her, she feels ready to put a plan into action. She is excited to start training, which will get her closer to the men holding her captive. She reminds herself that they may treat her well, and it's easy to slip into feeling comfortable, she is still their prisoner. Liz sits up, arms raised above her head, bruising healed enough to finally stretch.

The sharp knock from the door across the room causes her to jump out of bed. She quickly walks over to the door and throws it open, peering up at Riley. She follows his eyes down to her body. The loose robe nearly exposing her chest sends a wave of panic over her. She slams the door in his face, thinking it's only a matter of time before he comes in after her. She grabs some clothes and quickly gets dressed. Shocked at how well they fit.

She buries her embarrassment and channels the person they want her to be. If she has any intention of getting out she needs to push everything down. She has been hurt by too many men, endured too much at their hands. If nothing else, she is strong and has plenty of practice ignoring her feelings and pushing on like nothing happened. A fake smile spreads across her face as she prances back to the door.

"Damn," Mikey says with a low whistle. "I knew you were hot, but I didn't expect you to be this hot."

Riley stares daggers at him before going back to his cooking, not happy with his friend's shameless flirting.

"Thanks, sweetie," Liz says, practically skipping over to Riley at the stove. His jaw drops, having no idea what has gotten into her. She leans on the counter next to him— "Good morning," she says with a smile, batting her eyelashes up at him.

"Is that all I needed to do to get on your good side? Buy you things?" Riley asks, looking over her. Mikey was right, he realized, she looks amazing. A week of meals and hot showers brought some of the color back to her cheeks. She no longer looks so sickly. Something stirs in his chest at the sight of her, all cleaned up and acting like a person, not just a corpse going through the motions.

"Rude," Liz says, pushing off the counter and sitting at the table. "That's why you're my favorite," she says to Mikey with a wink.

"HA!" he barks, looking at Riley. "I'm the favorite." He beams with pride as he joins Liz at the table.

"I'm sorry, princess," Riley says, flipping the eggs he's frying. "Good morning." He loads up a plate with food and brings it over, placing it in front of Liz. Trying to shake the guilt she's feeling, she quickly thanks him.

"Maybe this will make you like me more, I have therapy sessions set up for you starting tomorrow."

"Oh, um, no thanks. I don't do therapy," she says, forcing herself to start eating.

"What do you mean you don't do therapy? You can't go through everything you did and not talk to someone about it." A deeply concerned Mikey says.

"Well when you cry about being raped and your therapist says it seems like you would be better off dead, it kind of makes you never want to do it again," Her shoulders slump, really not waiting to have this conversation. Liz knows they mean well, no one could have known that she doesn't trust therapists and her reasons why.

"Again, I won't force you into anything, but therapy can really help after something traumatic." Riley says, wanting to push the matter more, quickly thinking better of it.

"And being raped wasn't traumatic?" Liz sneers, "I will get through this the same way I have gotten through everything else in my shitty life, with my winning personality and can-do attitude." If her eyes rolled any harder they would tumble from her head.

They finish breakfast in silence, unsure of what they could possibly say to one another. Liz excuses herself to brush her teeth, when she comes back, Riley is nowhere to be seen. She tries and fails to hide her disappointment.

"Ry had some work to take care of. I'm in charge of training today, darlin." Mikey reaches for the door and undoes the three locks. Liz cranes her neck hoping to catch even the smallest glimpse of the numbers being punched in. Holding it open, Liz steps outside, the Nevada heat making her sweat. Mikey leads her down the narrow hallway, just as empty as the first time they brought her in.

She doesn't see another person during their short walk to the main door, just more doors on either side. Mikey opens the main door leading outside and Liz almost runs to get through it. For the first time in months, she is outside, and she can't even enjoy it because the sun hasn't come up yet.

Liz looks around, trying to take in as much of the small military base as she can. Even the smallest details will help if she's planning to escape. The door leads to a small parking lot with not much beyond it. The whole base is surrounded by a giant, concrete wall, guard towers every fifty feet or so, and right in front of her, across the parking lot, is a large metal gate, presumably to keep their enemies out, and her in. She makes a mental note to ask if it ever gets opened.

"Ready?" Mikey asks, getting in a few stretches. "I'll start you slow for now; we will just start with running the perimeter of the housing unit twice and walk it once to cool down." He takes off, sending Liz running after him, trying to keep up.

He looks behind him to see Liz throwing herself onto the lawn where they run, fighting to catch her breath. He turns around and jogs back to her. "You good, darlin?"

She looks up at him, desperately trying to catch her breath. "Do I... look... okay?" she says in between gasps. "I thought you were teaching me to fight?"

"How are you gonna fight if you can't even run?" he asks through a laugh. "It's been just over a week since we found you. I know you felt great after some sleep and food, but that's only because your body was deprived for so long. We need to work on building muscle and gaining stamina or you will be winded after a few swings."

Mikey reaches out a hand and she takes it, letting him pull her up. Liz thinks over each word he said. It all makes sense, how will she ever get free if she can't even jog around a building? As long as they continue to treat her the way they have, it won't kill her to build strength, biding her time. She stands, breathing finally steady, and starts again, this time at a much slower pace, more power walk than jog.

They stay silent the whole time they walk, when they finally reach the parking lot by the door for the second time, they slow to a relaxed pace. Liz fights to catch her breath, not used to this much physical activity. Every muscle in her body is screaming at her to stop. They continue their walk, not speaking to each other, Liz just silently observing. She makes a mental note of all the other buildings. Three large ones off to one side, and what looks like two airplane hangars to the other with parking lots and small fields sprinkled in between. Lots of places to hide once she finds a way out of Riley's apartment, assuming the whole place isn't swarmed with soldiers.

"Ready to head back?" Mikey asks, heading for the glass door.

She nods her head and follows him, feeling like she can finally breathe when she steps inside the cool hallway. She follows Mikey back to the room, surprised to pass a few people on their way. Each one goes out of their way to avoid looking at her. She wouldn't be surprised if word of whatever Riley did to the two men who escorted her got around, making everyone wary. It's better to know now that they won't help her when she escapes. Stepping into the apartment, she finds herself looking for Riley again, a little disappointed when she doesn't see him.

"He'll be happy to know you were looking for him."

"I wasn't looking for him," Liz snaps, a little harsher than she meant, still refusing to think about whatever feeling she gets in her chest at the sight of Riley.

"I'm going to shower." She walks to her room and closes the door behind her.

She gets into the shower, warm water washing away the ache in her muscles. She lowers herself onto the floor and just sits, allowing herself to enjoy the small luxury of hot water. Liz starts to think about her escape. It will never work if she doesn't get herself in shape, and fast.

Right now she is only allowed so much freedom, and being watched makes for a horrible escape. She runs through everything she can do in the privacy of her room. If she can be quiet enough: pushups, sit ups, crunches, or even just pacing in circles will help her build stamina. A weight lifts off her shoulders. When she is alone, she will spend all her time doing simple workouts. Any time spent with one of the guys her focus will be on gaining trust, doing whatever she has to in order to get it. Top priority is figuring out if the alarms are real, and if they are, she needs the door code. It will take time, being patient will be the hardest part. Liz smiles to herself, knowing soon enough she will finally be able to do what she has dreamed of doing for so long.

CHAPTER 13

It has been a month since Liz was saved and three weeks since she started training. The same routine every day: wake up, run, breakfast, hide in her room secretly working out until lunch. After lunch is hand to hand training with Riley. Then dinner, another secret workout, shower, collapse into bed. Every day for three weeks. The guys showed surprise at how fast her body adjusted to its new physical demands, having no idea about the extra work she was putting in.

The more she allows herself to open up around Riley and Mikey, the more Riley is willing to leave her alone while he and Mikey are busy. She doesn't let that time go to waste. Once Liz knows there are no cameras watching her, she gets to work trying to find where Riley keeps his weapons. By the third time being left alone, she stumbles upon a small gun safe tucked under the couch. She has spent every day since trying harder to see Riley put his code into anything that has one as an option. She makes a mental note of what numbers he uses, hopeful she can have it figured out soon.

Liz routinely asks about the general and his plans to let her go, but they just tell her it's going to be a few more weeks. She tries to wait it out and be patient, but she can't take it any longer. The more she's around them, the more she questions everything. They make her feel too comfortable, too cared for. She thought for sure they would switch up and start treating her differently the longer she is there but it is the exact opposite. Liz knows if she doesn't get out soon, she will lose her nerve and this will all be for nothing.

She glances at the clock next to the tv, knowing they will be back with dinner soon. She slides the gun case back under the couch and runs to her room, locking the door behind her.

"I'm back, princess," Riley yells, knowing the looks he's going to get for calling her that. The door swings closed and he walks to the small kitchen. Liz comes out to see him pulling containers out of a bag and setting them on the counter. The scent of garlic and marinara fills her lungs. Once all the food is out, Riley opens the cabinet above his head and pulls out two plates.

"I didn't think you even owned plates," Liz says to him, causing him to chuckle softly.

He sets the plates down and starts to open the containers, piling the food onto the first one. "Of course I do. I just thought you would break it and stab me with the shards... Again."

"I wouldn't have stabbed you if you didn't come at me first." Liz waltzes to the table and sits before quickly realizing she didn't make a plate. She moves to get back up, but before she can, Riley sets a plate in front of her, then a second. She looks down at the mountain of pasta, then to the salad on the smaller plate, eager to dig in.

"You haven't made a single plate since you've been here,

love," he says, carrying his own plates over to the table and setting them down across from Liz. "Don't try starting now."

Liz starts to blush, realizing he's right. She has always just had a plate full of food in front of her when she's ready for it. She looks over at him, his warm golden eyes meeting hers.

"Thank you," she says, smiling at him, wide and genuine. "For everything," she adds, avoiding the sinking feeling in her chest for what she knows is soon to come. Riley has been nothing but kind to her, taking care of her both mentally and physically, while juggling trying to get her home, deal with the general, and do his job. A job that is going to be ripped from him when she gets out. He will never forgive her.

Riley slides into the chair on the opposite side of the table, two glasses of wine in hand. He reaches over and hands one to Liz who is eyeing him like he's trying to poison her.

"It's safe," he says, noting her suspicions. He sets the glass down and takes a drink from his own.

"Are we on a date?" Liz blurts out before she can stop herself.

Wine flies out of Riley's mouth, covering the table. "What?" Riley asks, coughing.

Liz reaches for a napkin and starts to wipe up the mess. "Mikey's not here, you bring out a fancy ass dinner, on *plates*," she makes sure to add extra emphasis on the word. "And now you're giving me wine. Seems like a date to me." She sets the napkin aside and waits for him to respond, too nervous to eat until he does.

"No, it's not a date. You're married, remember?" he says.

Something about the way he says it makes her wary. He looks as if saying the words left a bad taste in his mouth. Her heart rate quickens, pounding in her ears. Before the panic has a chance to claw its way out, Riley keeps talking.

"I know the last few weeks haven't been easy, and I appreciate you putting your trust in me while I try to work things out, so I thought you deserved a better meal than commissary food."

"Oh... um, okay. Thank you," is all she can say before digging in.

Hoping the awkwardness is gone, they start to talk about training and what Riley's plans are for teaching her self-defense. They avoid anything to do with the general and getting Liz home, neither one willing to admit what that will mean for them and their blossoming friendship. Soon enough, the conversation turns from exercise and fighting technique to casual conversation and Liz trying to figure out how Rileys manages to date if he never takes his mask off. Without warning, Riley's head shoots to the door, hearing something Liz can't, seconds before the door flies open and Mikey runs in.

Riley is out of his seat in an instant, seeing his friend catching his breath has alarm bells blare in his head. He storms over to the couch, reaching for his carelessly placed gear as they wait for Mikey to explain.

"What's wrong?" he asks Mikey, pulling his vest over his shoulders. He starts strapping his gun holsters back onto his legs, tightening them as Mikey starts to talk.

"They found Dmitri. We've been assigned to bring him in," he says, eyes darting to where Liz sits.

"General called the rest of the force but sent me to deliver the news. He's briefing them now."

That's all she needed to hear. Liz knows they are talking but she can't hear anything. Everything goes silent. Her heart rate picks up, feeling like she can't breathe. Her mind drags her back to the horrors Dmitri put her through.

Liz was able to push those memories out of her mind for weeks. She buried them where they would never reach her. That one stupid fucking name is ruining everything. The men are talking, but no sound reaches her, she simply sits, staring forward, listening to the pounding in her ears as memories flash through her mind like the world's worst slideshow.

Eerie crystal blue eyes, one more white than blue where a deep scar runs through it. Those evil eyes watched her while she was beaten by someone new. A hard hand full of tacky rings slapping her across the face the first time she refused to apologize. Nausea rises with the feel of thick, sticky blood coating her mouth, the coppery tang that she grew so used to tasting.

Liz saw him watching with a sick smile when a pissed off little man came into her cell carrying a handful of old wire. He laughed the moment the first scream was ripped from her as those wires tore into her back. Even when he was not physically there, the men working for him made sure she knew they were doing it for disrespecting him.

Freshly beaten, curled in on herself bleeding, crying in pain when four men storm into her cell, chains in hand. She begged, for the first time she pleaded with them to leave her, that didn't stop the flurry of fists and feet before being chained to the floor.

Fear grips her and refuses to let go, forcing her to relive the memories she tried to hide from even before Riley saved her. Dmitri walked in with a man she had never seen following close behind, brown bag in hand. Her hands were in chains, she had nowhere to go, no way to hide. The man pulled a long needle from his bag, jamming it into her leg. Her eyes got droopy and the room started to spin. She will never know how long she was out, or what they did to her during that time, she never wants to.

"Head back, I'll be there in five," Riley says to Mikey, waiting for him to leave the room before turning his attention to Liz.

He will have to apologize for cutting off whatever his friend was trying to tell him, but once he heard Liz start to hyperventilate, that's all he can think about. He rushes to where she sits, standing in front of her, he gently puts his hands on either side of her face and tips her head to look at him. Green eyes staring right through him, filled with nothing but fear and panic.

"Breathe, love. I need you to breathe," he says to her, hoping to break through the thoughts swimming around her head. Her eyes find his and she takes a shaky breath, then another, and another, slowly bringing her back to reality. "Good girl," he says, eyes still locked on hers as she takes another deep breath. "Just like that, love, keep going." After a few moments of breathing, she opens her mouth to talk, but no words come out. She is paralyzed with fear, knowing the man who chained her up and tortured her is coming back into her life.

"Listen to me," Riley says, crouching so he can be face to face with her and in a moment of pure desperation presses his forehead against hers. "When we get him, I won't let them bring him here. He will never be near you again. I promise," he says, gently stroking his thumb across her cheek. "This is why you've been training, so he can't hurt you."

Liz just looks at him, tears welling in her eyes, knowing she needs to make a move tonight before Dmitri ends up here, with her. The plan she spent weeks working out no longer matters. All her calculations are out the window. Liz has one shot, she has to do whatever she can to get out. She can't move, can't speak. There is so much she wishes she could tell him, so much she will never get the chance to explain. She hates herself for what she has to do, but her time has finally run out.

"I have to go, princess," Riley says, hoping the nickname will annoy her enough to pull her from the panic attack. He only allows himself another second with her head against his, before getting up and opening the door. He looks back at her, hating himself for leaving her in the condition she's in.

"Half an hour, love. End of the meeting or not, I'm coming back to you in half an hour," he says, stepping into the hall, door closing with a loud thud behind him.

CHAPTER 14

As Riley disappears out the door, Liz sits, forcing herself to listen as his boots stomp down the hallway. When the sound finally fades, she lets the tears fall. She only allows herself a moment of weakness before she stands, wipes the tears from her face, and starts looking for what she needs.

She digs around in the drawers until she finds what she is looking for: a pen and scrap of paper. She will never forgive herself if she doesn't explain why she did what she's now forced to do. Tears drip onto the paper while she frantically scribbles. He needs to know this is not how she planned for her escape to go, in the end she trusted him to get her out, her plan was just a backup. She leaves it on the center of the table, hoping Riley will find it when this is all over.

Liz runs into her room. Ripping the pillowcase off her pillow, she stuffs as much as she can into it and tosses it onto her bed. She runs back into the living room, ripping the gun case from its hiding spot under the couch. She breathes deeply, trying to steady herself before punching in what she hopes is the code.

She watches, her heart pounding out of her chest, as a loud beep fills the quiet room, and the light next to the numbers turns red.

"Shit," she says to herself, knowing she won't have many more tries. If Liz can't figure out the code to the safe, she will never get out, or even worse, Riley will know what she was trying to do. Any trust he has in her will be gone. Everything they have spent weeks building will be ruined.

She can't fuck this up.

Liz takes another deep breath and tries a different code. The light is red, and the loud beep fills the empty room once more. She lets out a frustrated groan, standing to pace around the room. She was so sure she would get it right. For fifteen long minutes, Liz paces, going over everything she can remember. Thinking about what she has seen Riley do at the door a hundred times, her footsteps echoing throughout the room. She glances at the clock, if what Riley said is true, he will be back in less than ten minutes. She drops to her knees in front of the case, punching in one last code. Watching, unable to breathe, she hears a chirp and the light turns green.

Tears spring to her eyes at the sight of the case unlatching. She throws it open and looks at the gun sitting nestled into the plush black foam. She picks it up out of the case, not sure what she's even doing. She gives the small handgun a once over, pulling the slide and making sure it's loaded. Glancing back at the clock, she realizes she's run out of time. She pushes the case back under the couch and runs to her room, tucking herself into the darkest corner of her closet, praying one of the men comes looking for her.

Liz stays crouched in the corner running through every possible outcome of every possible way this could go. Each second that ticks by feels like an eternity. She tries to focus on the cold metal of the gun clutched to her chest. Then, she hears it, the sound of the front door unlocking. She breathes deeply, not at all ready for what's about to happen.

Riley and Mikey step into the room after their meeting with the general, both exhausted from all the information unloaded onto them. Riley looks around the small space expecting to see Liz waiting for him. She has been getting more comfortable being in the common areas of the apartment the last few weeks. She still stays in her room unless they are eating or training, but when he looks to the kitchen, she's not there. He notices her food still on the table. A sinking feeling grows heavy in his gut; he rushes to her door and knocks.

No answer.

He tries to tell himself she probably just went to sleep. She knew he was coming back, but something wasn't right. He throws open the door, needing to make sure she's in bed, but when he looks in, he's greeted by an empty room.

"She's gone," he yells, whirling to Mikey, panic flooding his voice.

Mikey's eyes widen at the realization. He starts looking around the room like maybe they just missed her, maybe she just doesn't want them to see her in the state she's in. Riley rushes into his room, checking everywhere before going into the bathroom.

When Riley storms back out, Mikey finally says— "Calm down, Ry. She's got to be here, if she somehow left the room alarms would be blaring right now. She probably just went back to sleeping on her floor. This has to be fucking with her head."

He strides into her room and over to the bed. Liz peers at him from where she is hidden. Carefully she tiptoes out, feet silent on the chilly floor. When she's not there, he pulls back the covers just as something pushes into his back, followed by the distinct click of a gun.

"I'm sorry. I don't want to hurt you Mikey," Liz says, voice quietly cracking as she struggles to control her emotions. "But I... I will if you don't do what I tell you... Tell Riley you found me and to stay where he is. Please," she adds, voice laced with sorrow.

"RY!" Mikey shouts. "I found her. Stay there, we're coming out."

Mikey puts his hands up in surrender. Liz keeps the gun to his back as they turn, not letting up as she guides him into the living room. She peers around Mikey's back over at Riley, seeing the hurt and betrayal in his eyes makes her sick to her stomach.

He fought so hard for her. He risked everything for her, and she betrayed him. The three of them stand there, no one daring to even breathe wrong. They are all painfully aware of how easy it would be to get the gun from her, but neither of the men are willing to harm Liz. They promised she would be safe with them, that they would never hurt her and it's one they intend to keep.

"Where did you get that gun?" Riley asks in a desperate attempt to distract her.

"I'm sorry," Liz says, a few tears slipping free. "I found the case under the couch, and I've been watching you, trying to learn the code."

"Why, darlin?" Mikey asks. Even with a gun to his back, he talks to her like a friend just attempting to understand why she is doing what she is doing. "We have been begging the general to let you go."

"We just needed more time," Riley whispers, taking a step closer, hands held up so she can see them.

She knows what he's trying to do. All these weeks she has let him get too close. She grew too complacent. Riley knows she could never hurt either of them and he's going to try and use that to get close and stop her. He's right, she can't bring herself to hurt them physically. If she has learned anything in all this time it's that they do care for her in some capacity. They have done everything in their power to keep her safe and out of harm's way. She may not be able to hurt them, but they want her alive, so she will have to hurt them another way.

She gives Mikey one big shove, before turning the gun on herself.

CHAPTER 15

Mikey stumbles forward, steadying himself as he turns back to where Liz stands. Both men stare in horror at the gun placed against her temple, her finger resting against the trigger.

Liz watches them, her heart shattering in her chest at the sheer panic etched onto their faces. They will never forgive her for what she is about to do and she will never forgive herself for forcing them to witness it.

"What the fuck is going on?" Mikey shouts, frantically looking at Riley, hoping he has some sort of answer.

"Just put down the gun. Talk to me, love. Please... Just talk to me," Riley pleads.

"We were trying to help you, Liz," Mikey says, voice low, fear lacing every word. "For weeks I have been trying to confirm your story, trying to get you free."

"I just wanted to leave, and you wouldn't let me, and now he's back. Why couldn't you just let me go?" Liz asks, tears forming a steady stream down her face.

Riley takes a small step toward her, then another. Her hand

starts to shake. The only thing keeping her from pulling the trigger is the devastation in Riley's eyes. "We're trying," he says, daring to take another step. "We have spent all of our free time trying to find out anything about you we can, but you haven't been very open about your past. I know there are things you want to keep from us, and that's okay... But it makes things harder." His voice raises slightly. Her eyes snap to his. He has never felt so awful for yelling at someone. Riley looks into her emerald eyes and all he sees is anguish.

"I just want to be with them," Liz says, barely more than a whisper. "I just want to be with them again and everyone keeps stopping me."

It's then they realize she's talking about going home to her husband, and the child she was ripped away from. They hadn't really stopped to think about the extent she would go to get back to her family. She never spoke about them and the few times she did it wasn't much. Liz never even told the men their names.

Liz closes her eyes and takes a shuddering breath.

Terrified, watching her finger tremble against the trigger, Riley rushes a few steps closer.

Mikey stays on the other side of the room, leaving his hands up in surrender, trusting Riley knows what he's doing. "We just need more time," Mikey says, trying to get Liz's attention on him and away from Riley who is still inching his way to her. "But if you do what you're thinking about doing, you will never get to be with your family again."

Liz looks at him, then to Riley, seeing the fear on their faces. She knows that look, she's had the same one. It's the look of a person losing someone they care about. She can't stop the agonizing sound that comes out of her, tears forming a steady stream down her face as she says through her sobs—

"This is the only way I will ever get to be with them again."

CHAPTER 16

Riley's heart drops into his stomach at the confession, finally understanding every look of pain, every avoidance of telling him about her family. He finally understands why she not only had no regard for her life but asked them to end it. He doesn't care about anything but getting to her, doing whatever he can to make her listen to him.

"Mikey..." Riley says, eyes still locked onto Liz. "Mikey, you need to leave. Don't say a thing to anyone, just go."

"I'm not leav—"

"GO!" Riley yells, interrupting his objections.

Liz watches as Mikey backs up to the door and silently slips out, knowing he's going to call for help; she knows she needs to make a choice.

Riley looks at Liz and knows the look she has on her face, he has seen it before after a particularly brutal mission. Her eyes are closed, every muscle in her face is relaxed, her lips curve upward in a serene smile, knowing she will be at peace soon.

"Eyes on me, princess," Riley shouts, riddled with fear.

Liz's eyes snap open, looking anywhere but at the man inching his way to her.

"Before you pull that trigger, you need to listen to me. You owe me that much." He looks at the gun, then the hand holding it as she starts to shake again. Riley knows he only has one shot at this, and he's going to make it count. "I've lost people too: a sister and a nephew." He takes a breath, trying to compose himself before continuing.

"They were the only family I had. After I enlisted, I didn't get to see them as much, but every day I had free, I would be there. When they promoted me to special forces, our helo got shot down, and I was captured. They found out who I was and went after my family. There was nothing I could do to save them."

Liz meets his gaze, his eyes reflecting her pain. He takes one last step, their bodies practically touching.

"It may not be my wife and child, but I carry that pain with me every day, and I promise, it gets easier."

He reaches his hand up, slowly, as if diffusing a bomb, and puts it on the gun. Liz loosens her grip, letting Riley take the gun from her hand. With record speed, he pulls it from her head, releasing the clip as he does. He pops the bullet out of the chamber and throws the gun into the void behind him.

He's on her in an instant, pulling her into his chest as violent sobs wrack her body. Liz lets him pull her in, finally letting out all the pain she's been holding. Riley holds her, making sure she is safe and cared for while she does. He rubs his hand up and down her back, trying his best to comfort her, his heart breaking a little more with each tear she sheds.

"It's going to be okay, princess. I'm not giving up on you," he says as he places a kiss on the top of her head. His words only make her sob harder.

Riley slowly moves them to the couch, his arms never leaving her as he sits them down. Liz curls into a ball next to him, softly sobbing into his chest, refusing to let her go. Eventually, her crying slows, and an eerie silence fills the room. Riley looks at the clock; 3:27 am. He yawns, the last nine hours have him utterly drained. He looks down at the woman sleeping on him, knowing she can't be alone right now, he stands, gently sliding her from his chest onto the couch, quickly picks up the discarded weapon and quietly goes to his room.

Riley takes a few minutes to grab her blanket and put it on his bed, then quickly strips his gear off. He takes his vest and tucks it back into his closet before sliding the door shut and locking it for good measure. He slips into a pair of sweatpants and a tight t-shirt before heading back into the living room.

Riley silently walks back to where Liz is still sleeping. Even in her sleep, her brows are pinched together, pain is etched into every line of her face. He bends down, slides one arm under her waist and the other under her neck, lifting her into him before carrying her to his bed. He lays her down as gently as he can, hoping she will stay asleep, and pulls her blanket over the top of her before walking to the other side of the bed and climbing in.

He lays in the dark room for a while, listening to the shallow breaths of the woman beside him, wondering how he's going to deal with this come morning. She will never forgive herself, that much he knows.

He could see her caring nature slip out every time they were together. Despite claiming to not care about them, she was always looking for Mikey if he wasn't around, and when he finally did come back, she would not so subtly make sure he ate that day. When Riley got his cheek cut open from letting Mikey demonstrate a new technique, she was right there making sure he was okay before scolding Mikey for being too rough. He saw the guilt that plagued her the first time she saw him outside of her cell, her mesmerizing green eyes shot right to that spot on his shoulder. Try as she may to hide it, she is full of compassion, driven to her breaking point by desperation.

Liz starts to stir, tossing and turning before finding Riley again. She scoots over and he instinctively lifts his arm where she wastes no time moving herself closer. She lets out a small whimper, nuzzling her head onto his chest and tossing her leg over his waist. Riley sighs, wrapping one arm around her shoulders, the other goes to her thigh, gently rubbing it, holding her close as they both drift off to sleep.

Riley wakes in his dark room to Liz still wrapped tightly in his arms. Not ready to let her go, he just lays there, listening to her dainty snores, gently stroking his hand up and down her arm. He runs through every possible scenario that could happen when she finally wakes, each one ending in Liz being hurt. Riley loses track of time, too focused on what needs to happen when Liz wakes up. He is only pulled from his thoughts when Liz starts to stir. She shifts, still mostly asleep, snuggling closer, letting out a happy sigh when she's satisfied with her new position. Her delicate hand strokes his broad chest, then goes deathly still.

Liz gives no warning before she jolts awake, scrambling to get away from Riley. Her breathing is rapid, like waking up from a nightmare. She freezes, trying to remember what happened the night before. She was holding a gun to Mikey, turning it on herself, and Riley taking it. She looks over to where he now sits.

The dim light filtering in through the cracked bathroom door provides barely enough light to see his eyes pinned on her, full of concern.

"Deep breath, love," he says, having no idea what he is supposed to say or feel.

She does what he says, taking a big breath in through her mouth, holding it in for a count of five, before letting it out through her mouth. Everything comes flooding back and there is nothing she can do to stop the fresh round of tears from flowing.

"I'm so sorry," she manages through choked sobs. "I didn't want to hurt anyone." She keeps fighting to breathe, doing anything she can to calm herself enough to explain. She needs him to know how much she regrets what she did before he turns her over to the general.

"I didn't... I didn't think I had a choice." She closes her eyes and takes a deep breath, needing to ask but scared to hear the answer. "Is Mikey okay? Did I... Did I hurt him?" she asks, opening her eyes and looking back to Riley. "Please tell me he is okay."

Even in the dark he can see how much this is hurting her. Each word she says makes it more obvious she is drowning in guilt. "C'mere," he says, moving closer on the bed, needing to hold her again. She quickly looks away, unable to face him after what she did. "I need this as much as you do," he says, hiding his pain.

She peers over at him, wiping the tears from her eyes before backing herself into his waiting arms.

"He's okay. I'm sure he will check in soon." Riley gives her a small squeeze before dropping his arms and pulling himself from the bed. He stalks over to the closet, unlocking it before sliding the door open. He bends down, shuffling through whatever is in there, before standing back up with his cell phone in hand. Unsure if the light should be on or off, he thinks back to all the times he fucked up, he didn't want anyone to see him so he hid his shame in the dark. Riley navigates the dark room back to Liz and sits next to her, causing the bed to dip just enough to force her to lean against him.

"When are you taking me to the general? Will I have time to apologize to Mikey?" Liz whispers, filled with shame. She pushes herself back and brings her knees to her chest, resting her chin on them. Riley looks at her sitting there staring at the empty wall beside her. The same way she did when he first brought her in, utterly defeated, and something breaks in him all over again.

Riley unlocks his phone, and types something in before tossing it onto the other side of the bed. Standing, he says, "I told Mikey to get here. When he does, we need to figure a few things out."

"I'm sorry, Riley."

His chest tightens hearing her say his name, the anguish in her voice enough to make him forget every event that led to this point. He shakes off the thought, standing and pacing the small room, happy he tossed his gear in the closet rather than the floor.

Liz dries her eyes and stands, willing her legs to move her to where he's pacing. He turns and almost walks right into her. She looks at him, green eyes glowing in the dark room, tears reforming. "I'm sorry. I'm sorry I broke into your things. I'm sorry I didn't trust you. And I'm so, so fucking sorry I broke your trust in me." Tears form a steady stream down her cheeks.

Riley takes a step, wanting nothing more than to tell her how much he understands her pain and why she did it, but before he can, a loud knock comes from the other room.

"Sit on the bed and don't move until I come back."

She watches him leave, closing the door behind him. Liz

breathes deeply, the smell of sandalwood calming her nerves slightly. She can barely make out what's being said, too scared to move.

Riley comes back in, seeing her sitting in the same spot he left her in, he says. "C'mon, we need to talk."

Liz follows him out of the room. Her eyes lock onto Mikey sitting at the table. He glances at Liz, his deep blue eyes meeting hers, and she doesn't miss the sadness in them. Mikey stands, walking into the living room, trying to meet them halfway.

Something breaks seeing him after everything she did. She takes one step, then another before throwing herself into him, wrapping her arms tightly around his waist, violently sobbing.

He reluctantly wraps his arms around her, lightly rubbing her back. She lets him go and tries to compose herself.

Deep breath in... Hold... Deep breath out.

"I will never be able to tell you how sorry I am," she begins, sniffling, hoping he will find it in his heart to forgive her before they hand her over.

"What I did to you was horrible, but I need you to know I would have never intentionally hurt you."

Deep breath in... Hold... Deep breath out.

"I thought I would never be let go, then you found him, and I was out of time. I needed a way out. I wish I could take back what I did to you, but I can't. I can only hope you will forgive me." Liz holds her hands out in front of her. Ready for what she knows is coming she quietly says, "I won't fight you. I deserve everything the general is going to do."

Mikey takes a step and wraps his arms around her, squeezing her tight enough to hurt. He places a gentle kiss on the top of her head before letting her go. "That dick won't ever get his hands on you, darlin," he says, forcing himself to continue at the sight of her crying again. "Believe me, I'm pissed you pulled that shit, but I know why you felt it was your only option." He walks to the kitchen, and pulls out a chair, loudly dragging the legs across the tiles.

"If we're ever going to trust you again, you need to tell us everything."

CHAPTER 17

Liz forces herself over to the table, sliding into the middle chair, Riley and Mikey joining her on either side. Liz looks at each of them, waiting for someone to talk. They look back at her, waiting to hear what she has to say, wondering what has led her here... to them.

"So, what do you want to know? I promise I won't keep anything out this time," she says, wiping crumbs off the table, trying to keep her hands busy so she doesn't panic.

"Everything," Riley says. "You need to tell us everything that happened leading up to Dmitri taking you."

"Okay, but I need you to promise not to get mad if I need time," she says, fully expecting them to already be mad at her for having demands.

"You pulled a gun on Mikey last night yet somehow you ended up in my bed and got *him* to feel bad for *you* after. I don't think you need to worry about us getting mad," Riley says, tone almost playful.

Liz takes a deep breath and begins to tell them everything about her past.

"Well, um, it was pretty much your typical, sad girl life. My parents were monsters, always fighting. If they weren't fighting each other, they were fighting me. I probably should have told you I have an older brother, he's been in jail more than out of it so there has to be some record of that, anyway, I'm pretty sure they only had me so the three of them had someone to take their anger out on. What my parents would do was nothing compared to him, though. They would encourage him to do whatever he wanted to me because, and I quote, 'he's our son'."

"I'm glad you're opening up, love, I really am, but we need to get to the part where you get taken," Riley says. Mikey shoots him a look, obviously trying to tell him to be quiet without saying it.

Liz looks over at him, crossing her arms and leaning back in her chair. "If you're not going to listen, I'm done talking. I know I fucked everything up, but this isn't easy for me. I have only told one person about my past and it got him killed," she says, glaring.

"Sorry. Continue," he says to her.

"Anyway..." She shoots him another look, hoping it's enough to keep him from interrupting again.

"I had a horrible family who liked to use me as their personal punching bag, except my brother, he used me for so much worse. Whatever you're thinking right now, he's done it. Not all my scars are from Dmitri you know, and I don't just mean the ones you can see."

"Jesus Christ, how old were you? How did no one help?" Mikey asks. Liz peers over at him, he is better at hiding it, but she can see the storm brewing in his mind.

"Honestly? I remember shit happening in preschool, it got worse as I got older, but those are the first real memories I have of my mom hurting me. She said my dad gave me too much attention, she slapped me so hard I fell out of my chair. I was so scared, I thought she felt bad when she came over, I cried for help but that just made it worse. She dragged me by my hair and put me in a closet, so that was fun," she jokes, using humor in a sad attempt to hide the pain. "I was in second grade when things got bad. It was the first time he hurt me, like that... he came into my room talking about how he learned about sex in health class, he told me he was going to be the first one of his friends to do it, then shoved his hand in my pants, I screamed and hit him. I thought my parents would keep me safe, but when they saw the red mark on his face...well, you learn pretty quickly to keep your mouth shut, take the hits and pretend nothing happened after" she stops, her eyes unfocus, staring far off, lost in the painful memory.

Riley watches in silence, filling with anger when he sees the agony fade to nothing behind her eyes. It's like she is so desensitized to her own trauma she can shut the pain off and become just a shell. He knows she is telling them the truth and it only fuels the rage building.

"Sorry, I'm rambling, so, I got out when I was sixteen. I jumped from one shitty situation to another, moving in with a grown man who promised me a good life. Big surprise, he was just as bad as everyone else, maybe even worse. After I got away from him, I was living in my car, working two jobs, trying to just stay alive. I had no one. Then, I met James, and I loved him from the moment we met. After our first date, we were inseparable. He took me in, taking care of me until we could take care of each other. We got married, and a few years later, we had Maria. I went from no family, to the most amazing one you could ask for. Our house was happy and always full of love. Even when things weren't perfect, the two of them made it seem like it was."

Tears roll down her face, dripping onto the table below. She takes a breath, wipes her face, and starts again.

"A few years ago, a woman reached out to me, saying she was engaged to my brother. It was his... sixth engagement, I think. I didn't keep tabs on him, but I would always find out when he got arrested. She told me she was going to be my sister-in-law and wanted to get to know me. The thought of him doing to her what he had done to me and so many other women made me sick. I looked at my own daughter, if she was going to marry a monster I would hope someone would try to save her. I told her she should get out before she ends up broken like the rest of the women in his life with a link to his latest arrest. His last fiancé was found in the woods, three missing teeth, a broken arm, broken eye socket and a bullet hole in her shoulder. Well, she must have listened, because after a couple days, I got a text from an unsaved number saying I was going to regret fucking up his life. I tried to ignore it, and after a while, I forgot and things went back to normal. I left James at home with Maria to go grocery shopping. When I turned back onto our street, I smelled smoke. There were flashing lights and sirens lining the road and our house was in flames."

Riley and Mikey both watch her, wanting nothing more than to reach out and take away her pain. Neither of the men knew what they were expecting her to say, but it wasn't this.

Liz takes a moment to compose herself, tears steadily streaming, dripping onto the table within silence. Mikey reaches out and takes her hand, giving it a gentle, comforting squeeze. A pang of jealousy goes through Riley at the sight of their joined hands, wishing he was the one comforting her. He's pulled back from his thoughts when Liz takes a shuddering breath.

"I only remember bits and pieces after that: screaming until no more sound would come out, trying to run to the house before an officer stopped me. From what I learned later, I tried to fight my way into my house. I remember one of the officers who grabbed me said they weren't in the house. I knew then, the look he gave me, I knew they were gone. I planned the services and got what little remains I could cremated, I mean the real way. Everyone knew it was my brother. My former in-laws hated me. They told me it was my fault for what happened, like I didn't already know. I tried so hard to get the police to listen, to get any kind of justice for them, but they wouldn't. The cops all told me I was lashing out because of my pain. Despite his mile long record of abuse, attempted murder, and literal fucking arson, they closed the case and let that fucking monster stay free."

They thought it couldn't get worse, but with every word she spoke, their hearts broke more for her. Riley had no idea she had been through so much, been forced to lose her family in such a horrific way. He was practically shaking with rage. Liz looks to Mikey who just gives her a nod, letting her know Riley will be fine, and it's safe to continue.

"James and I had made a promise to Maria; she had begged us to go on a big vacation. So, I put them in my car and drove. I couldn't stay in that town any longer. I forced myself to stay alive, every damn miserable day I fought the dark thoughts, for them. Every day for sixteen months... until the day came. I stumbled across the perfect spot to scatter their ashes. I hated the beach, but they loved it. Sometimes I would carry their tiny urns through the sand to make them happy, I lost track of what I was doing and ended up on this tiny hidden beach with the softest white sand. It was perfect. I swear I could hear them ask to be left there, so I did. I scattered their ashes on that beach so they could be in paradise together. I refused to taint their beautiful beach with my suicide. I already ruined their lives, I would not ruin their eternity too. I said goodbye and left them. I wanted to die the moment they did, but after two failed attempts I gave up until that day. I found a shitty part of town with a bar on a pier. I figured I could get drunk and drive off. It was deep enough no one could get to me and I would be drunk enough to not bitch out."

They both look at her intently, deathly still, waiting for her to finish.

"I went to the bar and had a couple drinks, that's when I was approached by a group of guys. They tried to buy me drinks and talk to me, but *he* wouldn't leave me alone, so I finally snapped, and said... something stupid that set him off. He got pissed, called me a pathetic, drunk, whore, but he left—"

"What did you say?" Mikey interrupts, knowing it's not important, but still wanting to know what could have set the Russian terrorist off.

"I told him... that he was a disgusting old creep, and I wouldn't suck his dick with his boyfriend's mouth and pointed to the bigger of his two buddies," Liz said with a smirk.

Riley watches her as she goes to a dark place, thinking of something she's keeping from them. He brushes it off. Opening up like this is hard enough for her. He will find out what she is thinking about eventually.

Mikey burst out in laughter, the booming sounds filling the apartment.

"Consider yourself forgiven, darlin. That's the best thing I've heard in weeks," he says to her before she continues.

"I kept drinking. I vaguely remember stumbling to my car, ready to end the nightmare that was my life. I think he was waiting for me in the parking lot, I don't really know. I remember someone pulling me into a car, something stabbing into my neck, then, nothing. I woke up in the cell, now I'm here.

I'm sorry, but I really don't have it in me to tell you more of what they did to me while I was locked up," Liz finishes, hoping they believe her. They have to believe her, she has never talked to another living soul about what happened; she's putting all her trust in them right now.

"Fuck," is all Mikey manages to get out.

Riley remains sitting in icy silence. He can't even look at Liz, scared for what will happen if he sees her in any more pain.

"So, this all happened because your brother is a pathetic piece of shit and you tried to save a stranger from his abuse," Mikey says, only half asking. He isn't sure what to think of her story; he never thought it would be as bad as what she just told them.

"Yeah, pretty much," Liz says, shrugging her shoulders, so desensitized by her brother's abuse she isn't left in shock when re-telling it.

"What's his name?" Riley asks. His deep voice is cold and dark, sending a shiver down her spine.

When she looks at him, their eyes meeting, she sees the anger he tries to hide. She thinks back to the first time they really talked. She thought he was joking about punishing the men who hurt her. Liz knew they faced consequences for their actions, she just assumed it was because they disobeyed orders. Now, looking at Riley, she knows it wasn't. He's looking at her like he is going to burn the world down just to keep her from being hurt again.

"I... I can't." she says, sounding almost scared.

Riley breathes deep, thinking the fear gripping her is his doing.

"I haven't said his name since I told the police... I just can't, the minute I do he becomes real again," she says, hoping they understand that by saying his name, she's giving life to the monster who took everything from her.

Riley glances down and notices the scrap of paper and pen on the table, he picks it up and reads the note, eyes softening as he looks at Liz. He rips a small part off and slides it over to her, slipping the other half into his pocket.

"Darlin, I know it's hard, but we need a name. It will really help us." He gives her hand another squeeze, needing her to understand they are both there for her. She blinks back the tears and reaches for the pen. Hand shaking, tears burning her eyes, she writes a name on the paper and folds it up.

As soon as her hand is free of the paper, Riley snatches it off the table. He stands so fast the chair he's sitting in goes flying behind him, hitting the cabinets with a loud crash. Liz jumps, never having seen him this angry. She's filled with worry that his anger is because of her.

Before anyone can try to talk to Riley, he storms over to the door, boots echoing through the room, and storms out. They stay there for a while, letting everything that has happened wash over them. Liz keeps looking at the door, waiting for Riley to come back. Mikey is the one to break the silence.

"It's not your fault. Ry just needs some time to process." He stands and walks to the fridge, grabbing a beer for himself. "It's been a long night, darlin. Why don't you try to get some more rest? I'll stay with you until he comes back."

Liz gets up, emotionally drained, and fighting sleep. She doesn't think about what she's doing when she walks straight to Riley's room and climbs into his bed, letting his scent carry her to sleep.

CHAPTER 18

Liz wakes to the smell of bacon. Opening her eyes and sitting up, she remembers she's not in her room, but Riley's. The last time she was in his room there was so much going on she forgot how curious she was to see what it looked like. Liz had expected it to be more personal. The room matches her own, the only difference being a bigger bed and a long closet on one wall vs her small one in the corner. She quickly gets up and cuts through the bathroom, hoping he won't be too mad at her. She changes and goes out into the main room where she spots Mikey in the kitchen, cooking breakfast, but still no Riley.

Liz strolls to the kitchen, asking if she can help, but Mikey refuses, telling her she had quite the day yesterday, so she can just sit and eat. The last forty-eight hours have been hell for everyone. There is a lightness in the air that hasn't been there before, like they needed to go through that to really trust each other and turn over a new leaf. She follows his orders and sits. He puts a big plate of bacon and scrambled eggs in front of her, then one at the other spot on the table before sitting down and eating his breakfast. When they finish, Liz cleans up the mess and heads back to her room, already ready for a nap.

"Get changed, it's run time," Mikey yells after her.

She stops in her tracks and turns on him. "I'm done with all that sweetie, no more training for this guy," she says, ready to go back to bed.

"You pulled a gun on me," he says to her, hoping the guilt doesn't eat her alive.

"You owe me."

"You said you forgave me!" Liz shrieks in return. Throwing her head back in frustration and letting out a groan, Liz walks into her room and digs out fresh clothes and her running sneakers. She gets dressed and meets Mikey at the door, stretching before they go. They walk down the hall and as soon as they exit the door, Liz breaks into a fast jog, needing the burn in her lungs and ache in her muscles to keep her thoughts from drifting to Riley.

They run their first lap, but by the second, Liz slows down. Her mind can't help but drift in wonder to where Riley went and if he really is mad with her. Mikey slows, noticing her pulling back into herself. He knows where her mind is going.

"Why are pirates called pirates?" Mikey says, looking at Liz, mouth pursed, trying to hold back his laughter.

Liz just glares at him silently, trying to make it through their run.

"Because they AARRR." Laughter flows from him.

Liz thinks there has to be something wrong with him for the way he's acting. After everything she did, he's still trying to make jokes. She sees his face drop before she picks up her pace and takes off in front of him. Her thoughts race, wondering what the hell just happened. She hears the heavy thump of his footsteps catching up to her. It hits her that he is trying to keep her distracted. He's not going to let her retreat into her head and continue to blame herself for every bad thing that has happened. They slow down, finally reaching the door.

Stopping for just a minute, they each take a long drink from the waters they left by the door. Liz starts her cooldown lap first, Mikey close behind.

He catches up and slows to match her pace. Even a month later, he's still getting used to keeping pace with someone so much smaller than him.

"How do you organize a space party?" Liz finally asks, breaking their silence.

Mikey looks at her, smiling wide, happy to have her back.

"You planet," Liz says, cracking a sad smile.

Mikey barks out a deep, rich laugh. Liz can't bring herself to say it, but she's thankful he is there for her, especially after everything she did to him.

"So, you're kind of Riley's best friend," she says, peeking at him from the corner of her eye. "He hates me, doesn't he? I know he regrets saving me now that he knows I got my family killed."

"Ry told you about his own family didn't he?" he asks, looking over at Liz who nods in agreement. "Do you blame him for what happened to them?"

"What?" Liz asks, confused.

"Do you think Riley is to blame for what happened to his family?" he repeats.

"Of course not. It's not his fault for what some psychopathic assholes did," she states, shocked he would even ask such a thing.

"Exactly," Mikey says, glancing over at her, her face showing no emotion. They walk in silence for a bit, Mikey trying to figure out how to explain the best he can. "Ry doesn't hate you, darlin," he says, stepping over and putting his arm around her shoulder, pulling her close to him. "I have never seen Riley act the way he does with you. He is the single most terrifying man I have ever worked with. His own shit keeps him in a constant state of being a broody asshole, but he has a soft spot for you. I think he sees a lot of himself in you. If it makes this any easier, it wasn't Riley who stormed out last night."

Liz looks at him with confusion, wondering what he could mean. She takes a moment to digest everything he said.

If Riley has such a soft spot for her, why would he get angry and storm out when she finally opened up? She starts to think back to all the other things he's done, always making her plates, buying her everything she needs, even bringing her into his bed so she wouldn't be alone. She never told him how much she needed that, he just knew.

"If it wasn't Riley last night, then who was it?" she asks, not sure she's ready for the answer.

Mikey looks at her, and she doesn't miss the fear behind his eyes— "Reaper."

CHAPTER 19

It's been three days since Riley left. Liz and Mikey fall back into a comfortable routine: eating breakfast together every morning before going on their run. Without Riley around teaching her to fight, Mikey has taken it upon himself to kick everyone out of the gym so they can get a real workout in. Liz cooks them lunch when they get back before she takes a shower and wallows in self-pity until dinner.

After dinner, Liz heads back into her room, ready to lie down and force herself to sleep, when Mikey asks— "Do you ever do anything for fun in there? Or do you just sit and stare at the wall?"

Liz looks at him, confusion plastered all over her face. "I mean, when I was planning my grand escape I would work out, but you do realize I have nothing, right? Just a bed and walls," she says back.

"I can think of a few things to do with the bed," Mikey says, winking at her.

"Pig."

"Oh, ew! I meant jump on it, you pervert! Save your gutter

thoughts for Riley," he says, feigning shock before Liz turns and strides back to her room. "Stay! Hang out with me tonight; we can watch a movie or something." He shouts to her, whining like a bored child.

Liz turns, eying him, not sure what to think of his offer.

He sighs and moves over on the couch, patting the cushion next to him. "Nothing weird, scout's honor," he says, holding up three fingers.

Liz rolls her eyes and goes back into her room. She quickly changes into a pair of bike shorts paired with Riley's hooded sweatshirt that somehow ended up mixed into her things. She pulls the sweatshirt over her head, smiling when it reaches her knees. She plucks the bottle of polish off her dresser before striding back out and tossing it to Mikey.

"What do you want to watch?" Mikey asks, flipping on the TV.

Liz flops onto the couch, propping her feet up on his lap, their friendship blooming effortlessly. "I haven't watched TV in years," she says , wiggling her toes. "You pick something."

They sit there, going back and forth, flipping through channels, trying to find something to watch. It's been so long, Liz groans loudly, not recognizing half the names that scroll past.

They keep going until finally one catches her eye.

"That one!" she says, snatching the remote out of Mikey's hand. She quickly scrolls and clicks on the channel. The room darkens with the dimly lit scene, the sounds of metal clanging and people screaming fills the air. A smile lights up her face, enjoying herself for the first time in years.

"You never told us you're a big ass nerd," Mikey says to her, surprised by how enthralled she is by the action on the screen. He cracks open the bottle she threw at him and starts to paint, hoping and praying she doesn't notice how bad he is at it.

"You never asked," she says, eyes never leaving the TV.

They watch in silence, simply enjoying being around each other. As soon as Mikey is done painting, he moves her feet onto the small coffee table. He gets up and walks into the kitchen, rifling around in the cabinets, looking for something. Soon the small room fills with popping and the smell of salt and butter. Liz turns and looks at him before going pale, her head snapping to the noise outside their door. Mikey follows her eyes to the door, finally hearing what she does.

"Chill, me and Ry are the only ones with access," he says, and she settles back into the couch, heart starting to race. Even after all the weeks she's been with them, Liz has never been outside her room other than to eat or train. She's not even sure she is allowed to be there if they aren't sharing a meal.

The door groans open, and Riley steps into the room. He quickly looks around, and when his eyes land on Liz curled up on the couch, swimming in his sweatshirt more relaxed than he's ever seen her, he doesn't give in to the pull. He wants nothing more than to take her into his arms, tell her he's sorry for leaving, and make sure she's okay. Instead, he just looks at her, sparkling emerald eyes meeting his.

"Get dressed, we're leaving." he says, before storming into his room, slamming the door behind him.

CHAPTER 20

When he finally emerges, dressed in full tactical gear, Liz looks at him, stuck between not wanting to make him madder than he already is and wanting to scream at him for abandoning her. Never one to make things easy, she decides to go with simply snuggling herself deeper into the couch, turning her attention back to the movie.

"Get out," he says, turning his anger on Mikey. Riley glares at his friend, the look alone enough to make him leave. Mikey heads for the door, knowing this isn't his battle to fight. "Gear up. Alex will brief you."

As soon as the door closes, Riley shifts his attention back to Liz. She tries her best to ignore him, even though every fiber of her being screams at her it isn't the time for being petty. She can't help herself. She opened up about her family, let herself be vulnerable with him, and he walked out on her.

"Get up and get dressed," he says to her again, not trying to hide his annoyance. He walks to where she sits, stepping right in front of the TV.

"No, thank you," she says, refusing to meet his gaze. "I think

I'm going to stay here and finish the movie." She peers up, batting her thick lashes at him. She can see his patience wearing thin already.

He picks up the remote, flipping the TV off, not in the mood to deal with her stubbornness. He glares at her, trying the same look he used on Mikey. Not surprised at all it doesn't work, he takes a deep breath, and says— "Princess, I will throw your fine ass over my fucking shoulder and carry you out of here if you don't get dressed and come with me." He hopes she doesn't call him out on his choice of words.

"Okay, so do it," she says, arms folding across her chest as she wiggles her hips deeper into the cushion.

A clear challenge to see just how far he's willing to go. He takes a small step, then another. Watching her watch him, a predator closing in on his prey. She allows him to take one last step before jumping up and skirting around him.

"Where are you taking me?" she asks, starting to worry he might be finally turning her in after everything she has done.

"Will you just change... Please?" he asks, tone softer, seeing the gears in her head turn.

She nods and walks into her room, not bothering to close the door behind her. She slips out of her borrowed hoodie and puts on a small, black crop top before peeling her shorts off. She stuffs her legs into a pair of tight black jeans before adding socks and the pair of combat boots Mikey gifted her. Liz goes back to the living room where Riley impatiently waits.

He looks her over, satisfied with what she put on, and simply turns and walks to the door, holding it open. Neither says a word as they walk down the hallway and out the glass doors. Normally, Liz and Mikey would turn right and start their run, but Riley just walks across the parking lot. Liz follows close behind, maintaining a safe distance, debating whether she should make a run for it or not. Recalling what happened last time she didn't trust him, she decides against it.

Riley stops in front of a big black truck, pulling keys out of his pocket, and pushes a button causing lights to blink. He goes over to the passenger side and opens the door. "Get in."

He holds the door, waiting for Liz to climb into the truck. She reluctantly obeys. The door closes and she watches Riley walk around to the other side, eyes never leaving him, as he opens the door and climbs in. The engine roars to life as he pulls out of the parking lot, flashing his lights when they pull up to the gate. It groans and slowly raises, making a ghoulish noise the entire time. When it gets just high enough, Riley starts again. Liz watches out the window as the base disappears behind them. She watches the twists and turns of the road, nothing in the distance but desert. When they pull off onto a well-hidden dirt road, her stomach drops.

"Are you bringing me out here to kill me?" She asks, only half joking. She looks over at him, back in the first mask she ever saw, showing just enough of his strong jaw line for her to tell he smiled. Whether it's from her audacity to ask or his excitement to end her life, she'll never know. Another turn and they are no longer on the road. Liz watches as they drive further and further from safety.

"So... I never pegged you as a Raptor guy," she says, trying to break the tension. Her anxiety running wild from his refusal to answer her last question.

"Oh yeah?" Riley responds. "What did you think I would drive?"

"I assumed you would have a sports car or something... flashier: Audi, Corvette, maybe even a sport bike, that's what all you military guys get," Liz says to him, turning her attention back to the window.

"Didn't peg *you* as a car girl," he says, glancing at her before turning back to the road.

"I've always liked cars. James and I even started rebuilding an old Impala together," she says, a small smile forming on her lips at the memory of her late husband.

He wants to ask more, learn more about her, but seeing her tiny smile fade into the pain she's feeling, stops him from saying anything else.

They drive another thirty minutes into the desert, nothing to see but rocks, dry bushes and the occasional cactus. Liz stays silent, running through every possible scenario in her head as the minutes tick by. When the truck starts to slow, Liz sits up more, looking for any sign of where they are. She doesn't see a lot, but off in the distance, she sees something that resembles a van. She starts to panic all over again. The closer they get to whatever it is they are heading toward, the faster her heart beats, and the harder it is to breathe. They finally reach the van, and Riley puts the truck in park.

"I won't go back with him. If you try to hand me over, I will make sure you're forced to put a bullet in my head," Liz whispers, voice cracking.

Riley shifts in his seat so he can face her. They lock eyes, just for a moment. Liz sees something in him she can't quite read. He reaches over, gently taking her hand in his, the glove he's wearing scratching her hand as he rubs his thumb in a small circle. "I need you to trust me," he says, squeezing her hand.

Liz nods, the only thing she can do while fighting off her oncoming panic attack. She goes back to staring straight out the window, not able to bring herself to look at him again.

"Just stay here, I'll be right back." He drops her hand and climbs out of the truck, shutting the door with a loud thud.

Liz watches as he strides to where three men get out to greet him. The first man is not much shorter than Riley with rich black hair, and full beard. Then she looks at the second man, deep brown skin with short black hair. When she looks at the third man, she realizes it's Mikey. Liz stays watching them, wishing she could hear what they were saying when the two she doesn't know both turn and look at her. She immediately ducks, trying to hide herself as if they don't already know she is there. Her heart rate picks back up, as she fights to catch her breath. The door flies open and she lets out a small yelp.

"Just me, love," Riley says, his deep voice sending shivers down her body. There is something different about it, harder than when he normally talks to her, like he's fighting against turning back to reaper again. "C'mon." He grabs Liz's hand and helps her down.

She lets him help her, and when she's out, he closes the door with one hand, the other still firmly holding hers. As he leads her to the men, he slowly interlaces his fingers with hers. When they reach the open space between the truck and van, Riley shifts ever so slightly, just enough for her to be tucked in close behind him.

"Hey, darlin," Mikey says, a wide smile on his face as he waves to her.

She gives him a small smile in return, still not sure what to think of what's going on. She sneaks a peak at the other two men only to find them already watching her. Riley gives her hand a gentle, reassuring squeeze, then steps to the side, bringing her fully into their huddle.

"Meet Alex," Riley says, nodding at the man with the full beard. "And Tyler." They both nod their head in greeting, unsure of what to say.

"These are the other men in Nemesis. I trust them with my life, and more importantly... yours."

Liz looks up at him, wondering if that's what he meant to

say. He must know by now her life is worthless. Before she can start to overthink as she so often does, Riley turns to her.

"I need you to trust us," he says, rubbing slow circles on her hand with his thumb again. He nods to the men and they all walk away, leaving them alone in the headlights. His eyes search hers for any sign she will trust him.

She can't stand him looking at her like that, so she quickly looks away.

"Bring it out!" He yells to his team at the back of the van.

The back doors creak open and Liz hears banging but can't see the source of the noise. Then, she hears it, the rattling of chains. Her breathing picks up, heart pounding in her chest. Too many thoughts in her head to fight it. She struggles to catch her breath, sharp pains pulsing through her chest. She looks to the source of the noise, seeing Mikey step from behind the doors, followed by a man with a sack over his head.

Everything slows, she watches the man, hands tied behind his back, ankles shackled, dust kicking up with every step he takes. Then Alex and Tyler appear, following closely, their weapons ready. She doesn't understand what is happening, but when she looks at the man, she gets an uneasy feeling in her gut. Something about him sends a chill through her body. Slowly, Liz turns to Riley, and asks, "Riley... who the fuck is that?"

Riley drops her hand and walks to the mystery man, his anger igniting with every step he takes. He approaches the man, stepping behind him and swiftly kicks the back of his legs, sending him onto his knees. He grabs the bag, roughly ripping it off. Liz looks on in horror, once again face to face with the monster who took everything from her.

CHAPTER 21

Mikey steps around him and rips the tape off his mouth. Her brother, Jeremy, wastes no time before the shit starts pouring out of his mouth.

"I'M GOING TO FUCKING KILL YOU!" he screams at the group of men surrounding him. "DO YOU KNOW WHO THE FUCK I AM?" He tries to stand.

Mikey pushes on his shoulder, keeping him kneeling.

He continues his rant, glaring at each of the men, personally threatening each one. He turns his head and does a double take, turning back to stare at Liz, ignoring the men completely. A dark, sinister smile spreads across his beat-up face. "Hey, sis. How's the family?" he asks, letting out a dark laugh.

Riley doesn't hesitate before swinging his fist into her brother's face, sending his head flying to the side, his body with it. Mikey reaches down and roughly brings the monster back onto his knees.

He spits a mouthful of blood at Riley's feet before turning back to Liz, smiling to reveal his bloodied teeth.

"Do you know the problems you caused me? Do you have

any fucking idea what happened when they ran me through their system? They found warrants and arrested me," he says, eyes growing darker with anger at every word that spews out of his mouth. "They dragged me back and threw me in fucking prison!" He screams at her, spraying blood and spit across the sand in front of him. "I guess it wasn't all bad. I met some pretty... interesting people there." Staring at her, smiling again as the tears roll down her face. Seeing her hurt and crying only motivates him to keep going, tied up or not, he's going to make sure she's in pain.

"But you already met my new friends, didn't you? I hear you're going to see them again soon. You all are." He cranes his neck to eye the men, who are exchanging confused glances, before turning his attention back to his sister. "She screamed for you, you know. Screamed for a mommy who never came to save her." His evil smile spread back across his face. "She screamed and screamed. James didn't stop fighting until I dragged my knife acro—"

He is cut off by Riley slamming his fist into his nose, a sickening crack echoing through the quiet night air. "Keep him quiet," Riley says to his team before running to where Liz stands.

She can't move, forced to stand there with her arms wrapped tightly around herself, a small stream of tears flowing down her cheeks. She takes a few deep breaths, trying not to vomit hearing about what he did to her precious girl.

"You're a fucking asshole," she says quietly as Riley approaches. "How could you bring him here after everything I told you? I know I fucked up. I made stupid choices out of fear and desperation, but this—" Liz waves her arm at Jeremy and the group surrounding him, "this is just fucking cruel."

She turns, intending to walk away, but something stops her.

She trusted him. She held back in the room when all she wanted to do was scream at him for leaving her. She put her trust in him, just for him to do this to her. She refuses to look at him, she keeps her back to him as she says,

"I trusted you, Riley. I trusted my whole fucking heart with you. I told you everything and you left me. I knew you had this reputation of some big scary soldier that everyone fears, the one who will do whatever it takes to hurt someone... but I didn't think you wanted me to fear you, too. I guess I was wrong."

Liz walks away, stopping next to the truck. She takes a second to think about what she's doing before she turns and walks into the desert. She doesn't make it far before she hears the soft *thuds* of boots crossing the sand. Riley catches up to her moments later, grabbing her by the arm to stop her. She whirls on him so fast her head spins. Every lesson they had floods her head as she swings her fist at him. Pain shoots through her hand as it connects with his jaw. Mikey yells something she can't make out, too flooded with anger to care about anyone else.

Riley lifts his hand in the air, signaling the rest of his team to stay put.

Liz pulls her arm back, attempting to swing again, willing to do anything to be free of him. Riley avoids her fist and grabs her other arm like it's nothing for him. She glares at him, nothing but pure rage in her gaze.

"I fucking hate you," she spits.

Holding her by both arms, he backs her up to his truck. She tries to pull her arm out of his grip. She didn't plan on fighting him. She planned on walking into the desert until her legs gave out, but he took the choice from her. She yanks on her arm, attempting to swing again.

"STOP!" he shouts.

He backs her up a step, then another. Before she has time to process what to do next, she is being slammed into the side of Riley's truck. Arms pinned at her side, she throws her leg out, attempting to kick him. All that does is open up space for him to slide his leg into, pushing her legs apart to keep her from kicking out again. He steps into her, bodies unbearably close together, pinning her in place.

"Look at me," he orders. The power in his deep voice sends a shiver through her. "Princess," he pleads softly, the pet name being her undoing.

She drags her eyes to his, opening her mouth to argue, but he cuts her off before she can.

"Shh... Just listen." He leans down, closing his eyes, resting his forehead against hers. The thin metal of his mask grounding her. "I'm sorry I left. I know I should have stayed. I should have been there for you. You needed me and I left—After hearing about what that fucking animal did to you, to them..." Riley lets out a breath, taking a second to compose himself. "I snapped. The only thing on my mind was finding him. I was going to kill him myself until I found him. You weren't lying about his record, I just wasn't expecting to see his name pop up in our K.E.I.M database. I think he planned your kidnapping."

He picks his head back up, searching her eyes for any sign she is really hearing what he's saying. He drops her arms, trusting her to not attack him again. Reaching down, a small pop echoes through the silent night. In that moment, he places all of his trust in her.

Liz takes a deep breath, pushing their bodies closer together when she feels cool metal sliding into her hand at her side. She looks down to see Riley handing over his gun.

"I didn't bring you here to suffer any more pain, love. I brought you here to finally end the cause of it."

CHAPTER 22

"You expect me to do what? Kill him?" Liz asks, looking down at the gun in her possession. She shifts slightly under the weight of him pressing against her. Riley reaches up, moving a stray curl out of her face and tucking in gently behind her ear.

"When I lost my family, all I could think about was finding the men who murdered them. I know you've thought the same, you're too much of a fighter to not think about ending him." He takes a breath, trying to figure out how to make her understand he knows what she's going through. "Everyone told me it wouldn't bring them back. That their lives weren't mine to take, and if I did, I would just have the weight of murder on top of the weight of losing my family. They were wrong. Taking a life stays with you forever. Knowing those men will never be able to hurt another person makes me carry that weight with pride," he says, the pain on his face visible, even with the mask covering most of it.

"So, what? Am I supposed to just strut over and put a bullet between his eyes? What happens after that, Ry? You are literally in the military, basically a super cop. I kill him and you lock me up for murder. If you don't, one of your friends will," Liz says, a slight tremble to her voice.

Riley takes a step back, freeing her from the truck.

"You think I would bring you all the way out here, risk everything, just to throw you in jail?"

Liz doesn't know what to say to that. Never in her wildest dreams did she think he would be delivering her brother on a silver platter, offering her the revenge she has always dreamed about.

"Look, princess, you don't have to do anything you don't want to. You can get back in the truck and wait, one of the guys can drive you back, hell, you can keep walking into the desert if you really need to, but he isn't leaving here alive."

Liz doesn't know how long she spends pacing around the truck, thoughts racing about what she is going to do. She thinks about everything that can go wrong, what will happen if Riley is lying about turning her in. She thinks about the new members of his team she met, wondering if they will turn her in if he doesn't.

Riley watches her, his eyes following every little move she makes. She stops dead in her tracks, turning to go back over to Riley, who's now leaning on his truck, arms crossed, waiting for her to collect herself.

Liz simply nods her head at him and he pushes off, meeting her at the front of the truck. They walk back, side by side. She looks over at her brother, blood dribbling from his nose, pooling in the sand. One eye is already bruised and swollen shut. She follows Riley's lead and stops when he does. He leans in close and shows her where she should stand to get a clean shot.

Her brother looks over to where they are standing. As soon as he sees the gun in her hand, his screaming starts again.

"YOU LITTLE FUCKING WHORE!" he screams at her, blood flying from his mouth with every word. "I'M GOING TO MAKE WHAT I USED TO DO LOOK LIKE A FUCKING GAME WE PLAYED AS KIDS!"

"Someone shut him the fuck up," Mikey says walking over to the van and rifling around in the back. Alex walks over with a ball of something, intending to shove it in his mouth but her brother continues his screaming.

"HE'S COMING FOR YOU ELIZABETH!" he screams, knowing she always hated it when her family used her full name, just another way to try and hurt her before the end. "HE KNOWS WHERE YOU ARE. I MADE SURE HE WILL COME FOR YOU IF I'M GONE. DMITRI WILL ALWAYS FIN—" He's cut off by Alex shoving the gag into his mouth.

Mikey emerges from the van, a roll of gray tape in hand. He proceeds to wrap it around his head too many times, making sure her brother's mouth isn't able to move again. Mikey looks to where Liz and Riley stand, Liz shaking and Riley fighting his instincts. He wants nothing more than to leave her side and take her brother's life with his bare hands.

Mikey jogs over, needing to figure out what the hell is happening and check on Liz. "You alright, darlin?" he asks, pulling her into a tight hug.

Liz shakes her head no against his chest before pulling away from him.

"They told you this wasn't a good idea, man," Mikey says to Riley.

Liz turns to him, meeting his big blue eyes full of worry for her. "I'll be okay sweetie," she says, flashing him a sad smile before turning back and looking at her brother, nothing but pure, uncontrollable rage in her eyes at the sight of him. "I have to do this," she says, voice low and raw. "For them."

Liz walks to where Riley showed her. Hands trembling, ever so slowly, she raises the gun and aims it at her brother.

CHAPTER 23

Liz looks down at her trembling hands, lowering the gun to her side, all too aware of the five sets of eyes watching her, waiting to see what she will do. She lifts the gun again, still unsure if she's holding it properly. Liz takes a deep breath, then lowers the gun once more. Turning to where Riley watches her, she walks over to him. Liz carefully extends her arm, holding the gun out to him.

"I can't do it," she mouths to Riley who now makes his way over to her. When he's standing in front of her, she looks up at him, reaching the gun even further. "I'm not strong like you, Ry. I can't do it," she says when he reaches her. She keeps her voice quiet, hoping her brother doesn't hear what an absolute coward she is.

Riley simply puts his hands on her shoulders and spins her around. He guides her back over, leaving one hand on her shoulder before looking to his team. He turns his attention to Mikey and waves him over. As soon as he reaches them, Riley turns to him— "Get them and go somewhere. In the van, behind it, take a walk... I don't care, just give us some privacy."

"EY-EY Captain," Mikey says, making a flamboyant salute before turning and jogging over to Alex and Tyler. After Mikey talks to them, the other two men look at Riley and give him a nod before walking to the back of the van and climbing in.

Riley waits for the loud bang, signaling the men are safely tucked away before turning his attention back to Liz. He takes his gloves off and tosses them into the sand before he takes her face in his large hands. Riley gently tips her head back. She looks up at him, her green eyes sparking in the moonlight.

"Will you trust me, love? No fighting me, no walking away, just trust?" he asks, his eyes searching hers.

"I'll try," is all she has to say before he steps behind her. She feels his hard, muscular body pushing into her back, strong arms wrapping tightly around her. His callused hands rub down her arms, leaving goosebumps in their wake. He wraps his hands around hers, bringing the gun back up, helping guide her aim. Riley lowers his head, warm breath tickling her ear as he says, "I know it needs to be you, but I'll be right here the whole time, helping you through it. I'm never leaving you again."

She can't form words with his body wrapped around hers like it is, so she just gives him a little nod.

He extends his thumb, pushing a tiny button on something attached to the top of the gun. Suddenly, there is a small green dot bouncing around in the distance. "Alright, make sure your sight is slightly above where you want to hit," he says, helping to guide the little dot until it's centered on her brother's forehead.

"Pull the hammer back," he says, their thumbs working together to pull it back. "Good girl" he says in her ear, sending chills over her body. "Now you really need to listen to me. I want you to close your eyes, and on three, we squeeze the trigger. Don't just pull it, slowly squeeze."

Liz nods her head, eyes closing tight.

"One... Two..."

"Wait" Liz whispers, turning her head to look into Riley's eyes. "I don't really hate you."

"I know, princess. I read your note," he says resting his head against hers. He drops one of his hands, wrapping his arm around her waist and holding her there. Liz turns back around and squeezes her eyes shut, waiting for Riley to begin again.

"One... Two... Three."

Together, they squeeze the trigger, a deafening bang ringing out before Liz hears the sickening thud. She can't move, she just stands there, tears pooling behind her closed eyes, stomach full of knots. Her hands shake uncontrollably when she feels Riley start to let her go. She wants to beg him not to, but she can't form words.

He slips the gun from her hand and quickly slides it back into the holster on his leg. His hands are back on her before she has time to miss them, turning her around and pulling her tightly into him. Liz lets herself cry, the reality of what just happened hitting her. Riley gives her the time she needs, holding her tight as he rubs her back.

"It's over, princess. You did it," he says, resting his chin on the top of her head, still rubbing circles on her back. She sniffles, desperately trying to pull herself together, another deep breath in as she takes a step back and looks up at Riley.

He lets go of her but picks her hand back up and walks her over to the truck, making sure not to let her see the bloody mess that used to be her brother. Riley opens the door and helps her into the cab. Liz hears the quiet chatter of the team and ducks down, not wanting anyone to see her after what she did.

"I'll be right back," he says to her before walking to where the three men are huddled together.

Liz can see them talking about something before Alex and

Tyler turn and head back to the van. Mikey and Riley walk together to the truck, but when they get to the front, Mikey goes to the driver's side while Riley strides back to Liz in the passenger seat. Liz scoots herself over to be closer to the edge where he is standing, and leans her head on his chest, numb from the events of the night, she doesn't fight what her body tells her to do.

"I have to take care of this. I promise, I'll be back as soon as I can." He strokes her back. "Get her home safe," Riley says to Mikey.

Even after everything that has happened, she doesn't miss that he called it home. Without thinking of the implications, Riley pushes his mask up just enough to lean down and place a kiss on her forehead before helping her settle into the truck. He closes the door and steps back, watching them drive away into the night.

CHAPTER 24

Liz sits in silence, staring out the windshield the entire drive back, replaying the night over and over in her head. The sound of the gunshot and body falling to the ground plays on a constant loop. She's relieved when they finally pull up to the large gate and it groans open. As soon as the truck is parked, Liz jumps out and heads to the door, waiting for Mikey to swipe his access card and let them in. They walk down the hall, side by side, completely silent until they reach the door. Mikey punches in a code and pushes the door open, the cool air and familiar smells of the apartment making Liz feel slightly less nauseous.

"You did great tonight, darlin," Mikey says, closing the door. "But you should try to get some rest. If you need someone to talk to, I'll be here all night." He pulls her into a small hug that she's quick to return.

She stays silent, too much going through her head to respond. She simply trudges to her room and closes the door behind her, leaving Mikey standing alone in the middle of the living room.

Liz walks straight to the bathroom, sits in front of the toilet, and vomits everything she's eaten in the past 24-hours. When her stomach is completely empty, she gets up and turns the shower on as hot as it goes.

Sitting on the shower floor, she brings her knees to her chest and rests her forehead. Tears flowing freely, she stays in the shower until the water runs cold. She stands, turning off the shower, and wraps herself in a towel, forces herself back into her room and sits on her bed. With no energy left, she simply sits, staring into the void of the dark room. The sound of boots stomping and people talking pulls her from her own head. She gets up and drags herself to the door, making her steps as silent as she can, hoping to hear what they are saying.

"It's done, I'll brief the general in the morning," Riley says, pacing to the fridge to grab himself a much-needed drink.

"Then what? Are we letting her go?" Mikey asks, voice full of concern.

"I don't know, I found her way out. We can't force her to stay any longer but if we let her go..." He opens his beer and takes a long drink. "If we let her go, she's either going to kill herself or Dmitri finds her, and she made it clear she would die before she goes back."

"You need to figure it out, Ry," Mikey says, flipping through channels on the TV. "The general is going to make it your call. He knows how protective you are of her and he's going to use that to force your hand."

"How was she?" Riley asks, eyes flicking to her door.

"Didn't say a word to me. She showered and went to bed, but I could hear her throwing up."

Riley sets his beer on the table and strides for her door. As soon as Liz hears him approach, she sprints to her bed and throws the blanket over herself, not ready to see him.

Riley gives the door a soft knock, and when Liz doesn't answer, he opens it and walks in. He tries to be as quiet as he can, not wanting to wake her, but his footsteps cut through the silence. He sits on the edge of her bed, hoping his weight doesn't shift it too much. He doesn't touch her, doesn't say anything, just sits in the dark with her for a few moments. Standing back up, he turns to look down at Liz curled into a tight ball.

"Please don't let this consume you, princess," he whispers into the empty room before turning and walking out, gently closing the door behind him.

"She good?" Mikey asks as soon as Riley emerges from her room.

"She's asleep," he responds, shrugging his shoulders, not sure what else he can say.

"She didn't wake up when you went in?" Mikey asks, shock plastered on his face. He knows all too well she wakes up at any little sound in the room, but he also knows she has learned their footsteps. They made a silent agreement to pretend they didn't know if she was awake or not, assuming her little charade just made her more comfortable. It only took a week for her to learn their footsteps, freaking Mikey out the first time she knew it was him from his walk alone. Mikey checks the time, groaning, and forces himself up off the couch and walks to the door. "She really trusts you. You need to talk to her, help her figure things out," Mikey says, before walking out, leaving Riley alone to think.

Liz spent that entire night lying awake, content to rot there until she heard Mikey come in and Riley leave. Curiosity getting the better of her, she climbs out of bed, still clinging to the towel she fell asleep in. She trudges to the bathroom and inspects the mess of tangles that is her hair and the large bags under her eyes. She sighs, putting her hair into a messy bun before getting dressed. She slips into the pair of Riley's sweatpants she refuses to give back and a plain black tank, and heads to the kitchen.

"Good morning, sunshine," Mikey says, flipping something in a pan.

Liz looks at him, narrowing her eyes, noting something is off but can't figure it out. He flips whatever is in the pan again and again. "How are you cooking with the stove off?" she asks, eyeing the knobs on the stove.

He flips it one last time before sliding it onto a plate. He walks it over to the table and sets it next to the rest of the feast he's laid out. Liz looks at the table overflowing with food. She can't hide her stomach grumbling.

"I can't cook," he says, chuckling to himself. "But you deserve a big breakfast today, so I improvised."

"You've cooked for me before," she says, confused.

"Wrong. I have pretended to cook for you before," he jokes back.

"Where's Riley?" she asks, rolling her eyes and sitting down to eat.

"He had to meet with the general, should be back anytime." Mikey pulls two plates out of the cabinet and sets them on the table.

She eyes the plates for a second before getting up and pulling a third one from the cabinet. Liz turns back to the table and starts piling the plate high with food. Pancakes, bacon, sausage, eggs, potatoes, everything she can see. She carries the plate to the microwave and sets it in before turning back and sitting at the table. Mikey watches her the whole time, a knowing grin spread across his face, but the look Liz shoots at him has him thinking twice about saying anything.

They sit and eat mostly in silence, both making a few sad attempts at small talk, the events the night prior weighing heavy on their minds. They are almost finished eating when the door opens and Riley strides in, looking defeated. He isn't standing as tall, normally bright eyes seem duller, the confidence he usually struts around with is missing.

Liz notes the disappointment that flashes across his face at the sight of the empty containers on the table, and it's gone before she's even sure that's what she saw. She slides out of her chair and goes to the microwave, pulling out the plate she saved. She sets the plate at the empty seat at the table. "I don't know what you like so I took a little of everything. I hope that's okay."

He looks down at her, trying not to get lost in her shining emerald eyes. "Thank you," he says, eyes still locked on hers. The look in his eyes says he's smiling under his mask.

Mikey clears his throat in an obvious attempt to remind them they aren't alone. Riley turns and glares at him before pulling out his chair and sitting.

"Go get dressed. I'm working you out today," Riley says to Liz, causing Mikey to choke on the last bite of his breakfast.

The soft giggle Liz lets out makes the whole shit show worth it. Riley looks over and winks at her behind his mask before she prances to her room to shower and get dressed.

CHAPTER 25

Liz is ecstatic when they walk out into the bright morning air. They usually begin before the sun comes up and she's stuck in the room for the rest of the day, only leaving to walk to the weight room with Riley. Seeing the sun shining has been a rarity over the past few months. She heads to her and Mikey's usual starting spot and begins stretching.

"Over here, princess," Riley calls out, walking to his truck.

Liz looks over at him, confused, before she jogs over to where he is waiting for her. He gives her a look and she groans, opening the door and climbing up. Riley gets in and starts driving, heading to the large gate once again. Once they leave the base, Liz excitedly looks around, not having seen much outside of those white walls for months.

"So... you want to work me out?" Liz says, eyeing him playfully. She looks him over, never having seen him with just a neck gaiter on. She is surprised at the effort he puts into his hair, his crew cut spiked up just right.

"I uh... was just fucking with Mikey for eating all the food," he says, stumbling over his words.

"Oh, too bad. It's been a while since I've been... worked out," she says, her tone slightly sensual, setting Riley on edge. She watches as Riley shifts in his seat, his knuckles turn white as his grip tightens on the steering wheel. Not ready to tease him too much, she tries to change the subject. "What was your meeting about today?"

"That's classified."

"Was it about me?"

"Yeah, part of it."

Liz doesn't pry, but as they drive her mind wanders, wondering what they were talking about. Part of her hopes the general finally decided to let her go but another part, a part bigger than she's willing to admit, is hoping he fights for her to stay.

They pull off onto a dirt road, passing a big sign that reads "Knoll Trail". She looks around at the mountain they approach, in awe of how utterly beautiful it is. She absorbs everything as Riley continues down the road before pulling into a small dirt patch next to what Liz can only assume is the start of the trail.

"Thought you might like a change of scenery today," he says, watching her practically vibrate with excitement. Liz looks over at him, not sure how to thank him for bringing her here, for getting her out into the open air and sunlight.

"Lead the way." Her smile spreads across her face as she follows Riley up the start of the trail.

They hike in silence for some time, Liz was just happy to be breathing in the fresh air, enjoying everything the tail has to offer. While she spends her time silently watching the flowers dance in the breeze, Riley watches her prance her way up the trail, keeping quiet.

"I take it you used to hike?" Riley asks, trying to figure out how to bring up what he wants to talk to her about.

"Never, but after being locked away for god knows how long, this is my new favorite thing. What about you? You seem... outdoorsy."

"I used to hike with Sara when I would visit. I wasn't crazy about it, but she was, so I went along with her. We would pack up Sammy and her dogs and spend the whole day on a mountain."

"You're a good big brother," Liz says through a sad smile.

Riley doesn't miss the sadness in her tone. He wonders to himself if she's also thinking about what could have been if she had been born to a different family, to have a brother who did abuse her in every way.

They stay quiet for a while, both lost in their own thoughts, content just being in each other's company.

"What will you do when you finally get to leave us?" Riley asks, breaking their silence. The question has been heavy on his heart since he set foot in the general's office that morning, terrified of her answer.

Liz looks over at him, wondering what brought it on. She thinks for a minute, not sure how to respond. "Honestly... I don't know. I have no family waiting for me, and I don't even have a home to go 'home' to. I have no job to get back on my feet if I even wanted to, and you can't even find proof I exist. I have nothing left, Ry. If you want the truth, I will just pick back up where I left off." Liz says, kicking a small rock along the trail. Riley knows exactly what that means. His heart shatters.

When they finally reach the top, Liz walks to the edge, looking out at the land that stretches for miles. She takes a deep breath, letting the fresh mountain air fill her lungs before finding a flat rock to climb up on.

She looks around, waiting for Riley to join her, when she spots him by the edge of the cliff, stripping off his sweatshirt. Liz has never seen him like this. She doesn't even realize she's starting to stare.

He's dressed in shorts and a loose tank, arm holes stretched to almost reach his waist, the tan skin of his chest peeking through; his blonde hair turns golden in the sun. Tattoos she can't quite make out covers his muscular arms. She tries to look away, telling herself she's being creepy, but she can't help but focus on the way his defined chest is showing through the sides of his shirt. She's always been drawn to him, attracted to him by nothing more than his personality.

At first glance he seems strong, loyal, fiercely protective and maybe a little arrogant, but the more she got to know him the more he became so much more than that. He is attentive and dedicated, always keeping himself in check when she is scared. The times where he was flirty or teasing her, letting his playful nature show were some of her favorites. She is attracted to who he was at his core, she never stopped to think about how hot he is under the mountain of gear.

"Enjoying the view?" Riley asks, walking to where she sits. She was so consumed by him that she didn't even realize he had turned around to catch her staring.

"I just... didn't know you had tattoos."

He flexes his large tattooed arms, making the muscles bulge, sending Liz's stomach into knots. She quickly looks away, not willing to risk staring at him again. He climbs onto the rock that Liz is sitting on, settling next to her.

"How are you handling everything?" he asks, genuinely concerned for her mental health, knowing how hard last night was for her. He waits for her answer, hoping she will talk to him, let him help her through it.

"Well... I killed someone... so I'm going to go with not good."

"We killed a someone, not you, us, and he was a fucking monster."

"He was, but now I'm no better," Liz tells him, picking up tiny pebbles and throwing them off the rock they are resting on.

"Do you regret it?" Riley asks, building a small pile of pebbles for her. She opens her mouth to answer before snapping it closed again. She picks up another pebble, throwing it off into the distance.

"Not even a little. That's how I know I'm no better... Shouldn't I feel bad? Killing him felt good, and I hate myself for feeling like that."

"Would you have felt bad if you killed Mikey that night?" Riley asks, eyeing her.

"Don't even joke about that!" she says, voice raising slightly. She picks up one of her small pebbles and throws it at him watching it bounce off one of the grey skulls adorning his arm.

"Exactly. You wouldn't be able to live with yourself if you hurt someone. Your brother was a piece of shit who deserved to die. He abused you, abused other women. He killed your family over a warning, and when that finally caught up to him, he joined a fucking terrorist organization to get back at you... You don't feel bad because you know he deserved it."

Liz lets every word he says sink in. She lies down, turning her head to face Riley. Her eyes roam over the expanse of art covering his skin, wondering if they mean anything. She lingers on the small dove mixed into the smoke and skulls. When she looks closer she spots a second smaller one and her heart sinks. Liz doesn't need to ask to know who that one is for. She turns away, throwing her arms over her eyes and lets the sounds of the wind and wildlife occupy her mind while she basks in the sun like a lizard. She gets lost in the serenity when something next to her vibrates. She moves her arm and peeks at Riley to see him texting someone before he gets up and climbs off the rock.

"Mikey sent an S.O.S. You ready to head back?"

"Is everything okay?"

"Yeah, I'm sure it's just the general being an asshole again" Riley reaches his hands out to help Liz off the rock. She takes them, and once she is on the ground, she quickly drops his hands and starts down the mountain still embarrassed she got caught staring at his glorious muscles.

She slows, not realizing how much the altitude and sun would affect her. She drags her feet dramatically, kicking up dust as she does. Riley looks back, making sure she is keeping up, only to find her doing the opposite. He stops next to a smaller rock and waits for her to catch up.

"C'mon, princess, climb up," Riley says to her, backing up to the rock.

"You're not carrying me," she says, shooting him a look. As tempting as the offer is, she can't bring herself to be that close to him, not after how she's been drooling over him all day.

"I need a workout today. You're what, 5'2" maybe 110 pounds? I can carry you down and I will still need to hit the gym tonight."

"5 foot, thank you very much," she says, still not wanting him to carry her, but she's so tired she gives in and climbs up on the rock, jumping onto his back.

He wraps his powerful arms under her legs, and she tightens her arms around his neck, careful not to pull his mask down. A mix of cardamom and vanilla flood her senses.

Riley takes off down the mountain, walking faster than she ever could, and she realizes he was slowing himself down for her. She rests her chin on his shoulder, their faces almost touching.

"So why does everyone call you Reaper?" she asks sweetly, her warm breath on his ear.

He does everything he can not to think about their closeness, her thighs wrapped around him, breasts pushing into his back.

"I got captured by Dmitri when he was first starting out. He wasn't on our radar yet and we were getting too close to where he was camped. When we were flying over, they shot us down," Riley explains, gripping her a little tighter. "I woke up in a cage surrounded by corpses. He accidentally captured an American and thought it was going to make him a legend. I was forced to be on display like a prize. He wanted everyone to know what he was capable of. I was stuck in mud, surrounded by rotting flesh for weeks. Eventually, during a big storm, the rain washed some poor bastard's skull out of the dirt. By the time that happened, I was starting to go crazy, so I broke the skull and made myself a mask out of it, trying to hide myself from them like a fucking coward," he says, taking a small pause to collect his thoughts before continuing.

He has only told a handful of his closest friends and a mandated therapist what he had been through, but if anyone needs to hear this story it's the woman clinging to his back. Liz lifts her head from its resting spot on Riley and gives him a small kiss on the cheek, squeezing him tightly. No one knows the demons he's fighting in his own head better than her.

"A few nights later, someone came to throw scraps at me, but I was wearing the skull. I was completely coated in mud and filth. I didn't know it was Dmitri at the time, he was clearly drunk yelling about a reaper when he saw me. He stupidly unlocked the cage and came in. He told me he was banishing me to hell, like I wasn't already there.. When he got close, I attacked, I slashed his face open with a bone and ran. I got lucky, only one man was around when I started running. He tried to stop me and I beat him to death with that same bone."

Without realizing what she was doing, Liz nuzzles her head into his neck. Trying to get comfortable, acting like she's listening to a bedtime story instead of being carried down a mountain listening to someone's deepened trauma.. Riley did his best to ignore how close her face was to his, how one small turn of his neck would have his masked lips on hers.

"I don't remember a lot after that, I was running on pure adrenaline at that point. I somehow made it out of their camp and to a town, and a few hours later I was being loaded into a helo on my way back. Mikey told me I broke the nose of the first guy who tried to take it off, screaming about being the reaper. They decided right then it was my call sign and I've worn masks ever since."

"Damn... now I feel bad for always asking you to take it off," she mutters against his neck. It was a good thing they were almost at the bottom of the trail. "I didn't realize you went through so much," she says, giving him a comforting little squeeze. It's the best she can do while still clinging to his back.

"It helped me: my call sign, the mask, it all helped me get to this point. I became something everyone fears, and I use that fear to make sure what happened to me doesn't happen to anyone else."

Liz stays quiet, not sure what she can say. She looks up and sees they are standing next to his truck. She didn't even realize Riley had stopped walking. "You should have told me we were back," she says, wiggling her hips against him. He lets go of her legs and she drops from his back. Trying to hide her embarrassment, she waltzes over to the truck and opens her door.

"If I told you, you would have made me put you down, and

you never would have done that cute little wiggle," he says, chuckling at the pink creeping across her face.

Riley closes her door and walks to the other side, climbing in, and starting the truck. The air conditioner starts and Liz has never been more thankful for crisp, cool air. Riley pulls out, heading back the way they came, and Liz watches everything they are leaving behind.

"You ever think about enlisting?" Riley blurts out over the silence, still not sure how he should approach the topic especially after what he just opened up about.

Liz turns to him, a look of confusion and curiosity plastered on her face. She turns and looks back out the window, trying to absorb as much of the outside world as she can before it's gone.

"Is that what your meeting was about?" she asks.

"Depends on your answer."

"No, it's not something I've ever thought about. I mean, I'm 5 foot tall with an anger problem and mental health issues. Not sure I'm an ideal candidate."

"True," he says, laughing at the look she shoots in his direction. "But you're a fighter. You spent your whole life fighting for a better one. You fought Dmitri, and god knows you've been fighting me since the day I rescued you. You shouldn't stop now. You need to find something worth fighting for and hold onto that," Riley says, trying to gauge her reaction.

"How would that even work? You guys thought I was lying about my name for what... Two months now? I told you, I'm not even a real person anymore. How am I supposed to sign up for the military?" she says, peering over at him.

"You don't need to worry your pretty little head about the details, there is more than one way to join, the other ways are just kept hidden. I just need to know if you're in or not."

"I don't know, Ry," she says, scooting around so she can face him. Thoughts racing, she never imagined she would make it to adulthood, but she did. She never thought she would find love and have a family, but she did. She certainly didn't think she would survive losing her family, but she is, so maybe she can do this too.

"Where would I go?" she asks. "If I agree, I mean, I assume I'm going to get shipped off to do the whole basic training thing... that's kind of all I know about the military."

"You're not leaving me, love, that's part of the deal. Luckily, we're not just a spec ops unit, but one that technically doesn't exist, so adding a person who doesn't exist is kind of perfect."

Liz turns back around, the base coming into view. She stays silent, thinking and rethinking everything. They drive through the gate and park. Liz immediately jumps out and walks to the door, waiting for Riley to catch up. Her anxiety is at an all-time high with the base swarming with soldiers going about their day.

As soon as the door to the room opens, Mikey is on his feet, sprinting across the small space, and pulling Liz into a tight hug.

"You got my S.O.S! Welcome to the team, darlin" he says, holding her close.

"This is why you sent that?" Riley asks, frustrated their time was cut short for nothing.

Liz doesn't say anything, just slips from his grip and goes to shower and change into clean clothes. As soon as she's gone, Riley grabs a beer from the fridge and plops onto the couch.

"She said no?" Mikey asks.

"She didn't say anything," Riley says, before telling him everything that happened on the hike. As soon as the shower turns off, Riley gets up from the couch and goes into his room, closing the door behind him. He emerges a little while later, wearing his usual jeans, boots, and tight black shirt. Liz comes out minutes after Riley, hair braided down her back, wearing clothes not coated in sweat and sand.

"So," she says, walking to the couch and sitting down next to Mikey. "I've been thinking and you owe me some answers." She looks right at Riley. "I want to know what the meeting was about, since you said it was about me. I also want to know how this would work... if I say yes."

Riley sits at the table. Liz turns and lays across the couch so she can see him, kicking her feet up on Mikey's lap.

"I briefed the general on what happened with your brother. I made it clear to him you had nothing to do with Dmitri or his operation, but we learned your brother did, and he's the reason you ended up imprisoned," he explains. "I told the general I will continue to take full responsibility for you. Mikey, Alex, and Tyler all confirmed what your brother said. Even the general couldn't deny having someone solely trained by spec ops would be a huge asset, and at the very least, you're good for tight spaces," Riley says winking.

Hearing that has Liz picking herself up, bending over the back of the couch and leaning her arms on the table to be face to face with Riley. Mikey sits up straighter, his head bouncing back and forth between them, sure he missed something while they were gone.

"So, you want to keep me around... for my tight spaces?" she practically purrs. "I mean, my ability to get you into them?" she adds, batting her lashes, knowing exactly what she is doing to him.

The small expanse of skin showing on his face turns a bright shade of red at her words, his eyes following the curves of her body, jealous of the view Mikey has sitting next to her. He clears his throat and slides a small packet of papers toward Liz.

"Do I need a lawyer to go over these? Make sure I'm not agreeing to anything unsavory?" She teases, meeting Riley's eyes,

"You can read them if you want love. It's a slightly modified enlistment contract. If you stay like that I'll be happy to go over all the boring details."

"So y'all don't see me sitting here?" Mikey croaks, awkwardly watching the pair.

Liz bursts out in a melodic giggle fit while she reaches over, pushing her chest out, making sure she gives him a show as she signs the papers.

CHAPTER 26

The ink isn't even dry when an explosion rocks the building. Alarms blare, echoing throughout the room.

Riley and Mikey are on their feet at once, throwing on their gear and checking their weapons.

Liz jumps and sprints to her room, searching for her shoes. As she's bouncing on one foot, fighting to put on her second sneaker, Riley strides in, wearing the full suit of gear she first saw him in.

"Stay put," he says, before quickly walking back out.

Liz chases after him, seeing Mikey waiting by the door, also in full gear, gun slung across his chest. "You can't just leave me here," Liz screeches, determined to go with the men and help anyway she can.

"You're not going out there. We have no idea what we're dealing with."

She just looks at them, big green eyes shimmering with freshly formed tears. She gives them a small nod and starts to take a few steps back. They open the door and storm out into the stampede of soldiers. Before the door can close, Riley turns and sprints back in, pulling the large knife from the holster on his back and hands it to her. He disappears back out the door, Liz watching until it's fully closed. Keeping a tight grip on the knife, she walks into her room, trying to dress as close to what she sees Riley wear as she can.

She goes with her tight black jeans and combat boots, paired with a long-sleeved black shirt. She sprints to Riley's room, searching for anything to help, hoping he won't get mad she's invading his privacy. Liz finds an armored vest tucked into his closet and she slings it over her body, groaning in frustration when it's too big. She marches back to the living room, sitting on the couch, and prays her guys will be okay.

Riley and Mikey take off down the hall, hoping to make it to the central command center before all hell breaks loose. They navigate the hallways with ease and make it to the main door without much trouble, stopping to shout orders to the scrambling soldiers along the way. The second they step outside, it's chaos. Riley ducks behind the housing unit sign, only exposing himself enough to fire his weapon at the enemy men taking over the courtyard.

"Reaper!" Mikey shouts over the gunshots surrounding them. He ducks behind the sign next to Riley, taking turns firing at their attackers, slowly clearing the courtyard. Riley leans over, a bullet whizzing by his head. He fires again and sees the body fall to the ground.

"Commands not going to tell me shit. I'll keep pushing them back, you go find out what the fuck is happening," Mikey says, popping up and firing another round at a man who runs toward them.

Riley simply nods, looking for cover to get closer to the command building. Riley moves slowly, sticking to the shadows as much as he can while debris rains down all around him.

Mikey makes sure the small team of men keep the enemy busy to allow Riley to slip away, working in the shadows he prefers.

Riley crouches in the grass, hidden behind a small bush, and fires his gun at an enemy soldier, blood and brain matter spraying the door he was trying to enter. The man drops and Riley rushes over, kicking his corpse out of the way. He punches in his code and storms into the building.

He takes a quick look around, the glass-walled conference rooms filled with people hiding from the slaughter happening outside. It doesn't take long to spot the man he's looking for, barking orders, basking in being in charge. Riley pushes through the horde of people scrambling to get the base back under control. He pounds on the glass to get his attention.

The general stands, anger twisting his face, and storms to the door, holding it open for Riley to enter. General Scott looks around for someone who isn't there, before turning on Riley. "Where the hell is she?" he yells.

Riley pales, stomach in knots at the mention of Liz, wondering why the general would ask about her.

"She's safe. What the fuck is going on, General?" Riley barks, monitoring the cameras covering the fight erupting on the base. He spots Mikey, ducked behind a car, pushing his men to the massive hole blasted in the western wall.

"Dmitri," the General says, turning his attention to the wall of screens. "They are here for her. We need to hand her over and end this, Corson."

Riley fights every urge in his body to end the general's life for even considering handing Liz back over to the man who tortured her. His eyes flick to the screens, making sure Mikey is okay before searching for the housing unit, checking to see if men are advancing on it. Seeing what he is looking at, the general grows angry.

"This is exactly what she wanted! Dmitri wouldn't send his men to retrieve her if she wasn't working with him," the general says.

"She signed! Liz is one of us now and you're a fucking idiot if you still believe that she has anything to do with Komarov," Riley growls.

"I've let you have your fun with her, Corson! I allowed you to use her for whatever you wanted but she was never supposed to sign those papers!. I thought you would get tired of her and give her to my men, not become infatuated with the bitch," he shouts, trying to hide the tremble in his voice.

Riley doesn't hesitate, doesn't give the general time to react, before his hand is firmly wrapped around the man's throat, slamming him against the glass wall. Riley stares into his eyes, slowly tightening his grip. The general's face grows red as he gasps for air.

"You can act strong in front of everyone here, but we all know you didn't let me do anything, you're not really in charge, I just allow it. You and I both know what would happen to you if you tried to keep her from me."

Riley isn't someone anyone would want to go against on a good day, but when it comes to Liz and her safety; he becomes infinitely more dangerous. The general just stares, pure, unfiltered terror in his eyes.

"He has... a missile... aimed here. Thousands will... die," the general sputters, fighting to get air into his lungs.

"Then call for a fucking evacuation, General. What do you think he's going to do when he has her back, huh? You think the leader of a fucking terrorist organization is just going to take her, pull his men, and be on his merry fucking way? That missile is coming for us whether he has her or not," he screams at the man in his grasp, drawing the attention of everyone outside their glass box.

Riley loosens his grip, letting the man drop to the floor still gasping for air. Riley takes a step back, needing to put distance between them before he does something he may regret.

"If you won't hand her over, I will do it myself, Commander," the general snaps, rubbing at his neck.

The words are barely out of his mouth when Riley turns on his heels, slamming his fist into the general's face, blood pouring from his shattered nose. The command room goes silent, all eyes on them, terrified of what Reaper will do next.

"Call for the fucking evacuation," Riley says loud enough for everyone to hear. His caramel eyes are filled with nothing but loathing as he stares down into the general.

He turns his head and gives a slight nod to someone Riley can't see. Suddenly, the room shakes with the booming sound of a siren. Riley turns, storming out of the room, needing to protect Liz more than his need to end his commanding officer. As he's storming his way back out of the building, he gets on his radio, trying to reach Mikey.

"Tank, you have ten minutes to get as many people out as you can, if they can't leave, direct them to the bomb shelters. When that ten minutes is up, you get as far from this fuckin place as possible!" Riley shouts into his radio as he sprints across the courtyard.

People everywhere are scrambling to get somewhere safe. Everything seems to slow when an announcement sounds over the missile alarm.

"Ballistic missile inbound, fifteen minutes to impact. Seek immediate shelter."

Liz paces the room, filled with dread, when she hears a siren blare. Her heart drops from the sudden change. This isn't the same one that has been a constant ringing since the attack started. Mikey and Riley are out there somewhere, and she has no way of knowing if they are okay or not. A sharp knock on the door stops her in her tracks. She cautiously tiptoes to the door, heart racing, a thousand thoughts crossing her mind and not a single one good. She thinks back to what Mikey told her about how he and Riley are the only two with access to the room. If someone is knocking, it's not someone she wants to be dealing with. The person on the other side knocks again, louder this time.

"Open up," a familiar Russian voice commands.

Her blood runs cold. Liz backs away from the door, stumbling over her own feet, keeping the knife clutched close. Everything goes fuzzy, her head spinning when the knocking turns into pounding.

"Time to come home, pet," another voice yells from beyond the door.

The door begins to shake, deafening bangs filling the small space. She knows the men on the other side are going to break it down and take her back to Dmitri.

Liz forces herself to take a deep breath before running through the rooms, trying to find anything other than her knife to fight them off. She reaches under the couch for Riley's gun safe, telling herself if all else fails, she can end her life before they get their hands on her. She screams in frustration, feeling nothing but dust. She should have known he would take the gun after what she did.

The banging continues, Liz watches in horror as the frame of the door moves a little with each new impact. After coming up empty handed, she does the only thing she can do. She grips the knife like Riley had been teaching her and readies herself for a fight.

As Riley approaches the housing complex, he finds a small group of men trying to break the door down. He lifts his gun and fires off three shots. The men fall to the ground with a sickening thud, not dead, but they will be down long enough to get to Liz. Making his way across the small lawn, his only focus is getting to her, so focused on getting back he doesn't even hear the RPG until it's careening into the building, sending him flying through the air.

Riley gets blown into the side of the neighboring building. He forces himself to his feet. His head throbs, a sharp ringing in his ears. His whole body screams in protest, but he needs to get to her, he promised she would be safe. Riley sprints as fast as his legs can carry him, hurling himself through the hole in the wall where the door once stood, racing to reach Liz.

Liz watches in horror as the door lurches a little more with each kick, knowing it's only a matter of minutes before the men break their way in. Three is all it takes and the door flies open. Two men stalk into the room, heading right for her. She swings the knife at the man closest, barely missing his chest. He jumps back, avoiding her, as she whirls on the second man, attempting to drive the knife into his stomach. The first man uses that time to grab her arm, twisting it to the point she feels it's going to snap off, forcing her to drop her knife. She swings her other arm out, this time hitting her mark.

The man drops her arm but swings his large fist at her, connecting with her face. She is thrown back, pain blooming in her jaw, the coppery tang of blood filling her mouth. She spits a mouthful of red onto the floor, and launches herself, anger and adrenaline overtaking her training. She swings wildly at the men, fighting for her life like a cornered animal. She curses herself for not heeding her training. Quickly growing tired, Liz starts backing away, desperate to buy herself a moment to think. When a gunshot rings out, everything stills. Liz looks to see a third man she hadn't seen before fall to the ground, deep red pooling around him.

"The building was supposed to be clear!" the first man shouts in his thick Russian accent. The second man nods and runs to the door. The first man uses the small distraction to drive his fist into Liz's face again, sending her tumbling to the floor. Something in her tells her to stay on the floor, a feeling deep in her gut, the same feeling she gets when Riley tells her to trust him.

Another shot rings out, followed by another body hitting the ground. The Russian man stops, mumbling to himself, and pulling his gun out he slowly walks to the door. He looks around the narrow hall, surrounded by debris and bodies. He turns his attention back to Liz when he hears a distinctive click. He lets out a deep, throaty laugh.

"Out of bullets, Reaper?" The man bellows down the hall, looking around hoping to spot Riley.

Liz pulls herself up, head throbbing from the impact. Trying to be as quiet as possible, she inches her way across the floor to where the knife now lies. She peers over at the entrance, seeing the man still distracted by Riley. She silently picks up the knife and starts for the door.

"You or her, Reaper. One of you will die today," the man yells again.

Liz hears the crunch of concrete somewhere in the hall and her stomach drops. All her fears leave her when she hears that, all but one.

Him.

She won't let him do this. She stands, picking a path through the debris, careful to avoid any sudden movements. Liz creeps closer to the door, when out of the corner of her eye the man raises his gun, aiming at something she can't see. She throws herself into a sprint. The only thing on her mind is protecting Riley. By the time the man hears her coming it's too late. She throws her body into him, stabbing down with everything she has, praying she doesn't miss.

She pushes as hard as she can, forcing the knife into the man as they fall. Time seems to slow as they collapse to the ground. She yanks the knife out, his blood rushing out of the hole she put in him. Liz raises the knife above her head and brings it back down on him, using all her strength to push it through layers of clothing and flesh. Liz pulls it out again, readying for a third strike, when someone grabs her arm. Liz winces and turns on whoever grabs her.

She starts to swing again, not ready to give up on getting to Riley, when the overwhelming scent of cardamom and sandalwood hits her. She lets the knife drop from her hand. Tears spring to her eyes as he helps her up. Liz throws herself into Riley, wrapping her arms around his waist, his arms wrapping tightly around her shoulders in return.

"Did they hurt you?" Riley asks, trying to keep his voice steady. His hands go to her face, forcing her to show him the fresh bruises forming. Liz simply shakes her head, not wanting him to worry. He wipes some of the blood from her face before pulling her into his arms once more. Their reunion is short-lived when the alarm sounds again, the voice making another announcement.

"Ballistic Missile inbound. Five minutes to impact. Seek immediate shelter."

Riley lets go of her, darting into his room. He emerges seconds later, two bags in one hand, the other grabbing Liz and pulling her into a run. They sprint as fast as their legs will carry them through the hall, throwing the doors open when they reach the end.

Riley fumbles with keys in his other hand, refusing to drop hers until he absolutely has to. The truck roars to life as they approach. Riley drops her hand, letting her run and climb into the passenger side while he climbs into the driver's seat, throwing the bags into the bed of the truck as he does. They don't even get their doors closed when a stream of smoke draws their attention. A missile streaks across the pale blue sky, headed right for the base. Riley throws the truck into gear and drives, heading for the gate across the parking lot, now blown apart by Dmitri's small team. The roar of the missile grows louder, causing the ground to shake. Riley navigates through the destroyed gate, swerving to avoid the large chunks of concrete and mangled metal now scattered around the exit.

The impact is deafening, like nothing Liz has ever heard before. The shockwave of it sends the truck careening off the road. Riley doesn't let up as he gets the truck back under control, debris raining down on them as he drives away. Liz can only watch in horror as the base is reduced to nothing but rubble and smoke. Tears silently slip from her eyes, watching until there's nothing left to see.

CHAPTER 27

Liz isn't sure how long they drive, the only indication that time passes is the darkness that surrounds them. Still in shock from everything that happened, neither one can bring themselves to talk first. Liz lets her thoughts drift to Mikey, hoping and praying he was able to make it out safely. She looks to Riley, at the death grip he has on the steering wheel, still speeding down the highway, realizing she needs to be the one to break the silence.

"What the fuck is going on, Ry?" she asks, voice trembling.

"I don't know, princess," he says looking over at her, his eyes softening when they meet hers.

"I'm taking you home, then I'm going to find out."

"Home? I don't have a home, Riley," she says, hurt that he plans on getting rid of her after everything that happened just a few hours prior.

"Just try to rest. I'll tell you everything I know when we get there," he says, watching her purse her lips.

Something she only does when really thinking about something, he's come to learn. She scoots over and lowers her body across the seat, putting her head as close to Riley as she can without laying on his leg. She pulls her feet up onto the seat next to the door. Her hand finds its way onto Riley's lap, needing some sort of physical contact to keep her anxiety from running wild. Riley drapes his arm over her side, sliding his thumb back and forth, needing to hold her the same way she needs to hold him.

Liz opens her eyes, not realizing she had even fallen asleep and slowly sits back up. Rubbing the sleep from her eyes, she looks at the radio, rock music playing softly. She notices the clock, 1:37 a.m. They have been driving for over eight hours without a break.

"Where are we going?" Liz asks, looking out into the dark.

"I told you, we're going home—"

"And I told you, I don't have a home!" Liz shouts. Too much has happened in such a short time for her to keep her emotions in check. "That's not good enough for me, Riley. I need to know where you are taking me," she states, calmer this time, needing him to understand how much she needs the truth from him.

"Blue Mountain Montana, I have a house there. We should be there in an hour," he tells her, trying to understand how scary this may be to her. He has spent almost twenty years in the military, this is just another day to him, but it's not to her. She has spent the last nine months in some sort of captivity with people telling her what to do and where to go, not telling her what's going on.

She sits, quietly watching the trees grow thicker, nearly impossible to see anything past them in the dark. She doesn't notice when Riley turns off into the woods, a hidden road tucked into the tree line. She peers out the window, eyes straining to make out anything along the nearly black trail. Turning her attention to the road in front of them, she watches as they approach what looks like some type of cabin built under a tower so tall she can't see the top. Off to the side of the tower there is a barn. Liz starts to wonder if maybe it's a ranger station or a fire watch tower.

Riley pulls up to the side and parks the truck before jumping out. Liz watches as he grabs the bags and rushes around the front to open the door for her, ushering her out before the headlights turn off and they are left in pitch black.

She takes his hand and stumbles out of the truck. Her breathing quickens, heart pounding in her ears as she tightens her grip on Riley's hand. There is no way in hell she is going to lose him out here. Riley tugs her hand, pulling her against his side so he can wrap his arm around her as he leads them to the beat-up little house. She thinks to herself there is no way this can be his home. Riley pushes open the creaky wooden door and walks inside, pulling Liz along with him. He hits something on the wall and the small room illuminates with a flickering yellow glow.

Liz steps in and looks around the small room, in disbelief that anyone could actually live there. The space looks like something from a horror movie. An old brown couch sits against one wall, torn and covered in stains, under it sits a dirty rug. Like Riley's apartment on the base, a small kitchenette lines the far corner, oak cabinets hang on to their rusty hinges for dear life. A battered table and three mismatched chairs sit halfway between the couch and kitchen. A door, too big for the room they stand in, catches her attention, but she just assumes it leads to a bedroom. The whole room smells musty, like a slow leak has been keeping everything moist for far too long. Cobwebs adorn each corner along with a thick coat of dust covering every surface, still, it's better than what she has had before. She drops Riley's hand so she can turn to look at the rest of the room and turns herself right into a taxidermied deer mounted on the wall next to her, causing her to jump back with a shriek, slamming into Riley.

"You good?" he asks, trying to keep her from falling over. Once she's on her feet again, she rushes to the other side of him, needing to get the deer out of her line of sight.

"Yeah, taxidermy just really freaks me out," she says, a shiver running down her spine.

Riley doesn't say anything, he simply picks up her hand and gives it a small squeeze. He walks over to the too big door, Liz trailing right behind him, and pulls out a key. Riley unlocks it and gives the door a pull and it groans open. Where there should be a room, there is only what looks like the door to an elevator. Liz looks up at him, brows knit in confusion.

Riley pushes a hidden button and the elevator door slides open and he steps in without a word. He watches Liz, needing to know if she trusts him enough to follow him. Liz looks around again, having no idea what is waiting for her wherever the elevator goes. She looks at Riley, amber eyes sparking with each flicker of the lights, and she steps in beside him.

They stand in silence as the elevator closes. Once Riley pushes his thumb against a small square pad the elevator starts going down. Finally, it stops, and the doors slide open. Riley steps out, Liz right behind him, trying to comprehend what she's looking at. Liz takes another step, looking around the large open space.

The walls and floor are all the same deep gray shade of concrete, but somehow the lighting makes it more cozy than ominous. A small step down leads to the living area with a plush couch, big enough to fit Riley's entire team nestled inside. What looks like a fireplace built into the wall with recessed shelves next to it, filled with books and small decorations. A TV the size of a car is mounted over it. On the other side of the space is a kitchen with a large island topped with a stunning marble top, chairs lined against one side of it. Directly in front of them, across the room, is a hallway and another hall to the right of where they came in pass a dining table so big you will have to walk to the other side just to pass the salt.

"What is this place?" Liz asks, slowly spinning to take in as many details as she can. Despite being made from stone, the space is cozy and warm, leaving Liz feeling more at ease here than she has been in years.

"This is home. I had it built after Sara died. I needed some-place safe for myself and the people I care about," he says, walking across the room.

"If this is your home, why stay at the base?"

"Because that's where you were, princess," he says, striding to the hall, Liz following closely behind.

He points to the first door on the right, telling her that's the laundry room as they walk past. He stops at the next door, further down the hall, to reveal a bedroom. He walks in, and Liz continues to follow, not saying a word. He tosses one of the bags on the bed and turns to her.

"I hope this is okay. You have your own bathroom through that door," he says, nodding his head toward the door on the left wall. "You're free to wander or hang out, do whatever you want."

Free. She can't stop the tears that spring to her eyes. Riley had started giving her more freedom at the base, but she was still being watched, still wasn't free. Every step she took outside of her room felt wrong, like she shouldn't be doing it. She was still a prisoner. Here, she's just a friend who needs somewhere safe to sleep.

"What are all the other rooms? Anything cool?" Liz asks, sniffling as she wipes away her tears.

"Next room down is Mikey's. My room is right there." He points to the black door directly across the hall. "The others are just spare rooms in case someone needs a safehouse."

"That's... actually really nice," Liz says, looking around. The room is at least double the size of the room she had at the base, the plush bed doubled in size too. That's when she notices the bag Riley threw, it was the pillowcase she filled from the night she planned to escape.

"I'll give you some time to unpack... maybe wash up," he says, lifting her hand, stained red with the blood of Dmitri's soldier. "I know this is a lot, just... come find me when you're ready and I'll show you the rest of the house."

Liz paces the room, checking out the drawers in the dresser, then the closet. She walks to the bathroom and pushes the door open, her eyes go wide and takes in the size of it. The bathroom is almost as big as the bedroom, with a standing shower and a giant soaking tub. She would love nothing more than to take a long, hot bath, and let all the stress of the last few months soak away, but she settles for a quick shower instead.

Once the blood is washed off, she gets out and digs through her "bag", pulling out Riley's sweatpants and a crop top, quickly dressing herself. Eyeing the bed for a second, she tells herself she can't just take a nap and pretend everything is fine, so she walks out and heads down the hall from where they came.

Liz finds Riley looking through the cabinets, then the fridge, not noticing she's there until he hears a chair being pulled out behind him. He turns, giving her a look she can't quite read.

"You unpacked fast."

"I don't really have anything... remember?" she says, sadness flashing across her face. She hops up from the chair, looking around the room again. "Still want to show me the rest of your house?"

"Our house," Riley says, unable to hide his smile, even with his mask on. "You signed the papers, love. They may have been destroyed, but you still signed them, you are officially the newest member of Nemesis. I'll move back to base if you want me to, but I was hoping you would rather we stay here."

He walks over to the far side of the room, what Liz thought was a hall was actually a set of stairs. She follows him down to the level below, wondering how much bigger his house can possibly be. The stairs end and open to a small foyer completely empty of any furniture or signs of life. One wall is all glass, a personal gym behind it, the other two walls completely empty except for a large door on each. This hallway is easily the most ominous part of the house. Riley opens the far door, holding it open for Liz. She steps through and the smell of chlorine fills her nose.

"You have a pool... underground?" she asks, impressed by what he has managed to build.

"Yeah, it's nice after an intense workout," he says, turning and heading back out the door, his heavy footsteps echoing around the empty room.

Liz looks at the next door, expecting him to open it, but he just walks back to the stairs. She spots the same finger scanner sitting just above the handle as the one in the elevator. She pushes her bottom lip out and gives Riley a pleading look, and looking into her big green doe eyes, he caves. Riley walks back over and puts his thumb on the scanner, pushing the door open for her to go in.

Liz steps into the dark room, barely able to make out what looks like a long room with some type of bench in the front. Riley flicks on the lights, revealing the gun range he had put in.

"Is this safe to have in your house?" she asks out of genuine curiosity. He just laughs and turns to leave. Liz follows him out, trying to be patient for his answer.

"Our house, princess, and yes, it's safe. Your prints will also work for the door."

"You're going to give me access to your guns... after what I did?" Liz asks timidly, looking back to the door as they ascend the stairs.

"Not just the guns, the whole house. I told you, this is your home now too unless you want to go back to base—"

"No!" Liz practically shouts, not letting him finish what he was going to say. "Sorry, continue."

"I was saying, this is your house too now, just like it's Mikey's. He didn't have anything of his own either, now he has a permanent place here. I take care of my own, and you're now one of them." She doesn't want to go back to base, a building surrounded by people who don't trust her. She won't force Riley to endure that for her either.

"This is a safe place, the only ones who know about it are the ones I want to know, even Scott doesn't have access to it."

"You don't trust him do you?" She asks, lowering herself onto a stair.

"I never have. The only reason we found Dmitri and his operation in the beginning is because we got shot down and I was taken. When I was cleared to return to duty I fought to build a spec ops team to hunt him down," A quiet echo bounces around the walls as Riley paces growing more annoyed with each word. "I picked every member on the team, I trained them, I gathered intel, I did everything possible to end his operation.

When Scott caught wind of it he appointed himself head of the unit and declared he was in charge. It never sat well with any of us, and if he ever leads us into a mission that goes sideways, well, we reconvene here and figure shit out."

"Is that why he's scared of you? Because he knows you're the backbone of all of this?"

"I'm sure that's one reason." He chuckles walking over and joining Liz on the step. Warmth blooms in his chest when the weight of her head rests on his shoulder.

"I'm scared Riley." His arm finds its way around her shoulder, holding her tight.

"He hates me. He still thinks I was working with Dmitri. What if he did something to the papers you had me sign? What if he snuck something in saying I admit to being evil or something and I stupidly signed it?" Her fears come tumbling out.

"I drew up those papers myself, I read every word, then read it again just to be safe. You agreed to train and be part of the team, you will have to take your tests, but even those are being done in a secure facility with us by your side. The contract you signed is gone, but I will get you a new copy and you can read it, if it's still something you want to do, you can."

"Thank you, now, no more heavy stuff, finish my tour please." She says shimmying out of his arm. They head back to the kitchen and Liz slides into her chair, watching Riley as he leans against the counter, crossing his arms.

"Sooo," she says, dragging the word out. Riley sees nothing but mischief dancing in her eyes. "Do you swim with the mask on too? Or do you have like, a special swimming mask? Maybe one that makes you look like a shark? Do you ever take it off?"

"What's your obsession with my masks?" he asks, eyeing her.

She simply looks at him and shrugs her delicate shoulders.

"You get this cute little look every time you see a new one, ya know, you have since the first time I changed it," Riley says with a soft chuckle. Liz looks away, her cheeks turning a deep shade of pink. "To answer your question, no, it never comes off. I was wondering when you were going to ask."

"It just seemed like everyone knows that's your thing and not to bring it up. They're all scared of you, and it's in my best interest to stay on your good side... so I never wanted to ask."

"Are you scared of me?" he asks, raising his eyebrows.

Liz can't help but watch him as he strides to the other side of the island, leaning forward on both hands. "I mean... I probably should be, right?" Liz says, looking away from his piercing gaze.

"But?" he says, encouraging her to finish her thought.

"I'm more... intrigued by you. You're this big scary soldier, even General Douche Bag is scared of you and he's technically your boss, but I'm just... not. Even when I was scared, it was never you," she says, playing with a loose strand of hair, trying to do anything but look at him.

"Good. You're the only person who shouldn't be afraid of me," he says, causing her heart to race at the thought.

"You really never take it off? None of your friends know what you look like?" she blurts out, hoping to break the tension.

Riley lets out a loud, genuine laugh, cut short by the whirring sound of the elevator. Liz tenses, worried they found her again. She hops onto her feet, preparing for a fight. The noise stops and when the door opens, Mikey steps out, bags in hand. Liz takes off running, throwing herself into him. She didn't realize how worried she was about him until he showed up here.

"Aww, I missed you too, darlin," he says, dropping the bags and wrapping his arms around her.

Liz lets him go and walks back to the kitchen, hoping now that Mikey is here and safe, they will tell her what's going on.

Mikey picks the bags back up and brings them into the kitchen. They start unpacking and filling the fridge with all the food he brought.

"So, did Ry give you the grand tour?" Mikey asks.

"Sure did. He even took his mask off. Finally showed me his face," Liz responds, winking at Riley who glares at her.

"He showed you?" Mikey practically yells, turning to where Riley still glares at Liz. "It took me two years to learn how fucking ugly you are under there."

"You lied to me!" Liz shrieks, crossing her arms and sinking back in the chair. Riley looks to Mikey, then to Liz crossing her arms and pouting. Without a word, he heads to his room, emerging minutes later in loose shorts and a t-shirt.

"I'm going to work out, let me know when you two are done being brats," he says, walking past them. He looks just in time to see Liz stick her tongue out, and Mikey follows her lead. He simply shakes his head and disappears down the stairs.

CHAPTER 28

The second Riley is out of earshot, Liz whirls on Mikey with a speed tornados would be jealous of, her eyes swimming with excitement, watching as he continues to unpack the bags of groceries he brought. "Have you really seen his face?"

"Sure have, and no, I'm not going to tell you what he looks like." He puts the last of the food into the cabinet behind him.

"I wasn't going to ask," she says, shrugging. "I don't even want to know what he looks like."

"Sure you don't, darlin," he says with a wink.

"Maybe I like his masks, did you ever think of that? Maybe… just maybe, I find it sexy… Endearing! I meant to say endearing," she shouts, cheeks flushing. Desperate to change the subject before Mikey gets the chance to come up with a smart ass comment, she asks, "How's the whole training thing going to work now?"

Mikey walks over to the chair next to her and plops down. "Same as it has been. We can go to the gym and do our cardio before the rest of the workout, and Riley can keep doing hand to hand training."

"Okay, but why? What's the point? We both know I'm going to be useless. I don't have the physical ability to stop the baddies like you guys. I assumed I would be a super cool sniper or something," Liz says. She is still trying to figure out how they could possibly need her on their team. They are all highly trained, abnormally large men, what is she going to do? Scold the terrorists into submission?

"Look, darlin, I'm going to tell you what Riley's too afraid to. You're fuckin hot. Believe it or not, we can use that to our advantage. You can get close to people we can't. Men aren't smart. We don't really think about potential spies, or if someone is highly trained when we are looking at a nice pair of tits."

"So... you think I'm hot?" Liz teases.

"Ry is right, you are a brat," Mikey says with a chuckle as he gets up from his chair and walks back around to the fridge and takes out a beer for himself.

"Did you get unpacked?" he asks, popping the bottle cap off.

"Babe... I have four things, I have nothing to unpack," she says, getting up from her chair and walking to where Mikey sips his beer.

"I'll talk to Riley about that again," he says, taking a long drink.

"Don't bother, it's not like I have money or a way to go shopping. I still owe you guys for everything you got me. I'm good with what I have, promise," she says, smiling sweetly before wrapping her arms around him one more time. "I'm really glad you didn't die," Liz tells him before she turns and walks to her room, closing the door behind her.

She looks at the bag on the bed and trudges over, dumping it out. Liz picks up the few things she packed a week ago and puts them in the dresser. Sighing, she looks at the sad pile of clothes taking up not even half a drawer. She drags her feet to the bed and falls forward, letting gravity do the work. Groaning into the plush mattress, she wonders what the hell she signed up for.

CHAPTER 29

The next morning, Liz wakes to the sound of metal clanging together and Mikey's horrendous singing. She climbs out of bed, pulls Riley's sweatpants back on and storms to the kitchen to figure out what the hell's going on. Liz just looks on in confusion as Mikey is singing around the kitchen while Riley is attempting to cook breakfast.

"What... the... Hell?" Liz says, pulling herself into one of the chairs.

"Riley!" Mikey shouts. "Will you buy this woman some god damn clothes so she isn't stuck wearing yours again?" He walks over to the stove where Riley is trying to cook and slings an arm over his shoulder.

"Unless... you find it sexy when she wears them, kind of like how she thinks your mask is sexy?" he asks winking at Liz, giving her a thumbs up.

Riley stops what he's doing and slowly turns his head to look at Liz, whose mouth now hangs open. Face frozen in shock at the audacity, especially in front of Riley.

"Michael!" she screams.

"Endearing!...She meant endearing," he says, turning so he's face to face with Riley.

"I should have killed you when I had the chance," she mutters, cheeks heating. Knowing if she looks in the mirror right now her face will be bright red.

Riley laughs, shaking his head, and turns back to cooking. Liz lays her head on the smooth countertop, too embarrassed to see either of them right now. She just lies there, as Mikey and Riley dig out plates and start piling the food up, setting it all around her. The delicious smells overpower her embarrassment. She picks her head back up only to see Riley leaning on the opposite counter, arms crossed, watching her.

"So... my mask is sexy? That why you keep asking about it?" he asks, amber eyes lighting up at the sight of her cheeks flushing.

Liz lets out a loud groan, putting her head back down on the counter. She thanks the gods when a loud buzzer goes off, drawing their attention from her. Riley slides his phone out of his pocket and quickly looks at the screen. A minute later, the elevator doors are opening and two large men step out into the living room. Liz instantly recognizes the men from the night they killed her brother.

They walk over to the kitchen, and the bearded man, Alex, swipes a piece of bacon off the plate in front of Mikey.

"We need to talk," Alex says before looking over to Liz and adding, "alone."

The room goes silent, Mikey and Riley both look over to Liz, trying to gauge her reaction to the blatant disrespect. Already on edge from the events of the last twenty-four hours, Liz glares daggers at the man, not trying to hide how pissed she is they want her to leave.

"Here's a wild fucking thought... You could just try asking,"

Liz snaps, looking at him, waiting for a fight. Out of the corner of her eye, she sees Riley tense like he's waiting for her to lunge. She slides out of the chair and storms to her room, slamming the door behind her. She makes a mental note to apologize to Riley for her outburst.

Liz pushes her ear to the door, straining to hear what they are talking about.

"I can't believe you brought her here. I thought killing her brother was going to be the end of your little infatuation," Alex barks at Riley, grabbing a plate and loading it up with food.

Riley glares at him, quickly grabbing his own plate and filling it up before setting it aside. "She signed the papers, she's officially part of the team, and the team gets use of the safe house" Mikey says.

"Part of the team or not, she may be putting everyone in danger," Tyler says, stepping into the conversation, trying to keep the peace before Alex and Riley come to blows.

"How? Do you really need more fucking proof she's the victim in this shit show?" he shouts.

"I've been thinking about something her brother said that night. He said they already knew where she was. That Dmitri will always be able to find her," Tyler says to them, walking to the cabinet and taking out extra plates.

"What if she is telling him?" Alex snaps, eyes finding Riley.

"She's been under constant supervision, and even if she wasn't, Liz is not fucking working with him," Riley shouts, stepping closer to Alex.

"Thats bullshit and you know it, Riley. She tried to kill one of ours and you just let her fuckin walk!" Alex shouts back.

"Enough, Alex," Tyler says to his partner, stepping in between the men. "That's not what we came for... What if she's being tracked? Anywhere she goes, Dmitri and his men would be able to find her. That could explain why the base got attacked after she left, our intel says they have been working on shit like that," Tyler says.

"Okay, but what's the point of tracking her? There's no reason for them to care about where she is anymore," Mikey says, thinking about everything they said.

"Regardless of reason, her brother was confident they would always be able to find her. I didn't think much of it at the time, but I found something when I was trying to target where the missile was coming from," Tyler says, walking to where he tossed a bag onto the floor, trying to pick his next words carefully.

He takes a charred paper from his bag along with a small glass vial and brings it over, sliding it across the island. Riley looks at the picture, anger taking hold. He keeps staring at the photo. Liz on his back, her arms wrapped tightly around him, her beautiful face nestled into his neck while he carries her down the trail. Mikey picks up the vial, examining the small hunk of metal rattling around inside. "Look, your feelings around her are going to cloud your judgment, Ry. I don't believe she has done anything wrong, but, what if they did something to her while he held her captive. Liz could be risking everyone without even knowing it," he finally says.

"She's going to get everyone killed! She needs to fucking go!" Alex snaps.

After hearing her name one too many times, Liz can't help the anger building inside her. She rips the door open and storms back into the room.

"If you're going to accuse me of shit, at least be man enough to say it to my fucking face!" she shouts, heading right for Alex.

Riley doesn't let her make it far, his large arm wrapping around her waist as she storms past, lifting her feet off the ground like she's a child trying to go somewhere she shouldn't.

"Let me go," she says through gritted teeth, staring at Alex across the room.

"Absolutely not. You're not going to square up with a man twice your size, princess," Riley says. His fingers splayed across her hip, tightening his grip on her narrow waist. He sets her down, steering her to the island chairs and forces her to sit.

"Well, then maybe he should have some fucking manners." Liz sneers, staring daggers into the man. Riley lets her go and picks up the plate of food he had set aside and puts it in front of Liz.

"And you..." she says, turning her anger on Riley. "You keep saying you want me on the team, but you're letting them kick me out and keep things from me."

"You're right," he says, eying the men gathered around them. Tyler gives him a small nod, agreeing she should know what they learned. "Tyler and Alex have been thinking about something your brother said. They seem to think you're being tracked," he says, sliding the picture of them over to her. She picks it up, smiling at how happy they look before the dread of what that photo means settles in her gut. She looks up at Riley, eyes wide. He simply nods, confirming every horrid thought flashing through her mind. "I need you to trust them as much as you trust me and Mikey. You need to tell us everything, and I do mean everything Dmitri and his men did to you."

CHAPTER 30

Liz takes a big bite of potatoes, chewing them slowly as she thinks back to how much she told Riley months ago when they first brought her in. He only knows the bare minimum, that she was abused, he never asked about it again. She eyes the small group gathered around her, wanting nothing more to slink back to her room and pretend none of this happened.

"Okay fine," she says, scooping up another bite of food. "But if the big one says anything, I will absolutely be beating the fuck out of him." Popping the food in her mouth, she simply glares at Alex, who is now staring right back at her. Liz takes a deep breath, trying not to think about the new sets of eyes watching her. "I don't know what to tell you that I haven't already. He would come into my cell and beat the fuck out of me, if he wasn't the one doing it, someone else was. They spiked my food with something that would make me really sick. Dmitri told me he could make it stop if I gave him what he wanted, when I said no, they started starving me, blah blah blah," Liz explains.

"What about the day you fought back? You told me I didn't need to know what happened, but we might need to know now, love," Riley says to her, reaching out and taking her hand in his.

Liz takes a deep breath, not wanting to relive that day. "Um, he came in like normal, usually he had one or two people with him, but he had a whole crew that day. I knew something was off. His men held me against the floor. I tried to get away but couldn't. I was weak, and the guys were too big. He started talking about how he was tired of waiting and said something about what I had said to him at the bar." Liz watches as Mikey and Riley exchange a knowing glance. She looks to Riley, trying to focus on the different shades of brown swirls in his eyes instead of the three other men watching her. He squeezes her hand, keeping it held tight while she continues.

"They kept me pinned down. He took his belt off and unzipped his pants. I wanted to move my body, to fight them off, but I was frozen. I just remember screaming at myself to do something, to not let another evil man violate me like that again. One of his men grabbed my face, the one with the monster tattoo on his neck, he forced my mouth open and I snapped," Liz says, taking a shuddering breath in. "I panicked, more than I already was. I did everything I could to get away, but they just held tighter. I tried... I tried so fucking hard, Ry," she says, her eyes staying locked onto his as the tears spill.

"It was too late. I did the only thing I could think of. I bit down as hard as possible until all I could taste was blood and didn't stop until everything went black. I woke up, they came back in, beat the everloving shit out of me, and chained me up,," Liz tells him, tears now forming in her eyes.

Riley takes a step closer and pulls her into his arms, stroking her back while she composes herself. He only lets her go when she starts again.

"The only time I saw him after that was when he came in with some kind of doctor. After that every few days someone would sedate me, making sure I wouldn't fight back again. I turned into their favorite toy. If they got bored with their fists, they used whatever they had with them at the time. When that stopped having the effect they wanted, they had some guy come give me some kind of injection."

Liz takes another second to compose herself, looking at Riley, seeing his jaw clench under the mask. She looks away, pushing food around her plate. It's Mikey who speaks first.

"What do you mean injections?"

"I don't know. Just injections. I would be really out of it for a few hours, but not really calm like being sedated. Everything would get fuzzy, almost like it was out of focus and I would have no energy. I could still scream, and try to fight, but it was almost impossible to move my body. I think they were testing it so they could finish what Dmitri had started that day. I know what they were planning."

The four men exchange looks, putting something together that Liz doesn't understand. She just looks at them, the silence causing her anxiety to run wild.

Riley walks over to the chair next to her and sits. "What do you mean, love? How do you know?" he asks, worry never leaving his eyes.

She just looks at him, continuing to focus on him instead of all the other men watching her.

"They talked about putting something in me, it just wasn't ready. I assume it was some kind of birth control or something. The day you showed up, someone really panicked came in and gave me one of those injections then left. Around the time I started hearing gunshots, some new guy came back in with another needle, but it hurt so much more than usual. He was mumbling something about hiding... I can't really remember, I was still pretty fucked up from whatever they put in me the first time,"

Liz takes another second, really thinking about what they were doing to her when she was in that cell.

"You said it hurt more. Did they do anything differently?" Alex asks, watching her carefully.

"I mean, it was in my leg instead of my arm or neck, but I just figured I was fighting so he did it where he could, it wasn't the first time they stabbed me in the leg. It also got really bruised. I must have had a bad reaction because it swelled up and there was a small bump for a while."

"Did the bump go away?" Tyler asks cautiously.

"Yeah, I mean, I can still feel the scar or something if I touch it, but that's normal for that kind of thing," Liz says. Her heart beats loudly in her ears. The way they are looking at each other sends her spiraling into a panic. They know something she doesn't, and it's not good. She looks at each of the men, remembering what Riley had said about being tracked.

"You need to show us the injection spot..." Alex says, staring at her, anger painting his face. "We don't have time to find a medic we can trust. We need to know if it's birth control. If it's not, you being here puts us all in danger."

"If it is a tracker they would have lost the signal ten miles out, you know that," Riley barks, knowing Alex is trying to intimidate her into giving in to his demands.

Liz looks around at each of the men again, thinking maybe if it was just Mikey and Riley, she would consider it. She doesn't know Alex and Tyler, and Alex clearly wants to get rid of her.

"No. I'm not taking my pants off, especially around him," she says, pointing at Alex. His face gets red with anger, he opens his mouth to argue with her but before he can, Riley speaks up.

"I'll take my mask off."

"What?" Liz says, whirling to face him.

"Just me and you. If you show me what they did... I will take my mask off."

"Oh my god, you're serious," Liz says to him, unable to hold back the nervous laughter that comes out of her mouth. She eyes him, wearing one of his masks that cover his whole face, just leaving his defined jawline exposed. She can't help the warmth that takes over her cheeks as she looks at him. She can't form words, just looks into his caramel-colored eyes and gives him a small nod.

Alex and Tyler try to divert their attention, feeling awkward from the intimate moment while Mikey just watches, smiling like an idiot. Riley steps back, allowing Liz to stand before he picks up her hand and leads her down the hall.

CHAPTER 31

When they reach the bedroom doors, Liz tries to go into her room, but Riley is quick to stop her. He throws open his own door and pulls her in, closing it behind them. Liz takes a slow lap around the room, not at all what she thought it would look like. It's more put together than a typical man's room.

A large bed with black blankets sits in the center of the far wall, a plush black rug underneath it. One wall has a door to what she assumes is his bathroom, the other has rows and rows of masks neatly hung up. She continues looking around, turning to the last wall, a simple dresser with a few trinkets laid out on top with a large TV mounted above it. Riley clears his throat, startling her. Liz looks over at him, leaning against the door frame, arms crossed, watching her explore his room.

"You're not really going to take your mask off, are you?" she says, looking away from where he's leaning.

"Why wouldn't I? You were right, you're part of the team, and if you're going to put your full trust in me, I should do the same. That means letting you see my face," he says.

She listens to his footsteps bang across the floor until they stop when he steps onto the rug in front of her.

"You really don't have to. I've seen your jaw when you were wearing these masks," she says, looking up at him, gesturing to the one he's currently wearing. "And the other ones show your eyes... So, that's pretty much your whole face."

"Worried you're going to find me just as sexy with it off?" he asks teasingly.

"No, I just don't think you'll be able to control yourself without it. You think I don't see the way you look at me?" Liz says, looking up at him through her thick lashes.

He lets out a small groan and takes a step into her. Her breath hitches at their closeness. Riley reaches out, not thinking about what he's doing, and takes her hand, pulling her fully into him, her hands resting on his hard chest. A shout from down the hall pulls them back to the task at hand. Liz steps back, quickly looking away.

"You need to turn around so I can take your pants off, I mean my pants, the ones you let me wear, not the ones on your body–" she shuts down her rambling before she makes it worse from her nerves on edge in anticipation for what's about to happen.

"I've seen you without pants, love. You didn't seem to care the other night when you changed," he says. His eyes darken as they drift down her body, stopping at the lush curves of her hips before snapping back up to her face.

Liz just glares at him, pretending she's not blushing from his gaze. Liz shoots him the same exasperated look she used to give James when she needed him to focus. He holds his hands up in fake surrender and turns around.

"Use my blanket to cover anything you're not comfortable with me seeing," he says as she slips out of her pants.

She quickly backs up to the bed and sits, pulling the corner of his blanket over one of her bare legs.

"Okay, you can turn around now," Liz says, her voice trembling.

Riley turns and stalks to the bed, sitting next to her. He peers at her exposed leg, trying to see anything abnormal. His eyes roam her leg, covered in scars. He takes each one in, wondering which ones were put there by Dmitri and which ones are from the monsters who raised her. His eyes dart from one to the next, some small, some larger and jagged as anger floods his soul. Trying to focus, he fights past the animalistic need to hunt down anyone who has ever hurt her and make them suffer for it.

"Where is it?" he asks, reaching his bare hand out to inspect her leg. He catches himself before he touches her, remembering how much has been done to her without her consent.

"It's um... more on my... inner thigh," she says.

Looking away, she pulls leg onto the bed beside her, hoping that's enough. She reaches down and feels around for the small lump under her skin.

"Right... there," she says, wincing.

"I can't see anything like this," he says, sliding off the bed and onto his knees in front of Liz. The sight of Riley on his knees in front of her sends her head spinning. "Can I touch you?" he asks, looking up at her. Hoping she can't tell what being on his knees before her is doing to him. "Your leg, I mean, to try and feel what you do," he quickly adds.

She nods her head and he wastes no time running his calloused hand up her leg. Liz looks away from his hand, trying to ignore how good it feels gliding against her skin. She lets out a breath, and Riley mistakes her arousal for nerves. Thinking he needs to do something to distract her, he stops moving his hand and looks up at her.

"Take it off, love," he says, her eyes meeting his. She slowly moves the blanket covering her other leg, exposing herself further.

"I meant the mask, but I won't say no to that coming off, too," he says, nothing but want in his eyes. He shifts, trying to hide the bulge growing in his pants. Taking his hand off her leg, he picks her hands up, placing them on either side of his face, curling her fingers under the sides of his mask.

"Do what I tell you, princess," he says, his eyes never leaving hers. "I'm going to touch you again, and when I do, I want you to take my mask off."

Liz nods and Riley puts his hand back on her leg, gently sliding it up her inner thigh. He starts rubbing his thumb around, trying to find the spot she was talking about. Liz gives in and starts to pull the mask up, his short facial hair scratching her fingers as she does. Halfway up his face she stops, dropping her hands to his shoulders. She never imagined seeing half of someone's face would have such an impact on her. Her eyes roam, trying to take everything in. His short, light brown stubble covering his chiseled jaw, full lips snagging her attention. He rubs his thumb a little higher and her thoughts snap back to where his hands are.

She shifts nervously, apprehensive about what she's about to tell him.

"Umm... it's a little higher up, closer to my... um... just... higher," she says, cheeks a bright shade of red. He flicks his tongue out, licking his lips while his eyes drift to where she's talking about. She sucks in a sharp breath, tipping her head back.

"If you need to move my leg or something just do it. I trust you, Ry," she says, bringing her head back down to look at him. He flashes her a small smile, and she tries to focus on that impossibly beautiful smile instead of what he's doing to her.

"When I move your leg, you need to rip my mask off. If you're going to be this exposed, so am I."

He grabs her leg and pushes it over as she tugs the mask off his head. She gently sets it down on the bed next to her, unable to take her eyes off him.

Seeing his full face has her stomach in knots, not expecting him to be so unbelievably attractive. Her eyes roam his face, not sure what to focus on. Her eyes dart from his chiseled jaw to his beautiful amber eyes, back to his full lips. She looks at his nose, slightly crooked from being broken so many times, a jagged scar running over the bridge. She follows that scar up to his forehead, cutting through his eyebrow. His hand roaming her leg draws her back in, hoping he doesn't notice the wetness he's dangerously close to. He rubs his thumb over her leg again and she flinches, jerking her leg away.

"Is it that?" he asks.

Liz gives him a small nod, not daring to open her mouth for the fear of what will come out. He rubs his thumb over it a few more times, dragging a small breathy moan from Liz. He shifts on his knees, cock growing uncomfortably hard at the sight of her moaning from his touch.

"This might hurt, love," he says before pinching the spot on her leg, his knuckles brushing against her center. He stops what he's doing, feeling the wetness seeping through the small panties she has on, and quickly pulls his hand back.

"Well it's definitely not a scar. Tyler should have something to see if it is what we think it is."

Riley stands and quickly turns, striding for the door. He takes a second to adjust himself before turning back to Liz. Trying to avoid looking at her, he simply says, "You can put your pants back on if you'll be more comfortable, but I'm going to need to see that spot again when I come back."

He opens the door and steps out, closing it gently behind him. The second the door is fully closed, Liz throws herself back onto his bed, groaning in frustration. She lays there, in his bed, surrounded by his scent, and can't stop the thoughts that flash through her mind. Powerful hands gripping her thighs, Riley on his knees before her, his full lips crashing into hers. None of the thoughts are doing anything to stop the wetness pooling between her legs. So engrossed in her fantasy, she doesn't even hear Riley come back into the room.

"Comfortable, princess?" he asks.

She shoots back up, face so red she can't even look at him after the thoughts she was just having. She looks away as he walks to where she now sits on the bed.

"Sorry," she mutters, just loud enough for him to hear.

"Don't apologize. I love seeing you spread out on my bed, especially when you have nothing on," he says, eyes roaming her exposed body. He looks away, silently cursing himself for making her more uncomfortable than she already is.

"I'm sure you say that to all the women you bring down here," she says, more jealous than she intended. She didn't even hear him cross the room, but when she looks up, he's standing right in front of her. She can't control the flick of her eyes that goes right to his waist, eye level with what's already growing in his pants. Somehow, seeing the proof that on some level he's attracted to her makes her feel better about her own thoughts.

"No women," he says, chuckling at the jealousy in her voice. "You're the only one I've ever allowed in here."

She thinks about that for a second, shocked that with a face like his, he isn't bringing women home every night. She's positive that when he goes out, mask or not, women throw themselves at him. She doesn't think too much about it, letting herself feel special for being the only woman to be allowed in his bed.

He sinks back onto his knees in front of her and she sucks in a sharp breath. He looks up, her green eyes shining with lust as she looks down at him.

"Spread your legs for me, love."

Her eyes go wide. "You want me to spread my legs... for you?" she says, voice low and sultry.

"I need to see the scar again, but if you have other ideas, I would love to hear them," he says, swallowing hard, eyes drifting to her legs as she slowly spreads them, shaking her head in embarrassment. He licks his lips again as he moves his hand up her leg, looking for the scar once more. Seeing that sends Liz spiraling. The only thought in her head is his lips on her thigh, his tongue even higher. Luckily, the pain in her legs draws her attention from his mouth.

She watches as he pulls out a small device from his pocket and runs it over the scar on her leg. As soon as it goes over, it lets out a few sharp beeps. He moves it further down, then to the other leg, making sure nothing else is setting it off before putting it back over the scar, causing it to beep again.

He pulls it from her leg and tosses it onto the bed behind Liz. He keeps his hand on her, slowly rubbing his hand up and down, enjoying the softness of her skin. His eyes keep wandering to the red lace panties she has on, the ones he picked out for her. There is only one thought in his mind... pushing them aside and burying his face between her legs. His grip tightens and she doesn't try to hide her soft moan.

Riley removes his hand from her leg, standing to lean over her. He holds himself with his arms on either side, forcing Liz to lean back with him. His lips inches from hers, she looks up at him through thick lashes and lets out a small breath. He can't fight his pull to her anymore. Riley starts to lower his head, going agonizingly slow, giving her time to stop him if that's what she wants. His heart starts to race when she doesn't. He keeps going, lips almost against hers when there's a sharp knock on the door. Riley sighs, resting his forehead on hers.

"I'm going to kill whoever is on the other side of that fucking door."

"Are you guys good in there?" Mikey yells from outside of the door.

Riley groans, reluctantly pulling himself away from Liz. "We were until you fucking knocked!" Riley shouts. He turns back to see Liz sliding off his bed, knowing the moment they shared is over. "I'm sorry if I made you uncomfortable. My mask has never come off in such an... intimate way before. I got caught up in the moment."

Riley tries to avert his eyes from Liz who is still half-naked and standing by his bed. He fights the overwhelming urge to throw her back onto it and finish what they had almost started.

"Are you okay? Do the scars freak you out?" he asks, looking around for where his mask ended up.

She looks at him, eyes softening when she hears the insecurity in his voice. She starts to walk to him, before becoming painfully aware she still has no pants on. Turning around to look for them she says, "No, not at all. Honestly... I like them, they add to the whole rugged, Greek god thing you have going on."

Riley walks to where she stands, wishing the moment they had earlier had not been ruined. Still wondering what her soft, pink lips would feel like on his. His eyes drop to her perfectly round ass, now on full display before him, unable to keep from looking.

"I should probably put my pants back on," she says, glad he can't see how much she is blushing right now.

"Yeah, I don't think Mikey will be able to focus on anything else if you don't."

"Are you sure you mean Mikey? Don't pretend you haven't been staring at my ass the whole time I've been turned around. I can't say I blame you, all that training gave me the body of a Pixar mom," she says, bending over to pick up her pants, knowing he won't be able to stop himself. Liz slips into her pants and turns to see that she was right, he's watching her get dressed. She prances to him, more at ease now that she's fully clothed.

"I'll cover for you if you need to go take a cold shower," she says, glancing down at his pants, no longer hidden by being on his knees before her. She bounces on her tiptoes and gives him a quick peck on the cheek before opening the door and disappearing.

Liz heads back to where the men are sitting around the table. Legs still slightly wobbly from the way Riley touched her, she struts to the table and plops herself into one of the empty chairs.

"Where's Reaper?" Alex asks, already starting back up with his sour attitude.

"Riley just needs a minute to compose himself," she says, shooting a wink at Alex, just trying to piss him off.

He narrows his eyes and watches her, tapping his fingers on the table in annoyance. He only looks away when Riley comes walking back in, adjusting his belt as he does. That one simple motion got all eyes on him, looking at him like he did more than just look for some device in Liz's leg.

"Why the fuck is everyone staring at me?" he asks, not at all happy about the attention his team is giving him. He pulls out the chair next to Liz and sits, ready to get their meeting over and done with. "She definitely has something in her," he says, holding a hand up and turning to his friend. "Don't fucking say it, Mikey."

Mikey's mouth snaps shut with an audible click, not surprised Riley knew what he was going to say before he got to say it.

"It's some type of electronic and they made sure to put it somewhere that's not going to be found."

"It's got to be a tracker," Tyler says to the group. "After what her brother said, that's the only thing it could be. That also lines up with what Rocco told us. Apparently they know she's somewhere around here, and they are planning another attack," Tyler adds, not sure if it was the right time to drop that on the team.

The whole group goes silent, not knowing what to do with the information that they are being tracked or that Dmitri is planning another attack.

"We need to get that device out of her leg," Alex says, looking at Riley.

"What good would that do? They already know I'm here, even if you carve it out of me and fly it across the world, he will still look here first," Liz snaps at him.

"So, what are you suggesting?" Alex asks her.

"I don't know. Unlike you, I'm not some highly trained soldier. All I'm saying is he's not going to give up on coming here, even if I leave," she says, crossing her arms and sinking further into her chair.

They sit in silence, minutes ticking by, trying to think of a way to get Dmitri off their tails while they regroup and recover. A few different ideas float around, but nothing sticks, they all know they won't be able to pull things off with the resources they have right now.

"What if we lure him here?" Mikey finally says. "He's going

to track her. We let her out on her own, find a safe place she can go to everyday. He knows he crippled us with that attack, but we know he's in the same boat. It's going to take time for him to make a move. If he sees she has a pattern, he will use that, thinking he has the upper hand. It would make it easier for us to prepare."

"No way in fucking hell do we do that!" Riley yells, standing from his chair. The only thing keeping him from breaking Mikey's jaw for even suggesting that is Liz watching his every move. "She's not bait. Find another way," he says, storming down the hall and slamming his door behind him.

Liz wishes she could follow him and thank him for thinking of her safety, but she can't. Her safety isn't more important than theirs. Liz thinks about all the people who lost their lives during the attack at Fort Stryker, all because of her. She won't let these men risk her lives for her without risking hers for them.

"I'll do it. Enough people have died because of me. I'll try to talk to Ry when he calms down."

Alex simply nods before getting up and stretching. He looks at Tyler and they both walk to the elevator, stepping in without muttering another word.

CHAPTER 32

Mikey watches Liz, his heart breaking for her as she looks toward Riley's room. He can see how much she wishes she could go to him. He hates that it has to be this way after everything she has been through. He holds up his wrist and looks at his watch, it's barely noon, unsure of what to do with the rest of his day, he turns his attention back to Liz.

"What does a robot do after a one-night stand?" he asks, fighting off his laughter. "He nuts and bolts."

"Did someone drop you as a baby?" Liz asks, wondering what the hell he is doing.

Mikey bursts out laughing, rich and deep, unable to hold it in any longer. Liz just yawns in response, the events of the morning draining away any energy she woke up with.

"Go take a nap, darlin. When you wake up, we can hit the gym." Mikey gets up and goes into the living room.

Liz lingers in front of Riley's door before ducking into her own. She crawls into her plush bed and replays every detail of her morning with Riley, over and over again until she finally drifts off into sleep.

Sometime later, Liz wakes, the feel of Riley's phantom hands all over her body, lingering from the dream she was having. She climbs out of bed, quickly changes, and heads out of her room in search of Mikey, the house eerily silent. Looking around the living room, she doesn't see anyone hanging out, so she prances over to the hall and heads down the stairs.

As soon as she hits the landing, she sees Mikey on the treadmill, starting without her. She walks into the gym and heads over to the second treadmill when she spots Riley working out. The second her eyes land on him, it's like all the air is ripped from her lungs. She wasn't prepared to see him like this. No mask, no shirt, just a glorious expanse of tan skin, tattoos, and incredibly sexy scars.

Liz can't seem to pull her eyes away. She watches, jaw on the floor as he continues his pull-ups, large, tattooed biceps flexing every time he lifts himself to the bar. Her eyes start to drift lower, to his strong chest and well-defined abdomen, with a deep V leading below his waistline, a thin layer of sweat making him glisten.

"Enjoying the show, love?" he asks, pulling himself up again.

Mikey's laugh on the other side of the room makes her blush.

"I'm sorry, I didn't want to interrupt. Can we talk later?" she asks, hoping the flush in her cheeks is gone. He pulls himself back up and holds, looking down at her. He nods his head before slowly lowering himself. Liz gives him a small smile and heads to the treadmill.

"Don't fucking say it," she snaps, pushing buttons on the machine until it turns on.

The next two hours are spent doing an intense workout, simultaneously trying to listen to Mikey explain this is her new regular so she can pass the OPAT. She desperately tries to focus but finds her eyes drifting to where Riley is doing his own workout, smiling to herself when she catches him watching her.

Riley finishes his workout and leaves, not able to say anything to Liz while she's doing her squat reps, the image of her without her pants flashing through his head each time she drops.

"What did the fish say when he swam into a wall?" Liz asks fighting to lift the weights back up. "Dam," she says, racking the weight before the giggle fit hits.

Mikey just watches her, a big smile spread across his face, enjoying having someone to joke around with. When they finish their workout and head back upstairs, Liz goes right to her room, taking a quick shower to wash the sweat off. She leaves and heads next door to where she hopes Mikey is. Lucky for her, his door is wide open, and he is lounging, flipping through a small stack of papers. Liz waltzes in and throws herself across his bed as if they have been friends their whole lives.

"I'm bored. What do you guys have to do down here?" Liz asks, sounding frustrated.

"Nothing, darlin," he says, sitting up a little straighter to talk to her.

"Ry didn't build this for fun. I know it's home, but neither of us are here much, usually just a few days between missions."

"Oh," Liz says with a sigh adding, "Is he going to be mad if I use the pool?"

"Sweetheart, there isn't a single thing you can do to make that man mad," Mikey says.

Her cheeks flush and she gets a tight feeling in her chest at that. She gets up from his bed and walks to the door.

"Want to come play mermaids with me?" she asks, joking.

"I can't, darlin. I have human work to do unfortunately," he tells her, giving her a sad smile as she turns and walks out.

Thinking a lonely swim is better than nothing, she heads down the hall. Stopping at her door to change, she thinks about what she can wear but quickly remembers she has nothing. Liz starts again for the stairs, deciding to just go topless, hoping Mikey doesn't change his mind and come looking for her.

Liz makes it down to the pool, her footsteps echoing around the silent space. She finds a small stack of towels and takes one, walking back and peeling out of her clothes before diving in, temperature be damned.. Liz lets out a small groan, not expecting the water to be warm and feel so good on her aching muscles. For the first time in years, she decides to just relax, float around and let the warm water soothe her.

With no clocks anywhere, Liz loses track of how long she is floating around the oversized tub.

"You down here, princess?"

She hears a deep, velvety voice call out, unsure of how close he is to the pool. She rights herself, looking around for somewhere to hide. "Yeah. Hang on, I'm naked."

Heavy footsteps echo through the silent chamber as Riley approaches, growing louder with every step. Liz starts swimming for the edge, hoping to hide herself against it when the door opens and Riley strides into the room, eyes going wide before filling with want at the sight of her.

"I thought you were joking," he says, averting his eyes. He listens to the water sloshing against the pool's edge as she pulls herself out, her wet feet slapping on the floor. She quickly picks up her towel and wraps it around her body.

"This is why Mikey said I need to go shopping," she snaps, a little harsher than intended.

Riley turns to her, eyes dropping to the towel she's wrapped in, not leaving much to the imagination. She squeezes her arms tighter around herself, only causing the swell of her breasts to be more accentuated.

Riley quickly looks away, knowing he won't be able to stop himself from staring. He listens to her delicate footsteps splashing through the small puddles as Liz walks back to the pool and sits, dipping her feet and gently kicking them under the water. He looks back to her arms stretched behind her so she can lean back, long black hair falling to the floor.

"I'm sorry. I didn't mean it to come out like that," she says nervously.

"I'll take you shopping, love, just say the word," he says, his deep voice sending a shiver down her spine.

She tips her head back so she can look up at him. "No. I can make do with what I have. I still owe you for what you've already got me. Besides, I don't have money for a shopping spree," she says, smiling at him, trying to convince him she really is fine.

"You do have money, or will when the paperwork is settled, still, I wouldn't let you pay. It's the least I can do after causing all this."

Liz opens her mouth to question him about why he thinks any of what happened to her is his fault, but before she can, he steps over and sits next to her, putting his feet in the water.

"I think we should do what Mikey said, use me to get to Dmitri."

"I'm not going to put you in more danger than I already have."

"That's not for you to decide." Liz says, resting her head on his arm. "People died because of me. I shouldn't even be here, I should have died with my family years ago, if I did, none of this would have happened. It's not fair I get to keep going while they don't. If this is what it takes to make sure that doesn't happen again, then I want to do it," she explains, hoping he understands her guilt.

"Do you remember the day I found you? I remember every inch of that cell, every smell, every drop of blood that stained the walls. I remember how scared you looked when you saw me. I still see you bloodied and broken, clinging to life when I close my eyes." He takes a deep breath, growing uncomfortable with the openness she brings out of him.

"When I carried you out, I told you I wouldn't let anything happen to you again. I made a promise to keep you safe, and I already broke that. I hurt you when I found your brother, I let you get hurt when the base got attacked... I keep fucking up. If we do this, I have no way of keeping you safe."

"You're the one who wanted me to live, to find something worth fighting for." Liz looks up at him, his eyes dancing with the reflection of the water. She reaches over and takes his large hand in hers, interlacing their fingers. "Well, I found something. I can't really live if you keep me from this just because you're afraid of me being hurt."

"You're right," he finally says.

"If this is what you need to do, I'll support you in any way I can. Just know I'm going to train you twice as hard. I need to know if anything happens and I'm not there, you will be able to handle yourself."

Liz gives his hand a squeeze, and looking up into his eyes, she asks, "When do we start?"

CHAPTER 33

The next morning, Liz wakes up to an empty house. She goes out to the kitchen and looks around. With no sign of Riley or Mikey, she ventures downstairs, seeing if maybe they are getting in an early workout. She runs back up, looking at the clock on the stove it reads 7:18 a.m.

Liz tiptoes to Mikey's room, cracking the door open. She pokes her head in, seeing limbs sticking out of the big pile of blankets. Sure they will wake up soon, she starts digging around in the fridge and cabinets, getting everything together to make breakfast. Twenty minutes go by and Liz is almost done cooking. She puts the last few pieces of French toast on a plate and looks over the feast she made for them: two types of eggs, bacon, sausage, homemade hash browns. Both pancakes and French toast, toast with jam, and some fresh fruit she found.

She sets the table and piles all her food on it, hoping the smell will wake someone up. After a few minutes, she gives up on them coming out on their own, so she walks over to the start of the small hall, clears her throat, and lets out her best "someone save me" scream. Within seconds, both men are running out their doors, guns drawn, ready for anything.

Riley makes it to her first, alert and dressed for a fight. Mikey's not far behind wearing nothing but a pair of white boxers covered in yellow rubber ducks, sweatpants around one ankle, hair disheveled, still half asleep. They look around, seeing nothing but Liz smiling at them, the smell of her cooking wafting through the air.

"What the actual fuck, darlin!" Mikey shouts, still trying to pull himself together.

She just walks over to the table and pulls out their chairs, a clear order to sit. "That, my dear, was payback for all the times you assholes woke me up by kicking me."

"You were nudged with a foot to make sure you were alive that doesn't count as kicking, it's not our fault you napped so much when we first brought you in," Mikey argues "It's not like you didn't hear us coming–" he starts again before Riley turns on him, quickly getting him to shut up and finish getting his pants on.

Liz sits and piles food onto her plate, having decided she waited for them long enough. They storm over, hearts still racing from her little stunt, and slump into their chairs, grabbing plates and filling them up.

"It's Sunday, you couldn't let us sleep in? We never get to sleep in," Mikey asks through a loud yawn.

"How the hell am I supposed to know what day it is? I haven't known the date in literal years," Liz says, voice dripping with attitude.

Riley slides out of his chair and heads back to his room. Liz gives Mikey a confused look, but he just shrugs his bare shoulders and takes a large bite of eggs. Riley returns a minute later, a small box in his hand, tossing it onto the table in front of Liz as he sits back down.

"I was going to give that to you later, but I don't think you deserve what I had planned anymore," Riley says, digging into his food.

Liz eyes him, suspicious of what he could possibly be giving her. She slowly opens the box, a small, black rectangle inside. She pulls it out and squeals, not having access to any type of technology in over a year. She quickly stands and runs over to him, throwing her arms around his neck.

"Thank you," she says, kissing his cheek before returning to her seat. The little happy dance she does while eating sends Riley's heart racing, completely forgiving her for giving him a heart attack.

"Our numbers are already in there in case you need us and we're not with you for some reason." Riley takes another bite, unable to remember the last time he had food that good.

"Or if you're lonely at night." Mikey says winking at her.

Liz simply rolls her eyes and goes back to her breakfast. She peers over at Riley through her thick lashes, thinking about what Mikey said. What would he do if she *was* lonely at night? Would he come running to her? Or would he realize he had a moment of weakness, remembering that she's not worth the trouble she causes. Liz eats in silence, pushing the anxious thoughts out of her head, instead listening to the men as they talk about plans and how they need to inform the General.

"You want to get out of here for a bit, princess?" Riley asks. "No training, just something fun to do together." He makes sure to add.

"I didn't know you liked fun," she jokes. She takes another small bite of food, thinking it over. "Where are we going?"

"Don't worry about it, just give me a few minutes to get dressed."

Liz stands and starts to clear the table when Mikey grabs her arm, stopping her, quickly dropping it and stepping back when she flinches.

"Go relax, darlin. Let me clean up," he says, turning her away from the table.

Liz walks over and throws herself down on the giant couch, almost falling back asleep with how comfortable it is. Before she gets the chance, Riley comes walking back out and she pops her head up from the other side. She rolls herself off the couch and stands, prancing over to where he's waiting by the elevator. He pushes a button and they step in, quickly making their way through the small cabin and out to Riley's truck.

They spend the next forty-five minutes in silence, Liz just relaxing, eyes closed, enjoying the sun shining on her face. Riley pulls into a parking lot and parks. Liz finally cracks her eyes, the bright sign catching her eye, instantly bringing a smile to her face.

"You brought me to Target?" she says, unable to hide her smile.

He ignores her question, wishing he had a better place to bring her. He looks over at her face, at how happy she is, and hopes this is enough for now. One day, when this is all over, he will give her anything her heart desires, even if that means helping her start a new life.

"You brought your phone, right?" he asks, sounding a little worried. Liz lets go of the door handle and turns to him, confusion etched all over her face.

"Yeah, but you're coming with me, right?"

"I can't go in with the mask, stores don't really appreciate masked men in them."

"I would appreciate a masked man in me," Liz mumbles under her breath, hoping he didn't hear her. "So, you're not worried someone is going to come after me?" she asks playfully.

He looks over at her, eyes darkening, not a hint of amusement in them. "If your little plan is going to work, you need to be seen alone. I'm sure they started tracking you as soon as they could."

Liz's heart sinks as she realizes he didn't plan this for something fun to do, wanting to spend time with her. She quickly blinks back the tears forming, thinking about how stupid she is for thinking that night in Riley's room meant as much to him as it did her. Of course it didn't, he told her as much. He got caught up in the moment.

"So this was never about us spending time together? Just me robbing a store to get Dmitri's attention?" Liz snaps, crossing her arms, unable to look at him.

"Calm down, princess. This is just the beginning."

Liz peeks over at him when she feels the truck shift, to see him reaching for something in his back pocket. She continues to pout, even after a small black card is tossed into her lap.

"Go nuts. Make sure you buy everything your heart desires" Riley says to her.

"I'm not spending your money. I told you, I will figure something out."

"Look at me," he says.

Liz doubles down, shifting her body so she can look away more than she already was.

"Liz," he snaps. She turns, her eyes shooting to his, shocked at the sound of Riley using her name instead of one of the pet names she's come to adore. He ignores her and grabs her face in one hand. His eyes meet hers, something like want in them as they flick to her pouting lips before he drags them back up to her eyes. "Listen to me, I should have bought you all this shit months ago. You deserve to go buy everything you need. I can buy out this entire fucking store and my bank account won't even notice."

Liz opens her mouth to object, but he just gives her cheeks a little squeeze, smiling down at her.

"If you don't go shopping for yourself, I'll send Mikey to do it. I can't promise he'll buy you anything but lingerie and snacks," he says, dropping his hand.

"Fine... but I won't be a cheap date," she says, challenging him to change his mind.

"Date?" he says, eyes lighting up.

Liz can feel her face getting hot. She groans and jumps out of the truck, practically running from her embarrassment. Riley watches as she jogs across the parking lot, keeping his eyes on her until she disappears into the store.

Liz walks into the giant store, grabbing a cart. She heads to the beauty section, grabbing bottles and boxes, tossing them in, making sure to take anything and everything she could need. When she's satisfied with what she has, she heads over to the clothing department. Distracted by the home decor, she grabs a bedding set and a few little decorations for her room. When she finally makes it to the clothing, she fills her cart to the brim with shirts, pants, pajamas, bathing suits. Like Riley said, anything her heart desires.

As she's looking at shoes, she notices a man watching her from behind a rack of clothes, when she looks over at him he turns away, but she can feel eyes on her the moment she turns away.. Liz had seen him more than once around the store. She tried to ignore it, telling herself it's been a long time since she was in public like this. She goes from isle to isle, thinking she's just being paranoid. Wherever she goes, the man follows. She peers at him from the corner of her eye, watching him pull his phone out and aim it at her. She quickly pulls out her own, sending two quick texts to Riley.

Someone's watching me.

Taking pictures.

Stay calm. Finish up and get back here.

Liz tosses in another pair of shoes, trying to act as normal as she can. She looks over her cart, satisfied, she starts for the front to check out. She passes the intimates and stops dead in her tracks. She rushes over and quickly picks out some new panties and real bras. When she turns to put them in her cart, she spies a lacy thing hanging on a mannequin.

Riley flashes through her mind, the image of him on his knees, touching her. She rolls her eyes, knowing it is stupid. She is being followed and needs to get out of the store but she can't help herself. She looks for her size and grabs the bundle of red lace and straps, tossing it in before she can change her mind. She quickly checks out and wheels her overflowing cart back to where Riley waits for her in the truck.

He watches as she walks out the door, heading back before seeing the man behind her, looking around. His eyes never leave her as she starts walking faster. Riley gets out of the truck, rushing to the passenger side and popping open the door. As soon as Liz reaches him, he puts his hand on the small of her back and ushers her in, closing the door behind her. He turns and looks back to where the man was, glaring at him as he turns and walks in a different direction. Riley quickly loads up the bags, gets back in, and starts driving to his next surprise.

"Get everything you need?" he asks.

"Sure did, and I promise I'll find a way to pay you back," Liz tells him, gazing out the window as the town passes by.

"Will you stop? You're not paying for anything, love."

Liz scoots over on the seat so she's sitting next to him, resting her head on his shoulder. He reaches over and puts his hand on her knee, rubbing idle circles with his thumb.

"You know, Mikey's going to make you show him everything, right?" he asks, squeezing her leg, causing her stomach to do flips.

She pulls her head back, looking at him like he has two heads. "You're joking right? He's not going to care what I got," she says, nervously.

"Why? Something you don't want him to see?" he teases.

"What? No, I just don't know why he would care."

"He hasn't told you yet? You're his best friend, tossed me out the window as soon as you started telling him jokes," he says, chuckling to himself.

"You're an ass," she says, trying to scoot back to the passenger seat, hoping he won't let her. Riley tightens his grip, stopping her from going any further, pulling her back into him. The gesture sends her heart racing in the best way. Giggling, she lays her head back down, loops her arm through his, and closes her eyes, enjoying the lightness he draws out of her.

It has been so long since she felt comfortable around anyone, let alone a man, but Riley is different. He makes her feel safe and seen, asking for consent to touch her when he knows she needs to be in control. Even the times like now, when he grabs her like it's second nature, she knows in her soul he would stop in an instant if she showed even a sliver of discomfort. The respect he has continuously shown her since the day in the interrogation room has built the trust and respect she now holds for him.

"Hungry?" he asks, idly rubbing his thumb back and forth.

"Starving." Liz doesn't open her eyes until they pull into a small lot on the side of the road. A bar is tucked further back with a lot of men in uniforms standing around.

Riley throws the truck in park and Liz starts to wiggle her way back to the door. "Stay. I'll be right back," he says, opening his door and hopping out.

Liz watches as he disappears behind a banged-up wooden door. She looks around, seemingly in the middle of nowhere. Liz sees a few small buildings down the road, but nothing else around. A few of the men outside the bar start to look at her. She slinks down in the seat, silently begging Riley to hurry.

After just a few minutes, he emerges with a big bag in hand, quickly making his way back to the truck. He climbs in, hands her the bag of food, and pulls out, heading in the opposite direction. The smell of fried something fills the small space, making her mouth water.

"Why aren't we eating there?" Liz asks, fighting the urge to rip the bag open and dig in.

"I thought we could go somewhere more... private," he says, sliding his hand back onto her leg before quickly adding, "In case Dmitri makes a move to attack, fewer people will be at risk."

Something in her tells her that's not the real reason he wants to go to this secret place, but she's too content to question him right now. They don't talk, just stay cuddled close until Riley pulls off onto a hidden dirt road. Liz bounces around as he drives over holes and rocks, wondering why he would want to come out here. She looks over at him only to catch his eyes darting to her chest, jiggling with every bump he hits.

"Is this why you're bringing me out here? To watch my tits bounce?" she asks, giving him a playful nudge.

"You'll understand when we get there. I didn't know the road was this bad, but I'm not complaining," Riley says, winking at her.

Liz opens her mouth to respond, but she can't form words when she sees where they are. The road ends at a hidden grove with a lake and small waterfall.

CHAPTER 34

Liz stares at the small, grassy field leading to the lake the waterfall flows into. The whole grove is surrounded by a small mountain range, giant pine trees kept concealed. The field is teeming with wildflowers in full bloom.

Riley parks the truck and walks around to the other side, opening the door and helping Liz climb down. He grabs the food and leads her over to the field, sitting in the plush grass he pulls his mask off, tossing it to the side. He starts pulling food out of the bag and setting it in front of where Liz now sits. She takes in the breathtaking grove, swearing he pulled it right out of a fantasy novel, when her eyes land on him.

Liz sucks in a sharp breath, forgetting just how stunning he is without his mask. She looks down at the food in front of her and thinks back to all the times he's done this. In all the months she's been with them, she has only served herself food a handful of times. Liz looks over at him, lounging in the grass, butterflies taking over her stomach as she thinks back on how much he has done and continues to do for her.

"Stop looking at me like that, princess," he says, his eyes meeting hers.

"Like what?" she asks, smiling sweetly.

"Like you're starting to like me. Like I'm not the asshole who dragged you into this shitty situation."

Liz just looks at him, unsure of why he continues to blame himself for the situation she got thrust into.

"I do like you... I mean, you're an ass, but you're also really sweet, and we have fun... sometimes," she says playfully. "You're going to make a great boyfriend when I finally get you to take your mask off long enough to meet someone," she says, stuffing fries into her mouth.

"What makes you think I want to meet someone?"

"No one wants to be alone forever, not even you," she says, eyeing him as he thinks about what she's saying.

"I never said I did, but if I'm going to be with someone, it's going to be someone who doesn't give a fuck about it. Whoever I end up with is going to understand why I wear it, and who knows, they might even think it's sexy," he says, winking at her. "Who knows, maybe that person will stumble into my life and make me feel whole again, make me feel like I can live life without it, then I'll decide if I keep it or not."

He lays back in the grass, tucking his hands behind his head. Liz sits there, not sure what she can say after that.

They stay silent, listening to the sounds of the waterfall gently crashing into the lake, picking at the grass and tiny flowers around her, basking in the feel of it between her fingers. Never again will she take something as simple as sitting in the grass for granted.

"Is the lake deep enough to swim in?" Liz finally asks, curiosity getting the better of her.

"Don't know, I've never been in it."

Liz crawls over to where he is lounging and kneels next to him laying her head and arms on his chest. He looks up at her, a mix of shock and joy that she's comfortable enough to lay on him like that. She has come so far since that day in the cell. He can't help but stare at the beautiful woman before him. Her eyes narrow on him, wondering what he could be thinking.

"I'm going to jump off the waterfall," she says abruptly.

Liz goes to push herself off Riley, but his strong arms are around her before she can stand, pulling her into his body. She doesn't try to fight it, just letting him pull her further onto his chest. Perfectly happy to stay close to him all day.

"No you're not, we have no idea how deep that lake is."

She lets out a little huff, looking down, practically straddling him. She wiggles her body as much as she can in his grip, moving her thighs up onto his and kicking her feet in the air above them. Their faces are mere inches apart. Riley reaches up with one hand, his other wrapped firmly around her, and tucks a stray lock of hair behind her ear. His hand lingers on her face, so she rests her cheek against it, and ever so slowly pulls her face to his, again giving her time to stop him. He's close enough to feel her nose against his, her soft pink lips just out of reach when a loud ring blasts from his pocket.

Liz throws her head back and laughs, rolling off of him and onto her back.

"I'm going to fucking kill him," Riley says, reaching for his phone, pressing the ignore button on the screen. He takes a minute to look through his messages before standing, extending his hand. He pulls her into his chest and wraps his arms around her.

"We have to go home, don't we?" Liz asks into his chest.

He leans down and places a kiss on top of her head, smiling because she called it home. "Yeah, we need to go home, love"

CHAPTER 35

When they return to the bunker, Riley makes quick work of unloading all of Liz's bags, only allowing her to carry the lightest one. When the doors to the elevator open, they walk in the room to see four people all hunched around the table, talking over each other, papers scattered about, and the smell of Chinese food drifting to them. Liz freezes at the sight of the general there, her blood running cold.

Riley follows her gaze and places his hand on her back. She looks up at him in response and picks up her bags, storming to her room. Riley's not far behind, pulling his mask off and tossing it onto the couch as he walks by. He meets her in her room and adds his bags to the pile on her bed.

"Thank you for everything today. Even if it was just to get Dmitri's attention. I had a really nice time," Liz says as she pushes a bag out of the way so she can sit on the bed.

"Good. We're going to be doing that a lot if we want him to come after you," Riley says as he reaches for one of the bags.

"Want some help unpacking?" he asks as he starts to pull things out, not waiting for her response.

She looks over at him pulling clothes out of the bag, eyes going wide before she jumps up reaching for it. "No, I got it," she says, a little too quick.

"Oh you definitely bought something you don't want us to see," he laughs, peeking at the bags, wondering what one holds the mystery thing.

She follows his eyes to the bags, quickly realizing what he's going to do. She jumps up, grabbing at the bag Riley is reaching for, knocking another bag off the bed in the process. The over-stuffed paper bag goes tumbling off the bed, contents spilling onto the floor at their feet. She looks down in horror at the little bundle of lace she was trying so hard to hide.

He smiles wide, bending down and grabbing it. He holds it up and whistles. "Hot date you didn't tell me about?" Riley says, trying to hide the anger that flashes across his face at the thought of her wearing all those straps and lace for someone else.

Liz reaches over and snatches it out of his hands and throws it onto the bed. "Don't be a jerk... If you must know, I thought, maybe, it would make me feel better about myself."

"You don't like what you look like?" he asks, trying not to picture her in the tiny strappy outfit.

"I don't know... It's not so much my body, the whole big tits, small waist, nice ass thing is amazing, but now I'm covered in all these new scars... I just... I can't stand to look at myself anymore," she tells him, picking up the rest of the pile from the floor.

"I get it, I felt the same way after I got out, why do you think i'm covered in tattoos? Not that your feelings should be based on any man's opinion, but you have to know that any man would kill to be with you," he says, stepping closer to her. "I've almost killed a few recruits for how they talked after seeing you in the halls. Hell, I've almost killed Mikey for looking at you the way he has and he's like a brother to me."

"Don't say shit like that," Liz says, gently pushing him away. "I appreciate what you're trying to do, but I don't want you to be nice just to make me feel better. I just need to learn to be okay with the changes."

"Believe it or not, you're beautiful, princess. No scars on your body are going to change that." He steps back over to her.

Liz takes the last step into him, their bodies touching. He wraps his arms around her. She pushes herself onto her tiptoes, determined to finish what they started at the lake. She stops for a brief second, trying to gather the strength to do it, telling herself he wants it too, when the door flies open and Mikey strides in. They both quickly take a step back, looking at Mikey with nothing but contempt.

"Are you fucking kidding me?" Riley snaps at him.

"Sorry, am I interrupting something?" Mikey says laughing, quickly shutting up when he sees the look on Liz's face. "Everyone is waiting for you two to go over plans. The general was about to come in here himself. I'll tell them you're almost done fucking."

Liz grabs a pillow off her bed and throws it at his head, but Mikey is too quick, catching it and throwing it back onto her bed.

"Can I help you kill him?" Liz asks Riley.

Mikey just chuckles and walks away. She can still hear him laughing when the phone in her pocket buzzes, pulling it out, she opens it and reads:

What did Cinderella do when she got to the ball?

She gagged.

Liz just stares at her phone, unable to believe the audacity that man has. She tucks the phone back in her pocket, already thinking of what she's going to respond with. She looks at Riley and he gives her a sad smile, dreading this just as much as she is.

She grabs Riley's hand and they head to the door to get this meeting over with.

CHAPTER 36

Liz and Riley walk out together and take their seats at the table, all eyes on them as they do. Liz quickly looks around, eyes lingering on the general. She can't help but smile at the sight of his black eyes and bandaged nose. The general just glares at her, clearly holding back from saying what he wants to.

Alex clears his throat and starts. "We have intercepted intel by Dmitri's men. Mikey was right, they took a big hit when they attacked Stryker. It's going to take weeks for them to execute another attack, but they are definitely looking for Liz, although we still don't know why. The good news is, we were finally able to confirm your story entirely." Alex looks at Liz, his eyes soft and caring for the first time since they met.

Liz wonders if he feels bad for the way he treated her, now understanding none of it is her fault, or if he simply pities her after everything she shared about what she endured at Dmitri's hand.

"None of this would matter if we just handed her over!" the

general snaps, adding, "Dmitri wouldn't have a reason to attack."

Liz stares, green eyes boring into him as she seethes with anger. Her body starts to shake. Riley, still not the best at reading her emotions, confuses her shaking for fear, and reaches his hand over, placing it on her leg, slowly rubbing up and down. It's a small gesture, but the only one he can do. He's learned physical touch is the best way to ground her.

"General," Riley says in a deathly calm that is more Reaper than Riley. "Did you already forget what got you that broken nose?"

The general's face turns red, and he starts to mutter before snapping his mouth shut when he sees the violence churning in Riley's eyes.

"And let's not forget, if it wasn't for Liz we never would have known about her brother. He would still be out there aiding Dmitri," Tyler adds, giving Liz a small smile that she returns.

"So what is your plan... Reaper?" The general asks through gritted teeth.

"They already know where she is. A man was following her today, taking pictures. He only stopped when he spotted me, so we know the tracker is active. I think we keep going. Every few days I'll take her out, start building a pattern for him to plan his attack around," Riley says.

"And you think that will work?" The general snaps.

"We have been watching him for years. You yourself know how he treats things he believes are his. He thinks he has a right to Liz, thinks he owns her. We all know it's not just about her, it's about us taking her, stealing what he claims is his property... In no world would he just let that insult go," Riley says to the general.

He thinks on it for a minute. The silence draws Liz's attention back to the large hand currently rubbing her leg, getting dangerously close to the apex of her thigh. Liz can't help it, a breathy little noise escapes her. Riley stops and grips her leg, strong fingers digging in. It doesn't take long for him to start again, trying to drag that sound from her.

"I want Bert and Ernie to stay here, track his movements, and Tank, you need to get started on a plan of attack for when he finally comes out of hiding." The general says, using the call signs he only uses in anger. He quickly stands and marches to the elevator, leaving without another word.

Alex and Tyler excuse themselves to follow the general out and return him to the base. As soon as the three of them are piled into the elevator and out of earshot Liz whirls on Riley, a thousand questions bouncing around her head.

"Who the fuck is Tank? And Bert and Ernie? Who's who?" she shrieks, excited by the new information.

"Tyler's Bert and Alex is Ernie," Riley tells her.

"Are they.... ya know?" she says, making a little gesture with her hand. Mikey laughs and gets up, grabbing two beers from the fridge before walking back and handing one to Riley.

"Yeah, they are," Mikey says.

"General doesn't really agree with the whole equality thing, especially in the military, so he gave them the shittiest call signs he could think of. Dude wants to shame them every chance he gets," he adds, sad for his friends, for the bigotry they have to deal with every day.

"Now I get why Alex hates me. I caused all the shit that's putting someone he cares about at risk," Liz says.

"You didn't cause anything, darlin, and Alex doesn't hate you, he just takes some time to warm up to people." Mikey tries to reassure her.

"So... your nickname is Tank? I didn't think you would have

one so... cool," she says to him, struggling to find the right words.

"Want to know how I got the name?" Mikey asks, preparing to tell her the most extravagantly wild story he can come up with.

"Dumbass drove a tank into a building after he convinced everyone he knew what he was doing," Riley says laughing.

Liz looks at him, not sure if she should believe Riley or not, but the look on Mikey's face is proof enough that Riley is telling the truth. Before she can question it, Mikey blurts, "It was one time."

"Because you got banned from driving them again," Riley responds without missing a beat.

That's all it takes, Liz bursts out laughing, deep and true, causing the guys to laugh along with her. After a moment, she pulls herself together, stomach hurting from not laughing in so long.

Riley looks at her, reaching over and taking her hand in his, the happiness shining in her eyes mirrored in his own. She rests her head on his shoulder and closes her eyes. The excitement from the day mixed with the contentment she's feeling makes her very tired, very fast.

"You should get some rest, darlin. We're meeting in the gym at 0500," Mikey tells her.

She nods her head and gives Riley a small squeeze before dropping his hand and standing. She tells them goodnight and heads to her room. Shoving everything off her bed and onto the floor, she climbs up and gets snuggled in, wishing she dragged Riley with her.

Liz pulls out her phone, having the perfect response for Mikey.

> What's a tank's favorite holiday?

> Tanksgiving

She sends the text, listening intently to hear if he gets it. Liz smiles to herself when she hears the two of them outside start laughing. She puts the phone down, snuggles into the plush mattress, and lets herself drift off.

CHAPTER 37

5 a.m comes all too fast when you fall asleep emotionally drained. Liz peels herself from the comfort of her bed, slinks onto the floor and begins ripping the tags off all her clothes. She quickly gets dressed and heads to the gym, stopping at the laundry room on her way to wash everything not on her body. When she makes it to the gym, she instantly finds Riley mid-workout, eyes drifting to the hard ridges of his stomach.

"Whenever you're done staring we can start, darlin," Mikey yells to her, drawing her attention.

Liz can feel the heat rise in her cheeks as she rushes to the treadmills and tosses her water bottle on the floor. The next hour is spent running and trying to stop herself from looking in the mirror to wherever Riley is currently working out, failing miserably. When the hour is finally up, she gets off and takes a long drink of water, feeling Riley's eyes on her. She makes sure to turn away from him, knowing she won't be able to control herself while Mikey leads her through their light yoga stretches before they can move on to weights. She barely gets into her downward dog pose when she hears Mikey yell.

"Oh my god! Will you two just fuck already?"

Liz slowly raises herself back up, turning to him confused. Mikey just shakes his head, pinching the bridge of his nose, he motions for her to go over the weight rack and get started. She looks over her shoulder to Riley, who is finished and leaving. He shoots her a wink before disappearing out the door. Blushing, Liz turns back to Mikey who's rolling his eyes at them. She picks up the weights and does her sets, wondering what Riley could have been doing to get such a reaction. By the time they are done, her whole body aches.

When they finish their workout, Liz and Mikey head back upstairs to find Riley cooking breakfast for everyone. Tyler and Alex are setting up boxes upon boxes of equipment, quickly taking over the dining table. Liz greets them, unsure how to feel about two strangers joining them, quickly reminding herself that this is more their home than hers. She skips to the island, jumping into her usual seat. Riley turns, setting a plate full of food in front of Liz who smiles up at him.

"Thank you," she says, gently peering up though her long lashes at him.

He fills his own plate and they all eat in silence, listening to the sound of machines being built. Tyler and Alex are quietly arguing over where everything goes. The three of them hang out in the kitchen for a while, watching the men like an exhibit at the zoo, trying to figure out just what Alex and Tyler are actually doing. Eventually, Mikey and Liz head back to the gym and over to the mats, waiting for Riley to join them in hand-to-hand training.

"Why isn't Riley doing this anymore?" she asks, breathless, throwing another punch at Mikey.

"Have you seen how two guys look at each other? The man was about to rip a hole in your pants and take you on the gym floor earlier," he says, effortlessly dodging every move she makes. "If you two train together, Riley will be hitting something, but it won't be the pads." Mikey laughs to himself.

Liz goes quiet, embarrassed by his observations. She stays quiet and focused on the task at hand, trying to retain as much information as she can. Liz didn't expect training to get so much more intense than what they used to do. By the end of the two hours, Liz is on the floor, dripping sweat, fighting to catch her breath.

"This is it for me Mikey, this is how I go, just kill me quick and end this suffering," she pleads dramatically, rolling onto her stomach and resting her face on the dirty mat.

"Riley's waiting for you in the gun range, darlin. I'm sure you can stay alive for that." Mikey nudges her in the ribs with his foot.

"It's not going to be easy, but I guess I can try," Liz slowly inches her way back up, standing on wobbly legs. She walks out of the gym and crosses the hall, knocking on the door to the gun range. The door doesn't open, glancing down at the small pad on the door, Liz lifts her hand and presses her thumb onto it. The pad beeps and turns green, a soft click coming from the door. Liz squeals with excitement, turns the handle and rushes into the room.

She looks around to see Riley standing over a table lined with various guns. He looks up to see her walking over and wastes no time starting. They spend the next hour going over each gun. He shows her how to load and unload them, how to clean them, and how to hold each one. She watches him closely, absorbing every word he says, knowing this is some of the most important training she will have. When he is done explaining, he hands her one of the small handguns and walks her to the targets.

She does what he's explained to her, trying her best to remember everything and not miss. When her clip is empty, he hands her another one and has her go again, doing it as many times as it takes for him to be satisfied with her shots. Unsure of how much time goes by, she fires her last round into a fresh target at the end of the long room.

"I thought you would take longer to catch on," he says, impressed with her progress. "Go get ready for lunch, I'll meet you in an hour." Riley grabs the gun from her and walks it back to the table. She takes her earmuffs off and sets them down, before turning and walking out the door.

Liz runs to her room, stopping to grab her freshly cleaned clothes. She ties her hair up before jumping into the shower, trying to hurry so she's not late. Stepping out, she quickly grabs one of her new matching bra and panty sets and puts them on, putting pink floral sundress on over. Liz lets her hair down and fixes it the best she can in the short time she has. When she's happy with the way the curls cascade down her back, she slips into a pair of sandals and heads out to meet Riley.

Riley walks into the room and stops in his tracks at the sight of Liz standing there, waiting for him. She blushes, looking away when she sees the way he looks at her, his eyes roaming her body.

"Ready for our date?" she asks nervously.

Riley nods, unable to form words with her looking like that. He stalks over to the fridge and pulls out a small bag before walking to the elevator where Liz patiently waits for him.

They step into the elevator and he waits for the door to close before stepping closer to Liz.

"So, is this our second date?" he asks, nudging her with his arm.

"What?" Liz asks, eyes snapping to him, brows knit in confusion.

"You called it a date and said yesterday was a date," he says, teasing her for her poor choice of words.

"I didn't know what else to call it," Liz says, blushing and looking away.

"Date's good," he says as the elevator opens.

Riley picks up her hand and walks her to the truck. When they make it to the dirt road, Liz throws her arm over her chest, preparing for the bumps that never come. Riley catches her doing it and laughs to himself.

"I asked Alex to fill in some holes when he was out yesterday, dude loves busy work." Riley tells her.

She smiles over at him, grateful he got the road fixed. They pull up to the opening of the grove and Riley tells her to stay in the truck. He hops out and walks around for a second, looking for something. When he doesn't find what he's looking for, he walks back over and opens the door, helping her out before grabbing the food and a folded blanket. They walk over to their grassy spot and Riley lays the blanket out before plopping himself onto it. He unpacks the food and hands Liz a bowl. Starving, she thanks him and quickly starts eating the salad, watching the waterfall crash into the lake.

When they finish their food, they both lay back on the blanket, close but not touching. Neither one is willing to make the first move while everything is so serene. Liz rolls to her side, propping herself up on an elbow. Riley smiles and rolls to face her. He reaches over and starts playing with one of the long black curls pooling around her elbow.

"We should start coming out later," he says, seemingly from nowhere.

"Why?" Liz asks.

"Darks better for an ambush. If we come out at night, Dmitri may be more inclined to move forward with his plans. Especially if he thinks we're only coming here to be alone." He tickles her nose with her hair.

She bats his hand away and gives him a little nudge. "Will you still train me when this is over? Or are you going to admit you're sick of me and send me away?" she asks, trying not to sound sad.

"Clearly you didn't read those papers before you gave them back. You're under my protection, wherever you go, I go with you." He says watching her silky hair flow through his fingers. "Even if you chose not to sign them, I'm with you forever, love. I wouldn't be the same without you."

Liz looks over at him, heart racing, stomach in knots at his words. She wonders to herself if he meant to say it.

It hits Riley then, what he just said, still trying to hide just how much she means to him he pivots, quickly changing the subject. "I had Tyler look into the lake for you. It's deep enough for swimming."

Liz squeals, launching to her feet. She wastes no time kicking off her sandals and starting to pull her arms from the straps of her dress. She looks over at Riley, still laying on the blanket, not moving to join her.

"Are you coming?" she asks, wiggling her dress down past her hips. Riley watches her, eyes darkening as she undresses.

"Later, hopefully," he says, a sinful smile on his face.

"You're disgusting," she says to him, picking up her dress and tossing it at him.

"You strip in front of me and expect me to not think about burying my cock in you?" he asks, sitting back up, voice deep and full of want as he takes in every curve of her body.

"RILEY!" she shouts, jaw dropping at his bluntness.

"Don't act like you're not thinking about it, princess," he says, knowing he's right.

Not ready to acknowledge the truth behind his words, or the wetness instantly pooling between her legs, Liz turns, trying to hide her reaction. She quickly makes her way to the small, rocky beach leading into the lake. Riley's eyes never leave her body. She wades up to her waist, looking back.

"You really won't come in?" she yells, bouncing up and down from the cold.

"I'm enjoying the view, princess."

"You're no fun," she yells, backing further into the lake until it reaches her navel.

She watches as Riley adjusts himself, sending a wave of heat coursing through her body. She slowly walks out of the lake, water dripping off and causing her to glisten in the sun. Riley watches the seductive swing of her hips with each step she takes back toward the blanket. She sits and stretches out on her back, soaking in the warmth of the sun.

"If you want me to live my life, you could at least live yours with me," Liz says to him. "Or let Mikey bring me. He would have come in."

"Love, Mikey is my best friend, but I would rip his fucking eyes out if he saw you like this," he says, eyes dropping down to the swell of her breasts.

"That's not very nice," Liz says, crossing her arms to pout, his jealousy sending her heart fluttering. "I'm going to get you to jump off that waterfall with me."

The sound of a car in the distance sets them both on edge. Liz jumps up and starts pulling her clothes back on while Riley pulls his mask back over his mouth. They are on their feet and back in the truck in less than a minute. Heart racing, Liz moves over to the middle, getting herself as close to Riley as she can. He peels out of where they are parked and takes off back down the road, only reacting when a black SUV comes into view.

Riley slows even more, rolling his window down slightly while he grabs Liz's hand in an attempt to calm her. Her breathing heavy, head spinning at the sight of the man driving, the same man who was following her at the store. She grips his hand tighter, trying to stay calm at the realization.

"Lake's all yours," he says to the man before rolling his window back up and speeding off.

Riley drives them home as fast as he can, taking a few extra roads to make sure they aren't being followed. When they pull up, Riley leaves his truck outside instead of pulling it into the barn, ushering Liz inside. He lets out a breath of relief once the elevator doors open and they step in. He takes his mask off before pulling Liz into him, holding her tight. They only have a moment of peace before the doors open to pure chaos.

CHAPTER 38

The second the doors open, Liz is overwhelmed by people yelling and computers blaring. She looks around, trying to find the only person she's comfortable enough with to ask what's going on, but Mikey is too busy trying to make the noise stop.

Alex rushes over and starts talking to Riley. Liz utilizes the distraction to slip away to her room. She quickly changes into something more comfortable and throws her hair into a messy bun, telling herself if she has to deal with all this shit, she is at least going to be comfortable.

She walks back out and the room is just as hectic as when they first walked in. She looks around, all the yelling and noise quickly becoming too much. All the voices are pulling her in a thousand different directions. She can feel her heartbeat quickening, her vision going fuzzy, a stabbing pain starting in her chest.

Before the panic attack can take her, she takes one big, deep breath and shouts over the men. "Can you all just shut the fuck up!"

The room goes silent, except for the blaring of computers, four sets of eyes turning on her, utter shock etched on every face as they look to where she stands. She walks over to where they are huddled, figuring she better say something fast before they berate her for speaking to them that way.

"How is anything going to work if all you idiots are screaming over one another?" She strides over to the table scattered with papers and maps and sits. When she looks over to see them still standing around, looking at her with wide eyes, she simply says, "Sit."

To her surprise, they quietly walk to the table and sit down. She isn't sure what to say now, knowing her outburst was caused by anxiety and not necessarily wanting to take control of the situation.

Riley senses why she did what she did and takes over for her. "What happened?" he asks, looking at Alex.

"We got through the encrypted file he sent us," Alex says, creating more questions for Liz.

"And?" Riley urges, needing more information.

"There's still a lot to go through. But you were right. Dmitri is pissed you're keeping her." Alex looks at Liz. "He has been going crazy, killing his own men who don't agree with getting her back. I think if anyone but you took her, he could have let it go, but you humiliated him when he was fighting for power, just to go back and do it again," Alex says to Riley.

"There's more," Mikey interjects, looking at Tyler to finish explaining what they found.

"He needs her for something, we just haven't found out what yet. But, Sir... it's not just about you taking her, it's something much bigger, we just don't know what."

"So, why was everyone screaming when we came in?" Liz asks.

Mikey is the one to answer this time. "We got word they found you at the lake. We started trying to break through the files as fast as we could to see if they had something planned... It got a little tense."

"It doesn't help that the general is on his way and expects us to know everything happening in Dmitri's mind," Alex adds.

"Great. General Dickhead is coming back," Liz says with a huff, anger flooding her body. She stretches her arms out, resting her forehead on the cool table, defeated.

Mikey cracks a small smile, but Tyler and Alex look at her like she's insane. Never in all their years working under the General have they heard someone call him anything other than his name. Even Riley, who loathes the man with his entire being, doesn't refer to him as anything but General or Sir.

"What did you call him?" Tyler asks, trying to hide the smile creeping up on his face. Liz picks her head back up, smirking at him.

"General Dickhead. Because, well, he's a fucking Dickhead," Liz says without an ounce of regret.

"They don't exactly see eye to eye," Mikey chimes in.

"He called me Dmitri's whore. Literally said I was fucking the man who kidnapped me, chained me to a dirty floor, attempted to rape me, and let his men beat me every fucking day. I should have beat his ass the second those words left his stupid mouth." Liz snaps, anger only growing as she thinks back to the things the general has said to her. The large hand that grabs her leg under the table is the only thing keeping her from storming out.

"We're not disagreeing with what you called him. Just never met someone so willing to say it," Alex says.

"Who is bringing him?" Riley asks quietly, hoping to get her mind off of the misery his boss has caused.

"He can't drive himself?" Liz sneers.

"I'm sure he would if I would tell him where we are. I told you this bunker is meant to be a sanctuary. The last thing I will allow is for him to taint it," Riley explains.

"For one, you said he didn't have access, not that he doesn't know where it is, for twosies, he really has no idea we are here?" Liz asks sheepishly. She doesn't want them to see how much that small piece of information means to her.

"He knows the general area, but he is brought in one of my trucks. Signals are jammed and windows are blacked out. He has been trying to figure it out for years," Riley says with a smirk.

They turn back to the papers on the table as they wait for something to happen on the screens scattered around the room. The sudden whirring of the elevator draws their attention to the other side of the room. The doors open and out steps the general. Riley tightens his grip on Liz's leg, trying to keep her calm after setting eyes on him. He walks to the table where everyone is working, polished dress shoes clicking on the floor with each step.

"Hello, gentlemen," he says, glancing at Liz before darting his eyes away, intentionally ignoring her presence. "Status report."

"So, I guess you don't fucking see me?" Liz snaps, already fuming from the mention of things he has said. Before anyone has the chance to start briefing him on what they found, all heads turn to her, watching as she stares at the general, nothing but anger and defiance on her face.

"I'm sorry—" he shouts, face turning red with anger.

"Apology not accepted," she sneers before he can continue what he was saying. "You greeted everyone at this table, looked at me, and continued on like I'm not here."

"Reaper, get your little pet under control," he shouts, sending spittle flying.

"Maybe I'm wrong. Maybe I just didn't hear you say hello to me, it's hard to understand you with half your face being held together by tape." Liz jabs back, eyeing his bandaged nose. She notes how his eyes darted to Riley, a smug smile on her face knowing how much he fears him.

"Know your place, General. This is her home, and I'm happy to repeat what happened the last time you disrespected her," Riley says, rubbing up and down her leg.

"I have done nothing to you, and yet you treat me like a criminal who doesn't deserve to see the light of day, even after they all worked so hard to prove I'm innocent. You can't even be in the same room as me without disrespecting me in some capacity," Liz says to him, voice trembling.

The general sighs and looks around the table at all the faces looking at Liz, their eyes filled with sympathy. It dawns on him that she has turned his operation against him; he's outnumbered. He lets out an exasperated sigh and looks back to Liz.

"Hello, Elizabeth," he says through gritted teeth.

"It's Liz, but I'll let it slide this time." She reaches under the table and grabs Riley's hand, interlacing their fingers. The general doesn't try to sit, he knows he's not welcome. He keeps his distance, standing a few feet away from them as Alex reiterates everything they have learned.

"Keep digging in those files. I want to know what he's planning," he says to Alex and Tyler. "Riley and... Liz," he chokes out, like her name leaves a bad taste in his mouth, "keep doing, wherever it is you're doing. Make sure you check for bugs. Last thing I need is our intel getting out because you were too wrapped up in each other to do your jobs properly. Who knows what those men did when they saw you leaving."

He quickly turns on his heels and walks back to the elevator, getting in and disappearing. Liz lets out a breath of relief, happy he's finally gone. Alex and Tyler stand and go back to their computers, checking all the equipment, quietly fighting about how to make it shut up.

Liz looks around at everyone doing what they need to do and starts to feel out of place. She snuggles her head against Riley's shoulder. "Everyone's so busy; is there something I should be helping with?"

"I think we're all set. Ty and Alex will kill anyone who tries to touch their equipment and you're not quite ready to plan strategy with me and Mikey," he says to her.

"Do you mind if I head to bed? Today was kind of a lot," she asks, yawning.

"Of course I don't mind. Go get some rest, baby," he says without thinking.

His eyes go wide the second he realizes what he called her. Somehow, that one little word feels more intimate than anything he's said before.

Liz just smiles, still trying to hide the flush in her cheeks that drives him wild. He looks around the room, Tyler and Alex are still tinkering away, and Mikey is paying them no mind as he goes over the maps in front of him. Liz shifts, tipping her head back to kiss his stubbly cheek and head off to bed. Before he can stop himself, his hand finds its way to her neck, his thumb rubbing back and forth along her jaw.

She looks up at him smiling, her green eyes shimmering with admiration. With his heart beating out of his chest, he slowly lowers his head, giving her time to stop him if that's what she wants. He only stops when his lips brush hers, waiting for her to change her mind. Everything feels like it's going in slow motion

256

as he brings himself the rest of the way, placing a tender kiss on her lips that she's quick to return.

Fireworks bloom in his chest, feeling Liz start to smile against his lips. He pulls back just enough to kiss her again, letting his mouth linger on hers, not wanting to stop. It's not how he wanted their first kiss to go, but now that he did it, he couldn't imagine it going any other way. She lets out a tiny, happy moan before pulling away. As much as she would love to spend all night kissing Riley, she would prefer to do it without an audience.

Liz reluctantly stands on wobbly legs and walks to her room, staring at the floor to avoid any looks.

Already missing her lips on his, Riley sighs and stands, wishing he could follow her to bed. He lifts his head to find Mikey staring at him, mouth agape, eyes wide from what he just witnessed.

Riley walks over, ignoring the look on his friend's face, and starts shuffling through the papers in front of him. "I swear to fucking god, I will end you," he says, still not looking up from the mess covering every surface in his house.

Mikey snaps his mouth shut. There is no way in hell he will be keeping his mouth shut about this, but he cares about them too much to ruin a beautiful moment. It's not long before they get lost in what they are doing when Riley's phone buzzes on the counter. He grabs it, seeing a new message from Liz. He opens it, unable to keep the smile from spreading across his face while he reads the short text.

Goodnight <3

CHAPTER 39

Two weeks go by without any word on Dmitri, so Liz spends her days doing her normal routine. She works out and trains with Mikey, goes to the gun range with Riley, and every few days Riley takes her to their grove. Liz wakes up every day looking forward to going, just getting to enjoy her time with Riley. Although things never go further than a few small kisses, every time they go she feels closer to him after. The two of them spend hours talking, or reading, some days they just lay in the grass and don't utter a single word.

Liz wakes up excited for the day, knowing she gets to get out of the house. She quickly gets ready and powers through her training before rushing back to her room and changing to go out with Riley. Liz puts on a pair of small cut off shorts and a white crop top. She throws her hair into a high ponytail and slips her freshly painted toes into a pair of plain black flip flops before heading up to meet Riley at the truck. They hop in and drive over like they have for weeks, when halfway down the road the non-linear junction detector stuffed into the back seat of Riley's truck starts going off..

Liz and Riley look at each other, shocked that something has changed. They don't know whether to be thrilled at being one step closer to getting Dmitri or sad that their special time is coming to an end. Riley puts the truck in park and quickly checks out the machine beeping behind him.

"They definitely put something here. I'll have Tyler look into it, but we need to be careful about what we say," he says, quickly getting out of the truck and walking around to grab their things.

Riley carries the blanket over to their spot and lays it out, making sure it's perfect for when Liz reaches him. They sit and Riley cautiously looks around before pulling the small RF detector out of his pocket and setting it down in the middle. He looks at Liz, noting the fear in her eyes as she looks around, hating that this special place is ruined for her. Maybe he should have brought her somewhere else and saved this for when they would truly be able to enjoy it.

"I'm so sorry I got you into this, love" he says, reaching over and grabbing her hand. "I know this isn't how you ever saw your life going."

"Why do you keep apologizing like my shit luck is your fault?" she asks, sadness taking over his face. "Riley, you saved me. You risked your life for me to make sure I got out. I heard you guys that day. I heard Mikey tell you that you would die with me if you didn't leave," Liz says, stomach churning at the thought of what could have happened to him if she had fought back any harder.

"You did everything you could to save me. In return, I stabbed you, almost got you killed, almost got you fired, then almost killed again. I don't think I ever thanked you for what you did that day."

She watches him with those big green eyes he loves so much. "You shouldn't be thanking me. I could have done much more, *should* have done so much more. If I did, you would have never been taken," he says, looking anywhere but at her questioning eyes.

"What do you mean?" she asks, confused. "My brother had them go after me, he admitted that."

"It's my fault they met, and it's my fault they took you. I could have stopped it and I didn't."

"What the fuck is that supposed to mean, Riley?" Liz asks, unable to hide the pain in her voice.

Riley takes a breath, knowing it's time she knows the whole truth, so he tells her everything. "I was the one who put Ivan in the same prison as Jer– your brother," he corrects himself, knowing how much she can't stand to hear his name. "Ivan was one of Dmitri's top men, we managed to catch him while he was in the U.S on the hunt for missiles. I brought him where I was told to bring him and I thought it was the end of it. A few weeks later we started hearing chatter that Dmitri's men would be at that bar, meeting one of his contacts. I didn't know he would be there. We were given a description of who he was meeting, that just so happened to match you. We were assigned to watch him, get any information we could before bringing him in. I was camped on a building close by, eyes on him all night. I watched as you went into the bar, you matched the discretion, but something was off. I assumed you were just another woman going to get drunk and find a man for the night and matching a smuggler was just an unlucky coincidence." Riley pauses, knowing that telling her the whole truth is going to make her hate him as much as he hates himself.

"I watched him. He sat watching you for a while before finally approaching you. When he did, I thought I was wrong and you were the contact he was meeting. I sent Tyler a more accurate description and told him to find out who you were, but nothing came back, so I just kept watching. When I saw him get mad and storm off, I thought your deal went south. I kept tabs on you all night, but all you did was drink and leave."

Liz looks at him, tears beading in his eyes, still unable to look at her.

"Instead of watching Dmitri, I watched you. I needed to find out who you were. I was sure you were working with him. If I had been watching Dmitri, I would have seen him leave. The second they grabbed you, I called Mikey, told him to get to you, but it was too late. You were gone by the time he got out there. I gave our guy on the inside your description and told them to find out what he did with you. I looked for you on every mission. Every compound we raided, I searched for you. The last one we did, he found me and told me they were holding a woman who vaguely matched your description. I had to make a choice: get Dmitri or save you. Obviously, you know who I chose."

Riley lets out a breath, finally able to breathe with that off his chest. He looks at Liz, tears streaming down her face, and his heart shatters. He reaches for her, not wanting to admit everything they had was gone. He had so many chances to be honest with her and he was too much of a coward to do it. He selfishly never wanted to ruin the moments they shared.

"So everything you've done... it's been about easing your guilt?" Liz asks through her tears. She doesn't wait for his response before getting up and walking to the truck, slamming the door behind her.

Riley parks the truck and Liz jumps out, heading for the cabin, not bothering to wait for him. She heads right to her room once the elevator doors open, ignoring Mikey when he asks where Riley is, refusing to speak to anyone. Liz slams her door, pacing circles around her room, her thoughts reeling.

Riley had seen her before and had fought to save her all because he blames himself for her capture. If he didn't, would he have bothered to release any of the prisoners? She has spent months hating herself, feeling like she is betraying her late husband every time Riley makes her smile. That self-hatred only grows with every kiss they share. All the time spent together only made her fall for him more. Now she knows he never felt the same way about her, he just blames himself for her ruined life.

She stands, stomping to the bathroom and filling the tub with the hottest water she can stand, thinking the burn will help clear her mind. Just as she's about to climb into the sweetly scented bath, someone knocks on her door. Liz quickly puts a robe on and storms over to the door, expecting to see Riley on the other side when she throws it open.

"Hey," Mikey says, flashing her a sad smile. "What's wrong?"

Liz looks up at him, tears filling her eyes again. "You knew?" she says, letting the tears fall down her face. "You knew all this was because he fucking feels bad and you didn't tell me?"

"It wasn't my place to talk to you about it. Riley blames himself for what happened, he needed to tell you himself, in his own time." Mikey lowers his voice.

"I never asked to be his pity project. He could have just let me go," Liz says through her sobs.

Mikey closes the door and steps over, wrapping his arms around her, letting her sob into his chest.

"Listen to me, darlin, he found you because of guilt. I'm not denying that. Everything that came after was because of you. I've known him for a long time. We have freed hundreds of people together, and he always makes sure they get the help they need, but he has never cared for anyone the way he cares for you. He has never fought for anyone the way he fights for you. The second you stabbed him, his heart became yours," Mikey says, rubbing her back as her sobbing slows.

"You know, he refused to leave your side until he was forced to. He made the doctor stitch him up sitting next to you. Everyone who broke his orders that day is still healing from what he did to them. Did he tell you why he's always around? Why a top operative hasn't left to go on a single mission?" Mikey asks.

Liz just shakes her head no against his chest. Thoughts racing from one thing to the next, she's unable to form words, so she lets Mikey keep talking.

"He had orders not to look for prisoners, more specifically, you. The general didn't want to waste resources. Riley went against his direct orders to find you. He broke the general's nose for suggesting he hands you over, putting his seventeen-year career at risk to keep you out of harm's way. Don't think for a second anything he does for you is out of pity. That man is in love with you, he's just too scared to admit it."

Liz sniffles and steps away from him, thinking about everything he said. She looks to the bathroom where her steaming tub is waiting.

Mikey follows her gaze. He paces to the door, turning back to her as he opens it. "Go enjoy your bath, we have information you need to know about when you're done." With that, he walks out, closing the door behind him.

Liz soaks for what feels like forever. When the water starts to turn cold, she climbs out and gets dressed, not excited for what comes next. When she enters the kitchen everyone stops what they are doing and looks at her as she walks over to the table and pulls out a chair, taking the only seat left.

"Mikey said there's something I should know. Anyone want

to tell me what's going on?" she says, looking at Tyler and Alex, moving the papers on the table in front of her.

"We go—"

"Not you." Liz snaps, holding one finger up at Riley to silence him before he can finish his sentence, glaring at him, green eyes shining with the sting of betrayal.

"We got through the files," Tyler says to her. "Apparently your brother spent the last two and a half years working his way up the organization. Turns out he offered you up as a way to get to Riley, somehow using that to get closer to Dmitri. Last thing we know about is he intercepted a shipment of missiles and housed them until they were cleared to move."

Alex clears his throat, not wanting Tyler to have to bear the bad news on his own. He looks at Liz and slides a few papers over to her. She looks through them, something like text conversations printed out.

"Before we got to him, he sent some information to Dmitri, convincing him he has been in contact with you and you know everything about his part in the operation. We think it's code, but I don't know for what."

Liz goes deathly still, all the blood draining from her face. A slow shake starts to take over, and mad at him or not, Riley takes her hand. Liz shoots him a look but doesn't pull away, everything Mikey said still weighing heavy on her mind.

"So, all this is, everything that has happened is just him making sure I never know peace," Liz says to herself more than anyone.

Riley tightens his grip when he hears the pain in her voice. "One more thing," Riley adds, hoping she will allow him to talk. "Tyler confirmed they bugged our grove. Two cameras, one with audio."

"Anything else?" she asks, looking around the table.

When no one speaks up, she slides out of her chair and walks back to her room, not bothering to change before crawling into bed, fighting the sleep trying to take hold of her. Even with all the new information, there is only one thing she can't get off her mind. One thing that Mikey said, setting her heart on fire.

That man is in love with you.

CHAPTER 40

Liz wakes up the next day and checks the time on her phone. When her eyes adjust to the blinding screen, she reads, 3:12 p.m. She throws herself out of bed, unsure of how she could have slept so late. Liz doesn't bother changing, running out of her room and into the living room, looking for Mikey to apologize for being late to training. She stops and looks around, seeing the usually full space completely empty.

"Good morning, princess," Riley says from the plush couch. He sits up from where he lounges. He wants to go to her, to beg on his knees for forgiveness when he sees the mix of confusion and sadness in her face.

"Yesterday was a lot, so I told Mikey to let you skip training today."

"Oh... um, thanks," Liz says, walking over to the kitchen and looking for food. With four giant men all living with her, it's no surprise she can't find anything to eat. She closes the fridge with a groan.

"Alex thinks Dmitri is ready to move, so the next time at the lake needs to be our last for a while. We need to make him think we're leaving," he says, watching her rifle through the cabinets. "It's a little late for lunch, do you want to get dinner? We don't even have to take it to go," Riley says, hope flashing across his rich, caramel eyes.

Liz eyes him, still angry for everything he told her, or more so that he withheld it for so long. Her heart betrays her mind when it starts to beat faster at the thought of going out with him again. She sighs, asking, "Where would we go?"

"The bar has a small restaurant in the back, I thought we could go there and talk."

Liz just nods and walks back to her room. She digs through everything she has trying to find something to wear, unsure of what he wants to talk about. She opts for a plain pair of jeans and a cropped tank, slipping her high-top sneakers on. She looks in the mirror and thinks it's good enough for a bar. The next forty-five minutes are spent taming the mess of tangles on her head and twisting it into a claw clip. Just as she is finishing her makeup, Riley knocks on her door and enters.

She walks out of the bathroom to see him unbuttoning his sleeve and rolling it up his arm. She looks him over, wearing a nice button up and a pair of snug black jeans that drive her crazy. She looks up to his face, a matte black skull mask that only covers the top half.

"You said we are going to a bar," she says, rushing over to her closet and digging around for something to change into. She grabs a small pile and brings it to the bathroom.

Riley smiles and follows her. He crosses his arms and leans on the doorframe, watching her struggle to pick an outfit. "What you're wearing is fine, love. You look great."

"No, you look great. I look... comfortable," Liz says, pushing him out of the bathroom and closing the door.

She strips out of her clothes and squeezes into a tight black midi con dress with a slit up her thigh. She admires her toned, hourglass figure in the mirror before putting on a pair of strappy black heels. She takes the clip out of her hair, running her hands through it to make it sit just right and walks out of the bathroom. Heels clicking across the floor, Riley takes one look at her and practically jumps off her bed. He rushes over to her, hands going right to her lush hips, pulling her close to him.

"You look incredible," he says, looking into her eyes. "Are you still mad at me?"

"I was never mad at you, just hurt. Can we talk about it another time?" Liz asks, stomach grumbling loud enough for Riley to hear. Reluctantly he lets go of her waist, picking up her hand instead, and leads her to the elevator.

Liz doesn't miss the longing in his eyes when he looks at her. "Why do you keep looking at me?" she asks when she sees him do it again.

"I told you, you look amazing."

Liz looks away, trying to hide the red blooming across her cheeks. She forces herself to focus on how he hurt her rather than how her heart flutters every time she looks at him. When the doors open, Liz steps out and goes right into the barn, headed to where the truck is parked, but Riley stops her.

"I thought we could take my other car tonight," he says casually as he walks by his truck. Liz follows him past his truck, then Mikeys, when she sees the headlights of some type of sports car light up. The closer they get to the car, the more excited Liz gets.

"You have a fucking Audi R8 and you've been driving me around in a big dumb truck?" she shrieks at him, running over to the car. "I knew it! I told you, you give off sports car vibes."

He watches her with a mix of awe and confusion as he follows close behind. "I'll be honest, princess, seeing you this excited about a car is a huge fucking turn on." He strides over and opens the door for her.

Liz climbs in and gets settled into the soft leather. Riley climbs in, closes his door, and pushes a button, sending the car roaring to life. He quickly pulls out of the barn and heads toward town.

"So, why get all fancy to go to the bar?" Liz asks, watching the muscles in his arm flex as he shifts gears and the way his legs move when he presses the clutch.

"The back is nicer than the bar. Mitch built it for all the guys to bring their girlfriends when he got sick of them complaining about their girls not wanting to go to the bar, girls are happy and he gets to keep his clientele" he tells her, shifting again.

Liz tries to look out the window, but Riley's powerful arm shifting gears keeps pulling her attention back. She stays silent, admiring every detail of the beautiful car and equally beautiful man driving it. Before she knows it, Riley is pulling into the parking lot, getting them there in record time.

She reaches for the handle when Riley stops her, so she sets her hand back in her lap and waits for him to open her door.

As soon as he has the door open, he reaches out his hand and, to his surprise, Liz takes it and climbs out. They walk up the rickety wooden porch and Riley pulls the door open, trying to get her to the back as fast as he can, feeling his jealousy grow with all the eyes on her. With his hand on the small of her back, he ushers her to a white door at the back of the room. He opens the door and watches as Liz takes in the room before them.

They step through the doorway and Liz can't believe it's even the same place. Whitewashed brick walls mixed with black marble floors and twinkly lights lining the ceiling make it feel like an entirely different place. There are small tables with white cloths scattered around, two intricate chairs at each one. In the center of the dimly lit room is a table with a candle and deep red roses sitting atop it. Riley walks over and pulls out a chair. Liz smiles up at him and sits, heart pounding in her chest.

CHAPTER 41

"This place is beautiful," Liz says, still looking around. "I can't believe you kept this from me. I thought we were becoming best friends," she says playfully, hating how easy she slips back into being happy around him.

"I didn't know if you would like a place like this, but since you keep calling our time together dates... I thought I would take you on a real one," he says, voice slightly shaky.

"So, this is a real date?" she says smiling, blush rising to her cheeks.

"If that's okay with you?" he asks timidly, knowing she's still upset with him.

Liz smiles, nodding at him. As soon as Riley sees that he lets out a sigh of relief as he reaches up and pulls his mask off, setting it down on the table. He returns her smile and Liz watches him, Mikey's words flashing across her mind before her eyes go wide and she starts looking around the small room.

"Relax, love. The only person allowed in is Mitch and he knows me," Riley says with a light chuckle. "Are you ready for the next few days? Things are going to get intense," Riley asks, unsure of how to bring up what he really wants to say.

"Not at all. I've never done anything like this. What if I mess up and someone gets hurt?"

"I think about that any time I'm leading a mission. I worry about my men every time we head out, and I worry about you every damn day."

"Careful, Ry, it sounds like you may actually like me," Liz says, teasing him.

"I do like you," Riley says, reaching over and trying to take her hand.

"You pity me. You blame yourself for everything that has happened and now you're trying to make up for it. That's not the same." Liz crosses her arms and leans back in her chair.

"Is that why you're mad at me? Because you think I feel guilty?"

"I told you, I'm not mad. I just don't appreciate being treated a certain way simply because you blame yourself for everything that has happened to me. My piece of shit brother orchestrated the whole thing. You had no idea he was in that jail, or that he would join Dmitri and seeing me that day wouldn't have changed the outcome, only delayed it," Liz says with a small shrug of her shoulders.

Before Riley can process what she said, Mitch walks out with two steaming plates of food, setting them in front of them. Liz thanks him and he disappears back out the door he came in from. Too hungry for manners, Liz digs into the bowl of chicken Alfredo in front of her, eyes fluttering closed at the first bite. They continue to eat in silence until Riley can't take it anymore.

"You honestly think I treat you this way out of guilt?" he snaps, dropping his fork onto his plate with a loud *clunk*.

"Yes. You told me you blame yourself and you clearly want

to make up for it. I genuinely believe you are trying to give me as close to the life you think I could have had as you can, and that's not fair to either of us," Liz says, twirling the pasta around her fork.

Riley doesn't respond, he can't even begin to tell her how wrong she is about everything.

They finish their meal in silence, and when they are done, Riley pulls out his wallet and drops a small stack of money on the table. They get up and walk back to the car, climbing in and driving to the lake without muttering a word to each other.

CHAPTER 42

They pull up to the lake and Riley parks the car, opting to leave it running for the headlights, knowing it will be dark soon. He grabs their blanket from the back seat and gets out, walking to their spot... alone.

She quickly gets out and meets him on the blanket, feeling a little guilty herself for ruining the nice evening he had planned. They sit, watching the waterfall, not daring to speak.

"You're wrong, love. I'm not trying to make up some new life for you," Riley blurts out, looking over to Liz.

"What?" she asks, confused after not speaking for so long.

"I know I could have stopped it, I will always blame myself for you getting taken, but I'm glad they took you. I mean... I hate what they di—"

"You're happy... that my brother handed me over to a terrorist, to be used as his personal punching bag?" Liz shouts at him, seeing red.

"That's not what I mean. If Dmitri never took you, none of this would have happened."

"Well, I'm sorry my getting kidnapped caused so many problems for you," she seethes, anger flooding her.

"Will you fucking listen, princess," he snaps, standing and pacing in front of where Liz sits as she tracks him with her eyes. "If you had never gotten taken, you would have gone through with it, you would be dead right now. I would have never found you, never gotten to know you, never fell in love with you. The only thing I feel guilty about anymore is hoping I would be enough to make you want to stay alive," he says, voice cracking with emotion.

"I may have found you out of guilt but that guilt was gone the second you told me what you planned to do. Everything I've done for you, every meal, every look, every conversation has been because I stupidly let myself get close. Even when I thought you would be going home to a family, I couldn't stop the feelings for you from building." Riley lets out a deep breath.

He turns again, only to find Liz standing in his path. He paces back to where she is, watching the ground. Riley reaches out, taking her delicate face in his hand and tips her head up to look at him before dropping his hand.

"I hate myself for not telling you the whole truth and I know I should have done it sooner, but the way I treat you is because of the way you make me feel, that's it. The only guilt I have is for wanting you to feel the same way about me after losing the two most important people in your life."

Liz takes one small step into him, her arms wrapping tightly around his waist. She rests her head on his chest, listening to his heart beat wildly. Finally, he slowly lifts his arms and wraps them around her, pulling her in as tight as he possibly can.

"Thank you for saving me, in every way possible," she says, face still buried in his chest.

They stay like that, holding each other, emotions high, until the sun begins to set. Liz drops her arms from Riley's waist and steps back. She doesn't miss the sadness in his eyes before it's gone. Liz bends down and slips out of her shoes, tossing them onto the blanket.

"What are you doing?" Riley asks.

Remembering the reason they are there, Liz turns to him and says, "If we're going to leave soon, I'm jumping off that fucking waterfall."

CHAPTER 43

"Absolutely not. It's getting dark; you're going to get hurt," he says, concerned when she tries to reach the zipper on her dress.

"I'll risk it," she says, still trying to reach the zipper. She looks over at Riley, standing there watching her struggle. "Help me get out of this," she says, giving her hips a small wiggle.

Riley stalks over and gently places his hands on her shoulders, spinning her around so he can access the zipper. He slowly unzips her dress, sending a shiver of anticipation through her. As soon as he's done his hands are on her again turning her back to face him. Her eyes meet his, holding his stare as he reaches up and starts to pull the strap down her arm. She can't take her eyes off of him, the soft glow of the setting sun making him look more god-like than usual.

"What are you doing?" she giggles nervously.

"You asked for help, so I'm giving it to you," Riley says, eyes dropping to her other arm.

He reaches over and pulls the other strap down, causing her dress to fall and pool around her bare ankles. His eyes darken, nothing but want in them at the sight of her. She stands there, laid bare in front of him with nothing on but a small black thong, wondering if she's taking things too far this time. His eyes drop to her body, breasts put on full display before him, nipples pebbling from the cool mountain air.

"Fuck, baby," Riley says, taking a step closer to her. "I didn't think you could look any better, then you do this," he says, looking at her exposed body.

"I should probably go before it gets too dark," Liz says nervously, cheeks turning bright shades of red.

She ignores the wetness starting to grow between her legs, trying not to think about how much a single look from Riley sets her entire being ablaze. She strides to the tree line, hoping it will lead to the waterfall as she ventures in.

Liz didn't take into consideration how exposed she was going to be until she started walking through the trees, trying to pick a path that wasn't going to trip her up. She carefully navigates around the rocks and tree roots under her, avoiding as many low branches as she can. It takes longer than she had hoped, but she finally hears water and makes it to the small opening at the top of the waterfall.

She carefully makes her way over to the edge, looking down at the grassy field below, hoping to see Riley waiting for her. Her heart starts to race when she can't find him. She slides closer to the edge, hoping he just went to the car or somewhere else she can't see from where she stands, but still can't find him.

Liz paces back and forth, unable to think of anything but Riley. She stops dead in her tracks when she hears something snap behind her. She looks into the trees, looking for an animal that may have caused it. When there is nothing, she begins to panic.

Anxiety rising, Liz starts to wonder if Dmitri sent his men

after them. She takes a step toward the trees, still trying to convince herself it's just a bird or small animal, but small animals don't sound like grown men walking, and those footsteps don't belong to Riley. She can feel eyes boring into her back, watching her every move.

Liz looks around, thinking to herself. If she could find a trail, or spot a better way down, she may have a chance of getting away. If she walks back down, she runs the risk of the men being able to ambush her. She needs to choose, jump or run.

Her head snaps to the trees, footsteps growing closer. She realizes the fastest way to get away from whatever is watching her is to just jump. She will never be able to outrun them in the dark, so she steps up to the edge, takes a deep breath in and readies herself. She spins back around when she hears footsteps now charging. She doesn't have time to register what is happening before Riley wraps his strong arms around her waist, picking her up as if she weighs nothing, sending them both flying over the edge, careening toward the lake.

CHAPTER 44

They crash into the cold water. Riley immediately lets go of Liz, allowing her to swim back up. As soon as her head is out of the water, Liz pushes her hair back out of her face and sees Riley already waiting for her closer to the edge. She swims over and quickly sends a large splash of water in his direction, only causing him to throw his head back, letting out a deep rich laugh.

"You asshole, you could have killed me," Liz shrieks, splashing him again.

Riley makes quick work of swimming over to where Liz is trying to focus on treading water and stands in front of her, water falling to just under his pecs. Growing increasingly distracted with the water beading on his muscular chest. Liz just glares at him while she bobs up and down.

"I would never hurt you, love," he says, taking a slow step in her direction. "You wanted me to jump with you, and I wanted to make you happy. I wanted to have one last nice night with you."

Liz opens her mouth to talk, but not being the strongest

swimmer, starts to lose focus on the task at hand and snaps her mouth shut.

Riley just chuckles, reaching out and pulling her toward him. He helps her get situated so she can float next to him, one arm under her head, the other resting over her torso, just under her breasts, holding her balanced. He tries not to think about her, almost naked and glistening under him, or how the soft skin of her breasts would feel in his hand.

"Have you really been having a good time with me?" she asks, peering up at him, big green eyes sparkling under the light of the setting sun.

Riley sighs, not out of frustration, but contentment, his eyes meeting hers. "Being with you is the first time in a very long time I've been happy," he says, peering down at her.

Liz wiggles out of his grip, getting herself upright again, turns and looks up at him. He just laughs, knowing she still can't touch the bottom of the lake. Riley bends down and quickly wraps his large hands under her thighs and picks her up with seemingly no effort at all. Liz squeals and starts to giggle, but wraps her legs around his waist, throwing her arms loosely around his neck.

"I feel the same way. I never thought I would find happiness again, but every time I'm with you, that ache in my chest isn't as bad. I can smile, and laugh and enjoy the little moments again," she says, lowering her head so her chin is resting on Riley's shoulder.

He pulls one hand from her leg and wraps it around her back, pulling her in close, never wanting to let her go. They stay like that, wrapped in each other's arms, nothing but the sounds of the waterfall crashing next to them.

"Am I a bad person?" Liz asks, almost a whisper.

Riley just squeezes her tighter. "Why would you think you're a bad person, love?"

Liz starts to move herself back, so Riley drops his hand back to her leg. She leans and looks down to where their bodies are pressed together, trying to ignore the fact that her bare chest is still on display.

"You think you're a bad person because... you don't want me this close to you?" Riley guesses, sadness in his eyes. He drops his hands from her legs, not wanting to make her anymore uncomfortable, assuming she will let go and move away from him.

"Please, don't," she whispers, wrapping her legs tighter on his waist.

Letting out a small sigh of relief, his hands are back on her in an instant. Both arms wrapped tightly around her back, holding her close now that he knows she wants it just as much as he does.

"Tell me why you think you're a bad person," he says, more a command than a request.

Liz pulls herself as close to him as she can, nuzzling her head into his neck. "For caring about you... for wanting you... for finding happiness with you," she says, voice starting to crack from the tears she knows are coming. "I know my family has been gone for years, but every time I'm with you, I feel like I'm betraying them. I hate myself for having feelings for another man. I told you before, I should be dead, Riley. I shouldn't be here, happy and wanting to live when they don't get to," Liz says, warm tears streaming down her cheeks and onto Riley's chest.

His hand starts to move up and down, rubbing large circles on her back, placing a kiss on the top of her bare shoulder before saying, "Listen to me. You are a great wife and an amazing mother, nothing will ever change that. What happened to them is a horrible thing that should have never happened, but that doesn't mean you're a bad person for not giving up on your life. From what you've told me, James was a great man, and he died knowing you will always love him. I think, somewhere deep down, you know he wouldn't want you to give up. He would want you to find some way to be happy again, and he would be so fucking proud to see you doing that."

Liz wipes her tears, letting his words sink in. She knows he's right, so she stays there, wrapped in his warm embrace. Finally, when her mind is calm, she loosens her grip on his neck, leaning back slightly to look up at him. They lock eyes, and ever so slowly, Liz brings herself back up. Riley leans his head down to meet her, resting his forehead on hers. Everything is out in the open now. There are no secrets left to hide behind. Liz battles the thoughts running through her head. She can't keep fighting how she feels. She leans in and places a featherlight kiss on his lips before pulling her face back.

That kiss is Riley's undoing. He has never been so relieved to have forgiveness in his life. His hands drop to her ass, fingers digging into her soft skin. He lifts her higher before his lips are crashing into hers. Her hands find their way to his hair, grabbing a handful to pull him in closer, inciting a small growl, and sending chills down her body. Liz parts her lips, allowing their tongues to swirl around each other. Riley grips her tighter and their kissing slows, turning gentle and loving as he carries her from the water and lays her on their blanket. Riley pulls away, breathless, and starts a slow, steady line of kisses on her jaw, down her neck and back up again, while his callused hands explore her body.

He rubs up and down her side, across her flat stomach, drawing tiny moans from her with each caress. Her hands wrapped around him, delicate fingers digging into his strong back. He kisses his way back to her mouth and her lips instantly part for him, his tongue sweeping back in. Riley drags his hand up her side, agonizingly slow, before finally giving himself what he wants and taking her breast into his large hand.

Riley holds her, almost tenderly, rubbing his thumb over her peaked nipple before giving it a small pinch. Liz arches her back and lets out a breathy moan, mouth still locked with his.

Liz takes her hand from his back, sliding it down the hard ridges of his abdomen. Reaching between them in an attempt to grab what's been straining against his briefs since her legs wrapped around him.

He stops her, bringing her hand over her head where he pins it. Reluctantly, he pulls his mouth from hers and leans down, whispering in her ear, "As much as I would love to feel every inch of you wrapped around my cock... we're being watched, princess." Leaning down, he kisses her again, this time gentle, loving, sending butterflies through her.

"I don't care," she mumbles into his lips, kissing him back. She can feel his smile spread across his lips before pulling away and looking into her eyes.

"I want this as bad as you, love, maybe even more, but this isn't how I pictured it happening for the first time," he tells her, placing a tiny kiss on the tip of her nose.

"So you've thought about this?" she asks.

"There is never a time when I'm not thinking about it," he says, releasing her hand. He moves his hand to her thigh, rubbing up and down, gently sweeping his thumb over the place he's dying to touch. Liz lets out a breathy moan, stretching up to kiss him, sad knowing it's going to end.

"Can we come back tomorrow? Since everything's changing, I want one more night here with you."

"Of course, baby," he says, kissing her again before pushing himself up.

They sit up, Riley pulling Liz onto his lap, holding her close while they watch hundreds of fireflies dance around in the dark clearing. It's the perfect end to their day. Riley's gentle caress doesn't last long before he starts kissing every inch of skin he can get to, his hands roaming her body once more. It kills her, but she has to stop him. They reluctantly stand, quickly redressing before they can jump back into each other's arms.

Riley takes Liz's hand and leads her back to the car, opening the door and helping her in before he climbs into the driver seat and speeds back home.

CHAPTER 45

The elevator doors open and all eyes snap to Liz and Riley, walking hand in hand. They do everything to keep calm, ignoring the curious looks from their team. The pair simply walks over to the table, ready for someone to explain what is happening.

"Where the hell have you two been?" Mikey shouts at them.

"Exactly where we were supposed to be," Liz says, confusion on her face.

"You must have been pretty convincing tonight because Dmitri is mobilizing teams," Alex tells them.

"We did what we planned to do. Liz and I made it clear tomorrow is our last day going there. Give us a few minutes to change before pulling us back into the shit show," Riley says to the group, already dreading the long night ahead.

They head down the hall, hands still locked together until they reach their respective doors. Reluctantly, Liz drops Riley's hand and rushes into her bathroom, taking a quick shower to get the lake smell off her skin. She finishes her hair, washes her ruined makeup off, and gets dressed. No longer looking like a wet rat, she meets the team in the kitchen.

The hours drag by as Liz listens to them make plan after plan, trying to account for every possibility, when Liz starts to doze off, not yet trained enough to have any helpful insight into what they should do. Eventually, the team agrees they have a solid plan and begin preparing for the long days ahead. Alex and Tyler break off to inform the general and start preparing the small amount of soldiers they were granted. Liz, Riley and Mikey start scouring the base for any equipment they will need. They split up going room to room, grabbing all their bullet proof vests, a small arsenal of guns and knives, and a few other things their team may find useful.

"I think we're good," Mikey says, eyeing the layout of gear they accumulated. "I'm going to bed. You two should try to do the same," he adds, eyeing them with a playful smile on his face.

"Goodnight sweetie" Liz calls to him down the hall, watching him as he closes his door. Liz walks back to where Riley is going over papers and wraps her arms around his waist, resting her head on his back. His hand drops from what he's doing and starts rubbing the arm around him. He turns, bringing his strong arms around her shoulders and pulls her in close. Placing a kiss on the top of her head he tells her—

"You should get some rest too, love... C'mon." He drops his arms from her shoulders and leads her down the hall.

Missing his warmth already, she turns and trudges behind as he leads the way. When Liz turns to her room, Riley grabs her hand and pulls the other way, right into his open door. He wraps his arms around her, kicking his door shut as he does.

"Stay with me tonight," he mumbles into her hair, more a plea than an order.

Liz looks into his honey-brown eyes. She simply gets on her

tiptoes and kisses him, deep and full of passion before she reluctantly pulls herself from his embrace.

"I need to at least change," she says, motioning to the jeans and t-shirt she's wearing.

Riley walks over to his dresser and pulls out a large gray shirt, tossing it to Liz. "Will that work?" he asks.

Liz smiles at him and nods. She can't help but watch as he unhooks his belt with one hand, gently pushing his jeans down until he's only left with his tight briefs. She pulls her shirt over her head and tosses it to the side before slipping out of her own jeans. When she stands back up, she feels Riley's hungry eyes on her. Left in nothing but a lacy red bra with a matching thong and garter, the very one he dreamed of seeing her in, she looks over to find him shamelessly staring.

"Are you trying to kill me?" Riley asks, his eyes darkening as he drinks in every inch of her. "No," she says innocently, keeping eye contact, as she unhooks her bra, letting it fall to the floor. "I'm trying to fuck you."

Riley crosses the room, pulling his shirt off as he does, his mouth crashing into Liz's as soon as he reaches her. His hands grab her hips, forcing her back against his bed, roughly shoving her down when they reach it. He climbs on top of her, his mouth going right back to hers. He reaches down, tightly gripping her thigh and pulling her leg up, seating himself perfectly in between her legs. Riley kisses his way down her neck, then her chest, before finally making his way to her breasts. Riley starts to lose control of himself, biting her nipple harder than he intended to, causing Liz to let out a small yelp. That little noise makes him stop, and slowly climb off, worried that he hurt her.

"We shouldn't do this, love," he says.

"Did I do something wrong?" she asks, his heart breaking at

the sadness in her voice. He sits on the bed next to where she is still laying, gently placing his hand on hers.

"Of course not, baby," he says with a small reassuring smile. "I have no control of myself when it comes to you. I can't promise I'll be gentle... I just don't want to hurt you."

Liz sits back up, relieved to learn that Riley is just worried about hurting her. She slowly moves over and climbs onto his lap placing her knees on either side of his hips and drapes her arms around his neck. He lets out a low growl at the feeling of her soaked panties pushing against his hard cock. Even through his briefs he can feel how much she wants him. She slowly rocks her hips back and forth, teasing him with her pussy. She leans down, putting her lips up to his ear, and whispers.

"I don't like it gentle."

That's all it takes for Riley to let himself lose control. One hand goes to her perfect ass, gripping her hard enough to bruise. The other goes to her hair, grabbing a handful and pulling her mouth to his, forcing his tongue past her lips. Needing to feel him, Liz reaches between them, fumbling with his briefs, until finally getting what she wants. She takes his cock out and wraps her hand around the impressive length of him, gently stroking.

Riley moans into her mouth, her soft hand on him driving him wild. He drops her hair and moves his hand to her waist, grabbing her panties. He wraps the side around his hands and pulls, snapping the thin lace. He moves over to the other side and does the same thing, tossing the torn scrap of fabric away from them.

Liz lets go, bringing her hands back up around his neck. She rocks her hips, sliding herself against the hard length of him, trying to take what she wants. Riley reaches his hand up, wrapping it tightly around her throat and rolls Liz onto her back, climbing back on top of her.

Riley pushes one of his legs up, taking hers with it, spreading her legs for him as he nestles in between them. Riley releases her neck just long enough to line himself up. His hand wraps around her throat again as he starts to ease himself into her. She lets out a deep, breathy moan, eyes fluttering closed, when he stops.

"Eyes on me, baby," he orders.

Her big green eyes snap to him as he holds himself back, refusing to give her what she wants until she follows his orders. His eyes darken, seeing nothing but need for him reflected back in hers. With one hard thrust, he slams himself fully into her. She screams, a mix of pain and pleasure, hands flying to his back, nails digging into his skin.

"Fuck," he breathes. "You feel so fucking good." He's breathless, slowly pulling out before slamming himself back into her.

Liz digs her nails into his back, driving him crazy. He drives into her, harder, faster, trying to make it last. Liz fights for breath, the edges from her vision going fuzzy, unsure if it's from Riley's hand around her throat or the orgasm quickly building. Riley doesn't let up, bringing her closer and closer to the edge with every thrust. She can feel it building with every movement until she can't take it anymore. Liz screams out, her back arching off the bed, every muscle in her body tightening, legs shaking with her release.

"Fuck. You look so good coming on my cock, baby," he says, thrusting faster and faster until he finally reaches his release, slamming into her one final time.

He releases her throat and slowly lays himself on top of her, breathing heavily as he plants delicate kisses along her neck, knowing it will be bruised by morning. He rolls off of her and onto the bed, pulling her into his arms. He knows as soon as he lets her go and they go to bed, everything is going to change.

Liz stays nestled into his arms, placing little kisses on his hands until she starts to doze off.

When Riley sees how utterly drained she is he lets go of her and gets up, walking to the bathroom. Riley emerges a minute later with a small towel in hand. Walking over to Liz he sits on the bed, using the warm towel to clean her up before walking over and grabbing his shirt for her to wear. She sits up, unable and unwilling to take her eyes off Riley who just motions for her to lift her arms. She does as he asks, and he slides the buttery soft shirt onto her.

"Orgasms and aftercare? You must really love me," she says, smiling at him as he changes into a pair of loose shorts.

Riley walks back to the bed and climbs in, holding the blanket up so Liz can crawl in next to him. Liz rests her head on his shoulder, snuggling her body close to his. Her hand idly strokes his broad chest, watching as it moves up and down with each breath when she sees it: a small frame sitting on his nightstand with their picture from the mountain, nestled into the corner is a ripped piece of paper and three small words scribbled on it.

"Maybe I do," Riley finally says into the top of her head, placing another small kiss there. Liz jerks her head, attempting to get up, needing to ask about her note with the photo, but his arm just holds her tighter. His other hand comes over and pushes her head back down onto his chest.

"Sleep, love, you have a long day tomorrow."

Liz lays there, in the dark silence, with Riley stroking her back, listening to the steady thump of his heart until she drifts off into a deep sleep.

CHAPTER 46

"Rise and shine, you dirty little whores!" Mikey shouts as he bursts into Riley's room. Liz and Riley both shoot up, startling awake. The look on their faces has Mikey rethinking his wake-up call.

"If you survive today... I'm going to fucking kill you," Riley says to him.

"We... We are going to fucking kill you," Liz adds as she lays her head back down.

"It was either me or the general," Mikey says to them adding, "By the way... General's here. Dmitri is on the move, and everyone is waiting on you two, okay, bye."

Mikey turns and walks back out the door, closing it behind him. Liz rolls over and kisses Riley's chest, wrapping her arm around him, not yet ready to leave the comfort of his embrace. She can't leave him yet. It has been two long years without this kind of joy in her life and that could all be taken from her today, she needs to hold on to this moment just a little while longer.

He brings his arm around her, holding her tight, placing soft kisses on the top of her head while her hands trace the hard lines of his abdomen. They stay there, wrapped in each other's arms letting the minutes tick by.

"Good morning, princess," he finally says to her.

"Good morning, sunshine," she says, yawning.

Reluctantly, Liz peels herself away from Riley's warmth, stretching as she does, quickly realizing that's the best night of sleep she's gotten in years. Riley follows her lead and climbs out of bed, walking over to his dresser and pulling out clothes for himself. Liz scoots to the edge and stretches one more time before standing and picking her clothes up off the floor.

"You ready for today?" Riley asks, pulling a tight black long-sleeved shirt over his head.

"No... but I guess I have to be, right?" she says, heading to the door so she can go get prepared. She turns the squeaky handle, but before she can pull the door open, Riley's arms wrap around her, pulling her back against him.

"Will you come back when you're ready?" he asks quietly, nuzzling his head against her neck.

Liz giggles as his warm breath tickles her ear. She twists around, bringing her arms to wrap around his waist. She lifts herself onto her tiptoes and gives him a quick kiss. "Always," she says, sinking back onto her feet.

Riley lets her go and she rushes out the door and across the hall into her room, closing the door behind her. Liz takes a quick shower, sad about washing the smell of Riley off of her. When she's done, she pulls her hair into a braid hanging down the center of her back. She moves over to her closet, water dripping off her and onto the tile floors.

Liz picks out a pair of plain black pants and matching long sleeve black shirt, quickly throwing them on before stuffing her feet into her black combat boots and lacing them. She walks over to the mirror, footsteps echoing in the small room. Looking at herself, she doesn't recognize the person staring back at her, but she doesn't hate her reflection anymore. Liz gives herself a minute to take in her new look; she looks stronger, more sure of herself. She swears she can even see a little light behind her eyes again.

Liz hurries back into Riley's room, prancing to his bed and plopping herself down, ready to watch the show that is him checking his gear. He shoots her a confused look, and she simply shrugs her shoulders, telling him, "It's kind of hot when you're pulling at all those straps."

He just pulls on another one in response, winking at her. Liz shakes her head and stands, pacing around his room, full of nervous energy. He follows her with his eyes as he finishes checking his gear. When he's done, he goes to his closet and pulls out a small box. Riley brings it over to where Liz paces and holds it out to her, making her stop.

She eyes him, but slowly pulls the lid off, revealing what looks like a holster. She lifts the straps out of the box, seeing two small handguns sitting underneath.

"It's the best I could do on such short notice," Riley says, reaching for the handful of fabric Liz holds.

He gets on one knee and wraps the harness around her waist, buckling it in the front. He moves onto her legs, buckling each double-leg strap and tightening them for her. Liz takes the guns out of the box and slides them into their holsters, looking down while she does a little happy dance. He reaches back into the box and pulls out two small knives, sliding them into a hidden sheath built into the holster.

"There's a mirror in the bathroom," he says, his smile lighting up his face.

Liz sprints to the bathroom, squealing at herself when she sees her reflection with the new accessories Riley gifted her. She runs back out, getting into her firing stance, using both hands to make a pretend gun. "Do I look like a badass?" she asks.

"You look incredible, Baby" Riley says, eyes roaming over every inch of her, her excitement sending his heart racing.

Riley reaches out his hand and Liz takes it, interlocking their fingers. As he leads her to the door, she takes a deep breath, trying to calm her nerves. Liz knows no matter what happens today, everything is going to change.

They walk out and head right to the group of men sitting at the table, quietly bickering to themselves. Liz grips his hand tighter at the sight of the general sitting there with the rest of the men she almost considers friends. As soon as they get closer, it becomes obvious something isn't right. The energy of the room is off.

"They know about the ambush. We need to change plans, quickly," the general says, wrinkling his nose at the sight of their connected hands.

Without any hesitation, they sit and join the debate on what their next steps should be.

* * *

After two grueling hours of back and forth leading nowhere, Liz decides it's finally time to share her thoughts. She held off as long as she could, knowing she doesn't know a single thing about strategy and battle plans. She looks at Riley, heart breaking, knowing he is going to fight her on what she's about to say.

"What if I go alone?" she says timidly. All eyes snap to her, and before Riley gets the chance to object, she adds, "He needs me alive. We all saw those messages my brother sent. He thinks I can bring him to his missiles. If I go alone, he may think I'm running from everything. There's no chance he won't come after me."

Liz looks around the table, everyone looks to be considering what she says, even the general looks like he may think it's a usable idea.

"Not a fucking chance in hell I'll let you do that," Riley snaps.

"That's not for you to decide. You didn't even let me tell you my plan," Liz snaps back, challenging him to tell her no again.

"Fine, tell me, either way it's not happening," he says through gritted teeth. He can't bring himself to look at her, so full of anger at her willingness to put herself in danger.

"Call whoever you guys keep getting info from. Tell him I found out Riley was using me to get to Dmitri and that I'm done. If he can get that intel to someone higher in their little crime circle, Dmitri will make a move. I'll leave, make a big show of it, and go to the bar or something. You can send the guy working for you some recording of the fight; he can make it seem like they found us."

Liz looks around the group, waiting for someone to object or tell her the plan will never work. To her surprise, everyone keeps their thoughts to themselves, allowing her to finish.

"Once they see the tracker away from the dead zone, I'm sure one of his goons will find me, report to him I'm alone, and he will come looking for me. The sudden change will make him scramble, so you can send a team to deal with the men at the lake. If the guys at the lake don't see me with Riley, it will only strengthen the story that I left."

"Are you fucking insane? I thought you moved passed being suicidal!" Riley shouts at her, standing and breathing heavy. He looks at her, waiting for her to respond to his outburst.

Matching his energy, Liz gets out of her chair, stepping up

toe to toe with Riley. Looking up at him and crossing her arms. The rest of the table looks on in shock, never having met someone so willing to face off against Reaper.

"You do realize you have been training me for this right?" she asks, hoping he's smart enough to not answer. She rolls his eyes when he's not.

"That's not the po—" he starts to say before being cut off.

"The only thing coming out of your mouth should be 'yes dear'. You and Mikey have been training me for months. This is exactly what I have been trained to do," she says, voice raising in anger. She takes another step toward him, taking a deep breath to calm herself. Seeing the hurt and fear on Riley's face, she drops her hands to her sides. Trying to be understanding of what he may be feeling, Liz looks into his deep amber eyes, forgetting the small team watching them.

"Look, I love you, and I appreciate you wanting to keep me safe... but... if this is ever going to work, you need to trust I can handle myself and let me help. I can't go back to being locked away. Keeping me from fighting is just another prison, Riley."

He looks down at her, eyes softening at her confession. Riley opens his mouth to talk, needing to know if she meant what she just said. He looks at all the eyes on them, quickly realizing he needs to focus on the rest of what she told him.

"You're right," he says, backing down, still trying to process everything.

CHAPTER 47

Liz leaves the bunker... alone, driving down the winding road, running the plan through her head over and over again. Her eyes still sting from the "fight" she had with Riley. If there is one thing she's sure of, it's whoever hears that recording will believe she's done with him. She looks over at the small bag she packed, thinking back to the last time she had a bag packed to leave like this.

Liz pulls into the small parking lot off the side of the road, put off by how empty it is. She makes sure there is no one around before resting her head on the steering wheel and screaming, putting the last two years of pain and fighting into it. She keeps her head down, giving herself a moment to sob, letting go of everything she has been holding onto. She lifts her head, wipes her tears, and takes a big breath before opening the door and stepping out.

Liz nears the wooden porch of the bar, looking around as she walks up the creaky steps. A sense of unease stirs in her gut amidst the silence. She reassures herself it's just nerves, attributing her apprehension to the anticipation of her first real mission, and steps inside.

The bar is almost completely empty, a few people she's never seen before sitting at a table across the small room. Liz crosses the small space and sits at the bar, smiling at Mitch.

"Vodka cranberry please," she says, sniffling.

She watches him disappear down to the other end before coming back with her deep red drink. She thanks him and hands him some money before taking a long sip. As she's sitting there, trying to calm her nerves, her vision starts to blur, thinking she's already getting a small buzz, she pushes her drink away. Liz hears shoes clicking across the floor a second before the hair on the back of her neck stands up.

From too close, she hears a voice she hoped she would never hear again.

"I'm glad you accepted my drink this time."

Liz spins on the stool, turning to come face to face with Dmitri. She looks back to Mitch, someone she thought she could trust, understanding why her head is spinning; the bastard spiked her drink.

"You are free to go," Dmitri says, his thick Russian accent making her skin crawl.

Liz jumps from her seat, seeing spots from whatever was put in her drink. She reaches for one of her guns, but his men are too fast, grabbing her arms before she can. Dmitri walks over to her and pulls the guns from their holsters, tossing them behind the bar. Liz tries to fight her way away from the men, using every technique she's learned, only to be met with a hard slap to her face, sending her flying to the floor. One of the men picks her back up, whatever they drugged her with already making it hard for her to stand, luckily she stopped at a sip.

"What do you want with me?" she asks, trying to fight

against the drug seeping its way into her system. She knows if she can hold out for a little longer Riley will be here.

"Your brother told me all about you. Before someone killed him, he told me you know how to get me what I want," Dmitri says, walking to one of the empty tables and taking a seat, glaring at her through the scar across his eye.

"I don't care what he told you. We haven't talked since we were kids and I don't know shit about getting weapons," Liz says, still trying to rip her arms away from the men holding her.

"That does not matter, my pet. I'm not looking for weapons. What I really want... is that freak in the mask who took you from me and destroyed my home."

"That's what this is about? You want Reaper?" Liz asks, laughing through the panic. They all thought this was about her, that she would be safe because he needed her. If Dmitri doesn't kill her, Riley definitely will when he finds out how wrong she was.

Dmitri stands back up, pacing around the bar, his cheap, musky cologne wafting toward her with every step. Liz watches him, looking for any opening to get away.

"I had plans, pet. Big plans. And when that... thing... escaped, after trying to kill me, he started killing everything I was building. It took years to build my empire. When he came looking for you, he ruined all those carefully laid plans. He was not so subtle trying to find you, so I let it slip where you were. You're all fools to think I do not know I have double agents in my ranks. Even more foolish to think I don't have my own in yours."

Dimitri stops his pacing and snaps his fingers. The two men holding Liz push her over to the table and force her into a chair, tying her wrists tightly behind her. Liz takes a deep breath, trying to focus on anything but the ropes around her wrists. She can't stop her mind from going into the dark place she fought so hard to claw her way out of.

"I did not know what he wanted with you, but I let him have you. Lucky for me, I had someone watching your every move, making sure he felt like he needed to keep you around," he mocks. "I'll admit, he made more of a mess than I had planned, that's why it took me so long to get you."

He walks to the bar, his shoes clacking on the beat-up wooden floor. He pours himself a drink and paces back to where Liz is restrained. Stroking her braid, he continues, "I didn't expect you to be so well... protected. That was an unfortunate bump in the road, but now that I have my pet back, I will have a way to control your *Reaper*," he says the last word like it makes him sick. "You almost had me convinced, watching you at the lake, but it wasn't hard to get one of his men to talk. Poor little pet, falling in love with a man not capable of loving her back," he snickers at her.

"So, what's the point then, asshole? What's the fucking point of taking me again if you want him? You said it yourself, he's never going to love me back, so you taking me means nothing to him," she snaps before her head goes flying to the side, Dmitri's slap making her ears ring.

"Because, my pet, if I take you back, then everything he did was for nothing. All the people he killed, all his men who died, all the orders he disobeyed will have been for nothing. So, he will come for you, and when he does... I will kill him."

CHAPTER 48

Riley and his small team of men load up and head to where the ambush is planned, hoping to pick off any forces Dmitri planted there as fast as possible. Wearing the mask he made that night all those years ago, he speeds to the lake, parking a few miles away. Riley gathers his men and goes over the plan: they are to go in on foot, a small group going in from the other side, and when they are surrounded, start picking them off.

After what seems like forever of walking through the woods, Riley morphs into Reaper, needing to not think about anything but the task at hand. They push forward, picking off men here and there as they do. Luck is on their side because Dmitri's forces don't know they are there until it's too late. Riley watches as the last man drops, his phone vibrating in his pocket.

―――――

Liz watches as Dmitri takes her phone and pulls up Riley's number, letting out a little sigh of relief when she remembers she left him as Reaper in her contacts. He presses the button and puts it on speaker, setting the phone in the middle of the table.

"What the fuck is going on? You're not supposed to call me," Riley says through her phone.

"That's not a nice way to speak to your girlfriend," Dmitri responds.

"She's not my girlfriend."

Dmitri looks at Liz, a sinister smile spreading across his face as if he can see her heart shattering in her chest.

"Well, if you don't claim her, I guess I will take her back," Dmitri tells him.

"You can let her go or you can die, your choice, asshole." The deep, raspy voice coming through the phone is all Reaper.

"The only place she is going to is her cell. It's up to you how much she endures before then. You have an hour, Reaper. One hour to surrender and I will hand her over," Dmitri says, pushing the red button to end the call.

He walks over to Liz, fist slamming into her cheek before she can even register what is happening. Her head is thrown to the side, the coppery tang of blood filling her mouth. She clings to consciousness, spitting the blood onto the table. He motions to his men who untie her and pull her from the chair, holding her up so she doesn't completely collapse.

"You have caused many problems, pet," he says as he drives his ringed fist into her stomach, Liz is unable to even hunch over in pain.

He paces back and forth, growing more angry with each step. He looks at her, face bruised and bleeding, before he swings his hand into her stomach again. Liz fights back the vomit rising in her throat, each hit making her more nauseous.

"I have a new cage for you and since you gave that... thing... what you refused me, I'm going to give you to my men. You let him defile you..." he sneers, bringing his hand up and into her nose. "Now, I'm going to allow every single man in my operation to do the same."

Blood sprays everywhere, the pain blooming behind her eyes. Liz fights to keep herself standing. She keeps looking for a way out, telling herself if she can at least hold on Mikey is coming with his team and Riley will find his way to her, despite everything, he will always keep her safe.

Her thoughts are interrupted by one of Dmitri's men running in the front door, shouting something in Russian she can't understand. The men holding her up start yelling at each other, worried looks on each of their faces. Liz takes that as only meaning one thing, her boys have arrived.

"We will not leave! He will not send his men in if it means she will be harmed. We wait!" Dmitri screams at his men, causing them to all go silent when one brave man steps up.

"Sir, they are building a barricade across the road, guns trained on us. Their general is demanding they blow up the building," he says, voice shaking as he waits for the wrath of his leader.

"We wait!" He screams, "Her Reaper will come. Get our forces ready to move when he does,"

"Sir, the one with the mask, he took the lake, and all the men there are gone. We only have the ones waiting with us," the man bravely says.

Liz watches in horror as Dmitri turns back to her, sending his fist flying into her face again as he lets out a frustrated scream.

The end of the hour is closing in. Every minute that ticks by, Liz loses a little bit of hope that help is coming. She focuses her mind on everything they have taught her over the months, thankful she didn't drink more, allowing her mind to clear some. She makes plan after plan in her head, going over every possible scenario like she has seen Riley do so many times. The blood loss and pain makes all her plans seem impossible.

───

Mikey, Alex, and Tyler walk around the barricade, screaming orders at the soldiers running around, making sure their men get into position and stay there. So focused on keeping everyone from the general's orders, no one notices the truck barreling toward them. Riley doesn't bother to shut his truck off. The moment he stops, the door is thrown open, and Riley jumps out just in time to hear the general tell someone to ready the RPG. Everything goes black as Riley rushes for him, this time, he's determined to kill him.

CHAPTER 49

Three sets of arms are around Riley, pulling him back, slamming him into his truck. He tries to fight past the men holding him, doing anything he can to get to the general, willing to take out his friends in the process. Riley can't think, can't do anything but fight. He can't let them fire that rocket, not while she's in there.

"Unless you want to fucking die, unload that god damn launcher!" Alex screams to the group of men surrounding the General.

"Riley! Calm the fuck down!" Mikey screams over the chaos. He grabs Riley by the straps on his vest, slamming him into his truck. "She's in there, Ry... Liz is in there, alone with him. We need to get her out, then you can kill Scott," Mikey says, pushing him back as he fights his way forward.

The sound of her name brings him back. He looks around at his team, holding him down to keep him from doing something stupid. He nods his head, just once, accepting what they say, and they release him.

Riley stalks the length of his truck, fighting the demons

growing angry inside him, trying to figure out how to get her out. He's running out of time and they all know it. Plans are flying out of everyone, but nothing will guarantee her safety. The only option Riley has is to turn himself over. As long as Liz gets away safe, nothing else matters.

His friends argue back and forth with him, trying to get him to change his mind, knowing what will happen if Dmitri gets his hands on Riley. None of that matters to him. Riley has been captured and tortured before, he can do it again. He has faith that his men will find him, Liz will make sure of that.

Despite their best efforts, Riley storms into the street, everyone around him going silent. He gets to the middle of the road and stops, screaming to the man holding Liz hostage.

"Dmitri! I'm here, let her go!" His voice booms through the silent night air. He paces back and forth like a predator ready to pounce, waiting for Dmitri to emerge from the bar. He stalks back and forth, then back again, trying to hide how helpless he feels knowing he can't do anything to keep Liz safe.

His heart starts to race as the door slowly cracks open, one of the men with Dmitri walking out and over to the road. He stands there for a moment, watching Riley, taking in the small team of men across the street. When he can't take it anymore, he finally snaps, "Where the fuck is Liz?"

"She's alive, for now," the man replies. "Dmitri will speak with you after your men stand down. If they don't, she will die," he says.

Riley just gives him a small nod, willing to risk anything, even his own men, to get Liz back. The man's smile widens and he turns and walks away, back into the bar, door slamming behind him. Riley turns and walks to where the general is watching him, still unsure of what is going on.

"Stand down," Riley says as he approaches the team. They

all look at him wide eyed, not sure whose orders they should be following.

"And why would I want to do that, Reaper?" The general sneers at him.

Riley steps up to him, eyes darkening. He can feel his mind shift from Riley to Reaper, and with a deathly chill in his tone, he says, "Because General, if anything happens to her, there isn't a force strong enough in this world to stop me from what I will do to you. There is no corner of this fucking planet where you can run, nowhere you can hide that will keep me from finding you and ripping your fucking heart out with my bare fucking hands."

The General pales, taking a step back. He starts to mutter something but thinks better of it.

"Stand the fuck down," Riley says one last time.

"You better know what you're doing. If he tries anything, I will end both of you without a second thought," he sneers, turning to the men surrounding them, he says, "You heard him, stand down."

Riley quickly pulls Mikey aside, needing to talk to him before he turns himself over.

"I'm going to get her out. The second she's away from him, you get her in my truck and as far away from here as you can. Get that tracker out of her and keep going," Riley says, turning and making his way back to the street, not giving Mikey the choice of saying no.

"They're standing down. Let her go, Dmitri," Riley yells to the dark building.

Mere seconds later, Dmitri emerges, Liz with him, a knife pressed tight to her throat. His eyes scan every inch of her, his heart shattering at every new injury adorning her body. She walks, bloodied and bruised like the day he found her, only now, she has two men trailing behind with guns aimed at her head. Dmitri stops as soon as his feet touch the dirt, not willing to get any closer to the man there to take his life.

"Let her go!" Riley shouts. "You wanted me, you got me. Now let her fucking go."

"That wasn't the agreement, Reaper," Dmitri says mockingly. "I said you have an hour before I turn her over, I never said it would be to you. You have been ruining my plans for years, destroying everything I love. Now, you get to watch as I kill something you love," Dmitri yells over to Riley.

He stops his pacing and forces his breathing to steady. He knows what he is going to have to do, he just hopes she finally trusts him to do whatever it takes. Everything stills as the horde of soldiers stop what they are doing and watch Riley.

"I don't love her," he says, unable to meet her eyes, knowing everything he's about to do is going to break her heart. She may trust him inexplicably, but the things he's about to say would tear apart even the strongest hearts. "It was my fault she got taken, so I made sure to get her back. That's all," Riley says coldly

"If that is true, then why keep her for so long?" Dmitri asks.

"To get to you. You kept her alive for a reason. I figured we could use her to get you to come out of hiding," Riley says, shrugging his shoulders. "Obviously it worked because you dragged your ass across an ocean, risking being taken in to get her back," he adds.

"You claim you don't love her, but here you are, bargaining for her freedom," Dmitri says.

"I already had plans in place to get rid of her once we got to you, her finding out... complicated things." He keeps his voice steady, channeling Reaper to keep any emotion he has from showing. "Everything I have done for her is out of pity. The only reason I'm here right now is because I made a promise. I promised she would be free, and I intend to keep that promise."

He drags his eyes to Liz, hoping and praying he doesn't see heartbreak in her big green eyes. He quickly looks away, the tears streaming down her face too much for him to bear. He hates himself for confirming every horrible thing she has thought about him since they met.

"And what of your time together. Were all those romantic nights all a lie too?" Dmitri asks, baiting Riley. He thinks he already knows the answer, he just wants Riley to say it, to deliver that final blow.

"If I was going to be stuck with her, I at least wanted some pussy out of it, you get it," Riley says, the faintest smirk on his face.

That was all Liz could take, tears forming a steady stream down her face as she listens to the man she trusts most in the world say such horrible things. She wants to believe it's not true, that he's just doing what it takes, but Riley was too confident in his answers for any of it to be a lie. He couldn't even look her in the eyes.

Dmitri stays where he is, one arm around Liz's chest, the other still holding the knife to her throat, thinking over everything Riley has told him. He takes his time, knowing everyone is holding their breath, waiting to see if he will accept the trade.

"Do you love him?" he asks Liz, just loud enough for Riley to hear.

Liz looks to Riley, the hurt building in her chest. His eyes flick to her, slowly and very carefully, she nods her head yes, tears flowing again.

"Remove your weapons," Dmitri yells.

His men step off the porch, staying behind Liz, waiting for Riley to unstrap all his weapons. Liz watches in horror as he complies, knowing what he's going to endure if he turns himself over. She can't stop the screams that come out of her. Liz struggles to get free, the knife digging into her neck, blood slowly trickling out. Riley watches in horror, unable to help, knowing if he makes one wrong move Dmitri will finish dragging that knife across her neck.

"Stop! Just let him take me!" she screams at Riley, her voice cracking. "Blow the fucking building. Do something!" she screams, turning her head toward the general, only to see his sinister smile. Her heart drops, looking back to Riley, his weapons scattered all around him, utterly defenceless, everything suddenly makes sense.

"Someone fucking stop him!" she screams again, watching in horror as the general loads a small missile into his launcher.

Everything seems to slow as she watches him lift the rocket launcher, aiming it at Riley. Liz doesn't think, driven by pure adrenaline, she reaches for the forgotten knife on her hip. Swinging her arm around, she drives the knife into Dmitri. Her blade finds its mark right where his neck meets his shoulder. His warm red blood coats her arm. His knife drags across her neck, spilling her blood alongside his own as he reaches for the weapon protruding from his body. Liz runs, trying to get to Riley before it's too late.

She only makes it a few steps when she hears the sickening sound of the rocket being fired. She is overcome with agonizing pain as she is thrown through the air. Liz lands with a thud, black taking over her vision. She can't see, can't think, so she lays there, waiting for death to finally take her. She just hopes Riley was able to get away.

The impact was enough to send Riley tumbling backward,

away from where Liz lies, lifeless. He gets to his feet, picking up one of his guns, firing at anyone who gets in his way as he runs to her.

Mikey beats him to it, already trying to dress her wounds the best he can in the middle of the now raging fight. They scream at each other over the gunfire, trying to figure out what happened.

Riley pulls Liz's limp body into his arms, carrying her through the devastation forming around them.

"Stay with me, baby," Riley says, fighting back tears. He sees Liz try to open her eyes, only for a second before fluttering shut. Mikey opens the door, helping Riley to lay her across the seat.

"You can't fucking die on me now, princess. I never got to tell you how you saved me, too." He leans down, placing a kiss on her head. He turns to Mikey, knowing the choice he's about to make is going to kill him.

"You need to get her to the hospital," he yells over to his friend, taking a moment to fire his gun at the men swarming their barricade.

"What? No! She needs you!" Mikey yells back.

"You're the only one I trust with her, Mikey. I need to figure out what the fuck is happening and make sure that fucker never takes another breath," he says, trying to hide how much this is breaking his heart.

He knows she needs him, and he needs to be with her just as much. Riley looks at the death and destruction unfolding in front of him. He would never let Mikey give his life for him, and so, he's choosing to give up the life he could have had. He lets go of Liz, resting her head gently on the seat before he leans down and talks to her for the last time.

"I don't know if you can hear me, but I am so sorry, princess. If I'm alive by the end of this, you're going to kill me when you wake up, but this is something I need to do." He places a small kiss on her bleeding temple. "I love you," he whispers in her ear, praying she can hear him.

Riley stands, tossing his keys to Mikey, trusting him to get the most important thing in his life to safety. He picks his gun back up from where he set it, and storms back toward the bar, determined to end Dmitri for good.

CHAPTER 50

Liz wakes to the sounds of something steadily beeping. She lays there, listening to the strange sounds, trying to figure out if she's dead or not, wondering if it was all a dream. She tries to open her eyes but the pain radiating through her body quickly stops her. She takes a deep breath, wincing at the sharp pain in her chest. Then she feels it, a warm hand wrapping around hers. Something scrapes across the floor, a familiar, wrong smell filling her lungs. She takes a breath, dread rising in her chest.

She tries to open her eyes again, but everything is fuzzy and out of focus. Liz moves her arms under her, trying to sit up and get her bearings, but the hand on hers stops her from moving. She smells it again, like someone has been drinking in the woods. She blinks, eyes stinging in the bright light, trying to force her brain to focus. Liz turns her head, looking at the strong hand on hers, following his arm until finally, she lays her eyes on Mikey. She can't stop the panic that floods her body. The beeping on the monitors starts to get faster, but she can't stop it. Her eyes dart around the room, looking for the one who should be there. Why isn't he there?

"What happened? Where are we?" Liz asks, almost silently, knowing she doesn't want to know the answer.

"You got yourself blown up, darlin," he says with sadness in his voice.

"More," is all Liz can bring herself to say.

Mikey takes a deep breath, knowing what he needs to tell her could very well send her over the edge. He takes a minute, trying to figure out how to explain everything that happened without making her too overwhelmed. There is no way for him to tell her everything that happened to her, to Riley, without it killing her.

"You begged the General to blow up the bar... we all thought you were screaming at us to stop Riley, everyone was too focused on you two... no one saw Scott give you what you asked. I don't know why he didn't blow up the bar, it's like he couldn't decide between Riley and Dmitri so he went between them in the road.. Me and Riley got to you, got you bandaged up the best we could in the middle of the shit show. Riley... he uh... made me bring you here, said he needed to make sure Dmitri was dead," he says, sadness in his eyes.

"Why isn't he here?" she chokes out.

"Darlin, maybe we should talk about this later, when you're feeling a little better," he says, squeezing her hand.

"Where is he?" Liz says, barely above a whisper. "Is he alive?"

"We don't know. No one has seen him since that day. He's just... gone," he says, unable to meet her eyes.

Panic grabs hold of her and refuses to let go. Tears spring to her eyes. She doesn't bother trying to hold them back. He can't be gone. She remembers an explosion and talking to Riley.

He told her he loved her. She doesn't know what to think

anymore, maybe this is just a way of Riley leaving her behind without having to do it himself.

"We are all trying to figure out what the fuck happened. When the general fired that rocket, all hell broke loose, and apparently it got worse while we were here. Tyler said Dmitri had more men that came out of nowhere. They started to get overrun and that's when they lost eyes on Riley," he says, noting every change in her as he explains what he knows.

"How long?" Liz asks, knowing the answer is going to break her.

"Six days, darlin. You had some minor internal bleeding so the doctor has kept you sedated to heal. You've been in and out the past two days. I didn't want you to wake up alone, so I've been here. Tyler and Alex are doing everything they can to find Riley."

Six days.

Six days he has been missing and she's just been laying in a hospital bed. Her thoughts race. Liz gets her arms under her, pulling on the wires and tubes connected all over her body, and she pushes herself up. Mikey reaches for her, trying to get her to lay back down, but she bats his hand away.

"Liz, stop!" Mikey shouts. He jumps from his seat and grabs her hands, stopping her from ripping anything else from her bleeding arms.

"I can't! He's out there somewhere. I need to get out of this fucking bed and help. He saved me, Mikey, he saved me and now he needs me to save him," she screams, a steady stream of tears running down her cheeks. Mikey sits on the bed next to her, pulling her into him.

"I know, darlin," he says, rubbing her back, doing his best to comfort her. "I need to know that you are going to make it, then we're bringing Riley home."

EPILOGUE

FORTY EIGHT DAYS LATER

Liz sits by the cargo door, anxiously bouncing her knees, watching Alex pace up and down the narrow hall. Two rows of men and women line either side of the plane, carrying them to their next mission. Her heart sinks, thinking about the last two. Their teams raided two of Dmitri's camps with no sign of Riley. Everyday that they return without him Liz loses a piece of herself. Mikey reaches over and takes her hand, giving her a sad smile. Losing Riley has been hard on everyone, but no one is taking it harder than Liz.

"Mikey, Tyler, Neil, head to the main building, take the tunnels on the far side. There will be less resistance but stay alert. John and Lauren, lead your team around the other side. Make sure their path is clear when they get there."

He turns and makes his way next to where Liz sits, eyes falling to the large scar across her neck. He goes silent, reflecting on everything that brought them to this moment. No amount of intel or planning could have prepared them for what happened that day.

Liz tries to stay focused and listen to the words of their new leader, but finds herself drifting to a dark place, thinking back on everything Riley told her about his capture, thinking about her own. The thought of what could be happening to him makes her sick. The worst part is she has no idea if he is even alive. Her new found family all agree Dmitri would have shouted from the mountaintops if he had ended Riley's life. Until that moment comes, he is alive. The irony of what Riley once told the general is not lost on her, because now, there is nothing on this earth that will stop her from getting Riley back. She will make those men beg on their knees for mercy before she is done.

"Men on the ground, you will be clearing a path to the cells ahead of Liz and I. If you see someone being held anywhere other than the cells, get them out. Leave no prisoner behind. Understood?"

"Yes, Sir," the team says in unison.

He glances over to Liz who is watching him prepare their team. He can see the heartbreak in her eyes. She may be proud and appreciate how he stepped up, he knows someone else should be standing where he is, giving these orders. Alex walks to the back of the plane, pushing a big red button on the wall. The door behind them slowly falls open, filling the room with deafening winds. Everyone stands, forming two lines, ready to hurl themselves into the air.

"Riley is down there. He has saved every one of our asses more times than I can count. Right now, finding him is our top priority. The general doesn't know we are here, so let's keep it that way. We get in, get what we're here for, and get the hell out," Alex shouts over the wind whipping through the cabin of the plane. "You know your roles, don't fuck it up. Let's bring our boy home," he says, giving Liz a sad smile.

THE STORY ISN'T OVER

KEEP READING FOR A SNEAK PEEK AT
BOOK TWO.

HERS TO DEFEND

Riley screams as the rusty hook tears through the muscles on his back, mirroring the one already on the other side. Every thrashing movement opens the mix of cuts covering his chest and abdomen. Metal clashing rings out in the courtyard as he tries to pull his arms from the handcuffs holding him against the table under him. Cheers sound out, hiding his screams of agony.

Dmitri's forces gather around the man who has ruthlessly hunted them, eagerly watching their leader ready him to be strung up for their entertainment. Every day has been spent fighting off ruthless beatings from his captors. He can only fight back so much before the little strength he has is gone. A dangerous mix of starvation, dehydration, and delirium quickly threatens to ruin any plans of escape he has.

Today is not the day, Riley was so hopeful when they moved him from the makeshift jail cell to the courtyard. Those hopes died the moment he saw the crowd gathering around. He has no doubt he can free himself of his restraints, but with so many of Dmitri's men surrounding him, he will never make it far. Riley does the only thing possible, waits.

He endures everything they throw at him knowing every cut, every stab of the knife, every fist slamming into his already desecrated body, is one that Liz will never have to experience again. Riley swore he would never allow himself to be thrown back into this situation. Now his capture is a sacrifice he will happily make one thousand times over if it means she stays safe.

He blocks out the searing pain coating every inch of his body, pushes everything out of his mind but her. The way her silky hair feels twisting around his fingers or the way her eyes light up when he surprises her with her favorite snacks. The feel of her small, reserved hug when he carried her down the mountain, telling her about his past.

Weeks have passed since the day he gave himself up to make sure Dmitri couldn't get his hands on her. Every day has been an endless cycle of attacks. Dmitri visits each day trying to beat information out of him, but he doesn't break, he can't. Breaking means everyone he cares for is in danger, and if getting his ass beat from sun up to sun down is what it takes to keep his loved ones safe then he will take it.

His team knows to reconvene at the bunker and decide if they should rescue him, or admit that it is just too risky and leave him to die. Riley wishes they would pick the latter. Every time he thinks of the love he left behind, he knows she'll make every man on the team find him and drag him home, for no reason other than to tear him a new one for his capture.

Another scream tears from him as he is lifted off the table until he is upright, held up by nothing more than hooks meant for cattle carcasses. He sucks a sharp breath in, running every training technique through his head to fight past the pain and keep from passing out. Rocks crunch beside him, footsteps drawing closer. Face to face with Dmitri, Riley greets him with a smile, his normally brilliantly white teeth turned now a deep shade of red from the blood coating his mouth.

"Are you ready to tell me where you have hidden my pet?" he asks coldly. A sinister smile creeps up his face as his icy blue eyes dart from the various wounds peppering Riley's exposed body. "How about what your leader has planned? I–" Warm red liquid sprays over his face, stopping his rant.

"Why don't you go fuck yourself," Riley chokes out before a hard fist slams·into his head, sending him spinning in the air. Cheers from the men gathered to watch erupt around him. His head spins faster than his dangling body, the near constant abuse taking more of a toll on him than he will ever admit. Dmitri reaches a hand out, stopping Riley's slow rotation. His eyes simmer with contempt, glaring at the man hanging before him.

"I will make you an offer *Reaper*," He spits, "Tell me what I want to know and I will end this. I will grant you a fast death. I have many men who want to watch you bleed. You can make it stop, all I ask in return is information. A small price to pay I think."

An eerie silence takes over the courtyard. Every man huddled together waiting to hear if the man they have spent years fearing will finally break and accept the sweet release of death. A hiss escaped Riley's lips while his eyes sweep over the small crowd. The adrenaline that has kept him conscious is starting to wear down, leaving his vision fuzzy. He rallies every ounce of strength left in him to drag his point across one last time before he succumbs to the loss of blood pooling from his wounds.

With his head high, speaking loud enough for everyone to hear, he seethes– "You should kill me while you still have the chance. When I get out of here, and yes asshole, I will get out of here, I'll be waiting for you, right up there," He cranes his neck to look at the building towering beside them. The blood drains from Dmitri's face as Riley turns back to face him, "Waiting to flay the skin from your fucking bones."

Dmitri's eyes widen in fear as each word sinks in. Pride swells in Riley's chest watching the man reach up and gingerly touch the scar crossing his eye. A reminder of what Riley will do to be free. He knows all too well Riley feeds on the fear of others, he will become your nightmare just to watch you squirm before he takes your life. With a small shake of his head he tries to ignore the pit growing in his stomach. Plucking a rusted piece of rebar off the ground, he swings it into Riley's abdomen. Deep, guttural screams of agony fill the air like thunder. His ribs crack from the blow. The impact sends him swinging through the air, the metal hooks threatening to rip clean out of his back.

"You are never getting out of here again. As I told my pet, I have my own men in your ranks. I made sure your general will not send help, and your partners do not care enough to risk their lives for you. No, one way or another, you will die here." He sneers before turning on his heels and making his way through the courtyard. "Someone stop his bleeding, we wouldn't want him to die before we've had our fun." He adds without looking back.

This is exactly what Riley needed. Dmitri may have power amongst his organization, but he has never been a smart man. His anger and need to be seen as someone worth fearing has always been his downfall. He is too busy preening, thinking he has outsmarted his enemies to realize he is feeding information. He will take every beating with a smile on his face because when he does, Dmitri will do anything to wipe it off. Including telling him his next plan of attack, and just who he has working for him on the inside. He can only hope his team makes it to him before Dmitri makes good on his promise to end his life.

Once his cuts are glued closed, the bleeding slows. He is left alone in the dark of the night, hanging from the flesh of his back, fading in and out of consciousness. It's then that he realizes he may have pushed too far this time. Mentally, he can take whatever is thrown at him, but even he has physical limits that can't be ignored. A wave of regret settles over him. He pushed too much. All the information he squeezed from his captor will never be heard, all his work will be for nothing.

He thought Dmitri would keep him alive long enough for his team to find and extract him, but it's too late. His heartbeat thrums in his ears, a sad irregular sound mixed with a wheeze from every breath he draws. Riley quickly comes to the conclusion that his lung must have been punctured by the freshly broken rib. He allows his eyes to drift closed, his pain growing lighter as his thoughts flood with the memories he made with Liz. If he is to die tonight, her face is the last thing he wants to see. Shimmering green eyes flash before him, but they are not right. He was supposed to see her, glowing with happiness, living her life once more. Instead he sees her how she was when they first met, with blood running down her face, eyes laced with fear as she screams at him. Riley refuses to let that be it. He compels his mind to go utterly blank before his world goes dark.

RILEY'S BASE APARTMENT

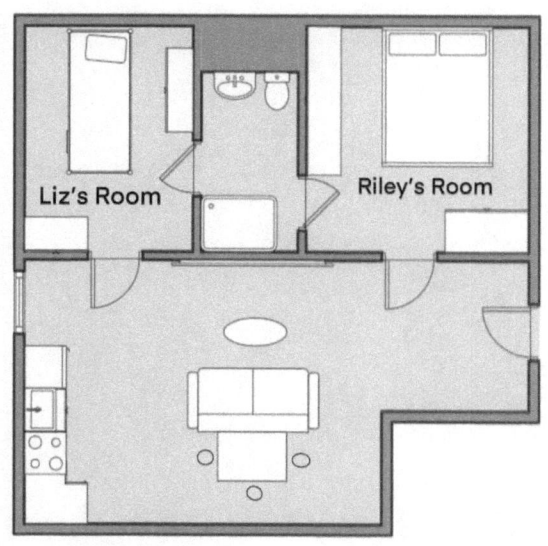

Liz's Room

Riley's Room

RILEY'S BUNKER - TOP FLOOR

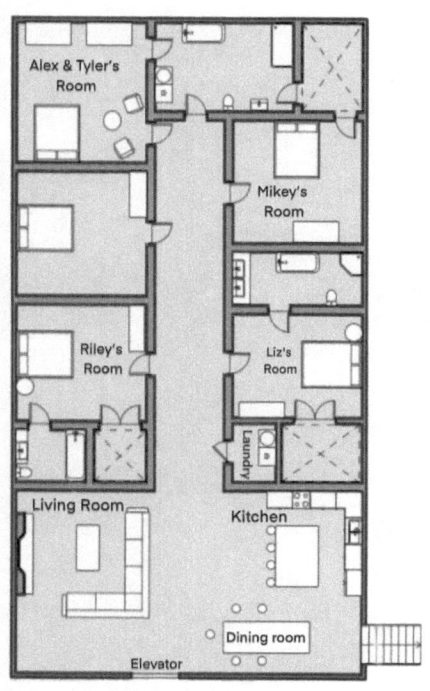

Alex & Tyler's Room

Mikey's Room

Riley's Room

Liz's Room

Laundry

Living Room

Kitchen

Dining room

Elevator

RILEY'S BUNKER- BOTTOM FLOOR

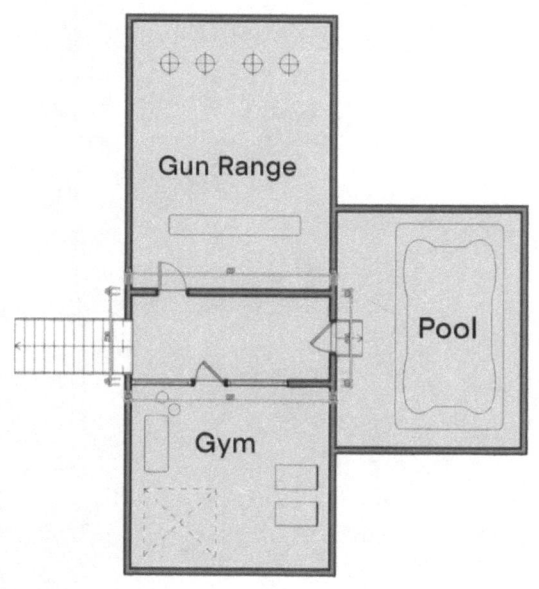

ACKNOWLEDGMENTS

To my incredible husband, Rob. This book could not exist without you pulling my dream of being an author from the dark corner I shoved it into. Thank you for being my loudest cheerleader and the voice reminding me I could do it. Through every re-wright, every meltdown, and every second of self-doubt, you have been my safe space, encouraging me to keep going. Every single word in these pages exists because you believed in me when no one else did.

To the friends and family who cheered me on, thank you for showing up and keeping mo moving forward.

And finally-

To my readers. I never thought I would get to say those words, but you took the chance on a debut author, and for that I am eternally grateful. Whether this is your first book or your hundredth, thank you for giving my story a home.

ABOUT THE AUTHOR

Ashley Davis is a debut author living in a small town in Western Massachusetts with her husband, daughter and two dogs. She has always had a deep passion for reading and writing, using writing to explore and work though traumas.

After being a stay at home mom for many years, she finally decided to take the leap and follow her lifelong dream of becoming an author. When she is not writing, you can find her building cosplays for her family or attending renaissance fairs.

You can find all her socials below.